PROVIDENCE

REN BROWNE

PROVIDENCE

REN BROWNE

CONTENT NOTES

The story you are about to read is a wild west tale with shootouts, chase scenes, and two outlaws who can't seem to stay out of trouble any more than they can stay away from each other. As a result, there are a number of mature themes in this story, including detailed sex scenes, on-page violence and death, instances of stalking, references to domestic violence and sexual assault, representations of mental health struggles, discussions of when a main character was being held captive and hurt, and use of derogatory language that may be triggering for some readers.

If you would like to view a more comprehensive list of triggers and tropes before proceeding, please visit RenBrowne.com.

If you're good to go, then by all means, ride on.

THE MIDNIGHT GANG SERIES

ADVERSITY

PROVIDENCE

PLAYLIST

Welcome to Hard Times — Charley Crockett

Cowpoke — Colter Wall

Man in Black — Johnny Cash

Way of the Triune God (Hallelujah Version) — Tyler Childers

Devil Always Made Me Think Twice — Chris Stapleton

Sleeping on the Blacktop — Colter Wall

A Horse with No Name — America

Big Iron — Marty Robbins

Dear August — PJ Harding, Noah Cyrus

Love on the Brain — Rihanna

Mama Tried — Merle Haggard

I Could Drive You Crazy — Sierra Ferrell

All I See Is You — Shane Smith & The Saints

Hollow Bones — Anna Graves

Oh My Days — Orville Peck

I Will Follow You into the Dark — Death Cab for Cutie

In Dreams — Sierra Ferrell

Wrong — Omar Rudberg

Pay No Rent — Turnpike Troubadours

For those of us who have lost faith.

May you find the person that makes you believe without question.

PART ONE

GAMBLER

CHAPTER 1
AIDEN
NINE YEARS OLD
PENNSYLVANIA

"Ten paces. I'll count it out."

I nod once, my fingers fumbling to place my gun in my right hand as the gruff voice at my back propels me forward. "One."

I feel him take a corresponding step, his impossibly large presence still covering me in his shadow. The evening sun casting it out in front of me as if to help guide my path. "Two."

The dry grass prickles my bare feet, a reminder that though the day had been warm, the plush green of summer is fading away. As are the endless, carefree days it offers. "Three."

I should have been back earlier. I was supposed to be, but I had been having too much fun—too distracted by all the things I *wanted* to do rather than what I *ought* to be doing. "Four."

On the next step, the last of the shadow from the man behind me slips away, my own breaking free. So much smaller than his, yet the darkness emanating from me is all I can see as I keep my eyes on the ground. "Five."

My heart is racing, my mouth too dry and my palms too sweaty as I try to adjust my grip on the pistol that feels too big for my palm. "Six."

I can't remember precisely what I'm supposed to do. He's so far away already. "Seven."

What if I get it wrong? "Eight."

Do I get to try again? "Nine."

Before he can give the final word, I turn, pivoting on my heel. My gun is already raised, my finger on the trigger before I've even completed the motion. "*Bang.*"

The man pitches forward, back still to me as he clutches his chest in indication that, *somehow*, my aim was true. When I see that his gun still hangs useless at his side, I grin broadly. "Gotcha!"

My opponent's expression shifts once he turns to me, his pained grimace immediately giving way to a smile that my mama always says is identical to my own. "That so?" His eyes narrow. "Come here, you little cheat."

My father sprints toward me, and I let out a holler in surprise, my carved wooden pistol falling to the dirt eighteen paces away from where he drops his as I make a run for it. My rapid footfalls are barely audible over the sound of his laughter.

"Run, Aiden!" A raised voice that still manages to sound soft calls out from the safety of the farmhouse front porch, her arms outstretched to welcome me as she watches us with a smile. "Don't look back! Run!"

I try to go faster, beelining straight for my mama, but I'm laughing too, so hard that I can hardly breathe through that suspended weightless moment. That one where you are still able to experience the frantic hope of evading an unavoidable fate.

I'm mere inches from sanctuary when I trip over nothing but myself. My long legs—still unfamiliar to me after my most recent growth spurt—go out from beneath me, sending me hurtling toward the ground before a strong arm around my middle pitches me sideways into a solid chest.

My father lets out a deep *oof* as he connects with the ground and absorbs the worst of our short fall, but he recovers quickly, already laughing again by the time I'm struggling back up. "Thought you wanted to be a cowboy," he teases as I untangle myself. "Seem more like a newborn calf to me."

I huff, brushing off the white chaps and the vest my mama made me and glaring up at him as he also gets to his feet. "I'll be a cowboy. There'll be stories about me. Just you wait."

My father arches an eyebrow at me, bending and picking up his displaced hat before knocking it against his pant leg to clear off the dust. Without it in its usual place on his head, it's easier to see how tan he is from spending long days working in the sun, his auburn hair shaggy and his gray-streaked beard scruffy with the demands of harvest season. The fields take up all his free time for trivial things, such as a haircut or a shave. Guilt swirls in my gut as I think about how tired he looks, now that some of the excitement from our game has faded. Another reminder that I should have been here.

"Sorry," I mutter. "For not coming back when I was supposed to."

"What about for cheatin'?" he asks, crossing his arms over his chest as he considers me. "You sorry for that, too?"

"I didn't mean to," I protest, my frown deepening as I avoid his gaze. "I was just—I couldn't remember if it was *on* ten or after. And I…I didn't want you to win."

He sighs, and I look up in time to see him give the ends of his hair a tug before he crouches, his blue eyes meeting my brown. The only thing about me that is unmistakably my mother instead of him. "If you have to cheat me to beat me, then I've already won," he says. "You want to be one of them cowboys in the paper? You gotta act like one. You gotta work hard. And you gotta be honorable. Right?"

"S'pose so," I reply, not wanting to admit the main appeal I see in the wild tales that make their way here from out west is not that they are *honorable*, it's that they are *free*.

No places to be. No chores. No rules.

"*Aiden.*" My father's voice turns sharp as if he can hear my wandering thoughts. "Son, there are a lot of things you can be in this life, but the most important is a good man. You understand?"

I nod quickly. "Yes, sir."

His mouth presses into a firm line but then he lays his hand on my shoulder and gives me a squeeze. "All right, then."

He heads for the porch where my mama is waiting, taking the same path I'd been on, but his steady strides somehow seem to be getting him there just as fast as my sprint.

"That's it?" I call after him. "Ain't I in trouble?"

He looks back at me, eyes dancing with amusement. "You want to be?"

"No, sir."

"You planning to shirk your responsibilities again?"

"No, sir."

"Then I'll take you at your word, cowboy." He meets my eyes, man to man. A good man to a boy trying to learn to be one. "Don't let me down."

I straighten, lifting my chin and feeling every bit of the weight that he undoubtedly intended with that statement settling on my shoulders. Still, I'm smiling again as I watch him reach my mama, wrap his arms around her, and give her a spin before placing her feet back on the solid porch boards. When he also places his hat on her head and bends to put his mouth on hers, she beams.

"Can't you do that in private?" I mutter, rolling my eyes as I drag my feet up the stairs. My protests only grow louder when my mama grabs for me once I get to the top, tucking me into her side so that I'm enveloped by the soft fabric of her dress, the gentle waves of her long black hair, the sweet smell of whatever she's been baking. Apples? Cinnamon? *Pie.*

My stomach growls and she chuckles, dropping a kiss on the crown of my head. Easier for her than it's been in the past since now I'm up to her shoulder, and I wonder how many summers it'll be before I'm as tall as her. Taller, even.

"Go on inside and get washed up," she says, nudging me toward the door, and I'm so absorbed by the aroma that's drifting from the kitchen that I almost don't notice the way my father has gone still beside us.

"Pa?" I look up at his face, the hard lines that are rarely ever there making an appearance as he stares at a figure approaching in the distance.

"You expecting anyone?" he asks, directing the question at my mother and me. We both shake our heads, and he takes a step toward the stairs, keeping his eyes on the visitor.

"Go on inside," he says, repeating my mother's words, but they sound completely different when my father is reaching for the pistol at his belt, the real one this time, instead of the wooden toy lying discarded in the yard. "Lock the door."

Later, I would remember having that sensation again. That suspended weightless moment where you are still able to experience the frantic hope of evading an unavoidable fate.

I would remember the way I tried to stay in that moment. To hide there. Even as my mother held my face and whispered, "Run, Aiden. Don't look back."

CHAPTER 2
AIDEN
TWENTY-SIX YEARS OLD
CENTRAL TEXAS

"You get kicked in the head recently?"

The damn kid just blinks at me, his mouth dropping open for a moment before he stammers out, "Wha—what?"

"Hearing loss? That what this is?"

He looks around, peering over his shoulder toward the rest of camp in the hopes that backup is coming. *Not a chance.*

Now that we've decided to stop here for a while, the only thing that's going to dislodge any other members of our party from their spot by the fire is their whiskey bottle running empty, and from the looks of it, they're just getting started for the day.

"Why are you askin' if—"

"Because I told you to get lost once already," I tell him, fixing him with a look that usually sends people on their way. "But here you still are."

His eyes widen a bit, and as much as it irks me, I do have to give him some credit for continuing to stand his ground when it looks like one strong spring breeze could blow him over. Brave kid. Stupid, with no survival instincts to speak of, but brave.

Guess he's not really a *kid*, though. As scrawny as he is, he has to be eighteen at least. Plenty old enough to be on his own.

Far older than I was…

The thought creeps in before I can bury it, and my teeth grind together with the effort of fighting off a memory that already cost me last night's sleep. Which isn't particularly unusual. You'd think at some point it would fade to something less sharp. That time would dull it, even if nothing else has managed to do so.

"I'm…I only…" The kid's mumbling again, and the overwhelming exhaustion I feel simply watching him struggle makes me finally pause my attempts to fix the busted pocket watch in my palm. I set it beside me on the fallen oak tree I'm sitting on rather than just hurling the fuckin' thing into the surrounding brush like I should.

Was a ridiculous purchase to begin with. It's never really worked right, and it seems unlikely to recover now that it's been stomped on by a sour bull that had been hoping to stomp me instead.

Close call, all things considered, even if living the way I do makes them an almost daily occurrence. Sometimes it's the animals. Sometimes it's the terrain. Although, more often than not in my experience, it's the fuckin' people. *Case in point…*

"The, um, the boss says he wants you in town with them tomorrow," the kid finally gets out. "Told me to tell you."

My glare shifts from him to one of the figures around the campfire, and I can tell from the tilt of his hat while he sips on his personal flask that Maddock is watching the exchange between me and the kid.

How very like him to send someone else instead of getting up and doing the job himself. He *knows* I don't do town. Nor should he, when it's barely been a hundred miles since the last one.

"Listen…" I look at the kid again from beneath the brim of my hat and take a stab in the dark. "Bucky?"

"Arty," he corrects, but then seems to regret it. "I mean, you *can* call me Bucky, if you want." Suddenly, he seems almost excited. "Could be a nickname or somethin'."

"Arty isn't bad enough?"

His shoulders sag, and I almost feel bad, but me being soft with him won't help him none out here.

"Listen, *Arty*, you tell the boss I'll pass. Someone needs to mind things with the herd."

"Well, uh…he said you'd say that."

"Good." I reach for the watch again. "Glad we're in agreement."

"So he also told me to tell you that if you don't come, he'll dock your pay."

I snort, shaking my head a little at this latest attempt to extort me. "He can certainly try. That all?"

The kid shakes his head, too, so fast that the smudges of dirt on his face blur into streaks, his unkempt blond hair flying out in a way that would be comical if not for the next words that come out of his mouth. "He said if that didn't convince you, then I should remind you of, um…"

He twists the hem of his shirt between his fingers. "That you ought to recall why he hired you. And that he still owns the horse." He pauses, chews at his bottom lip. "Say, is it true you—"

"Probably not," I tell him, not needing to hear the rest of the question to know I won't want to give him the answer. Especially since it's not just Maddock's first reminder but also his second that is making my jaw tick.

I glance at the young buckskin mustang grazing a few feet to my right. Making his way through the best patches of grass I could find for him as a reward for being the only reason my close call remained no more than *close*.

With a mean streak as dark as the stripe running down his back, the stallion had been passed to me initially as a means of welcome once all the other cowhands had declared him *unrideable*. As well as *not even worth the cost of the bullet to put him down*. Their way of saying welcome, I guess. And of trying to put me in my place in the herd.

Unfortunately for them, however, that horse and I have always gotten along just fine. And, fortunately for me, he's undoubtedly the best in the lot. Quick, solid, smart, and just the right amount of crazy to see a bull charging and think it might be a good idea to send hooves flying rather than running.

There's not a chance I'm about to let him go easy. Not after today, and especially not when I know how the rest of this crew tends to treat their own horses. Not a chance...and Maddock knows it.

"So then," the kid mutters, clearly ready to finish this conversation as he looks back longingly toward the fire, "should I tell him you're comin' or...?"

"If you think you need to," I reply, pulling a knife from my belt to pry the watch open and seeing him take a cautious step back. *Maybe not as stupid as I thought. Or as brave.*

"Got it," he says with his eyes on the blade. "Is that a yes, then? Sorry, I'm not sure if you're sayin' you will or you—"

I sigh and stand, which sends him stumbling back this time, fast and unsteady enough that his backside hits the dirt when he trips on his own feet. In response, a round of laughter breaks out from the direction of the campfire, but it dies off into quiet coughs the moment I turn my head their way. Once I'm certain I've gotten my point across, I slip my knife back into my belt and stash the watch in my pocket before I reach down, grabbing hold of the kid's forearm as he does the same with mine.

"I'll go," I clarify, letting him loose as soon as he's back up. "You can tell him that I'll meet them in town tomorrow."

"Oh." For one horrifying moment, he acts like he's going to tail after me as I start to walk away. "He was thinkin' that you'd ride there with them."

"Then maybe he's the one who got kicked in the head today," I say back, striding past the mustang who thankfully does turn to follow me as I move away from camp and out into the valley.

"Wait, don't you want to eat?" he calls after me. "Lunch should be 'bout done."

Already past my limit for conversation for the day, I don't reply. I'm more than fine with another serving of hard tack from my saddlebags if it means a bit of peace. Sure, a rogue bull or a protective cow may decide they want to kill you every once in a while, but at least they don't talk your fuckin' ear off with questions in the process.

Before I get too far, I look over my shoulder to make sure he's really gone, and I'm just in time to see him get welcomed back to the fire as a returning hero—Maddock giving him a pat on the shoulder and gesturing for the bottle to be passed his way. The kid takes a seat at the right hand of the king, an unknowing pawn that, for a brief moment, gets to look like a knight.

Only for an instant, my steps slow, but then I'm moving again. I don't need to be getting *involved*. He's not my responsibility. No one is.

And that's precisely how I want to keep it.

CHAPTER 3
AIDEN

"All right, boys, get yourselves something to eat and meet at the saloon in an hour, ya hear?"

Maddock Douglas makes his announcement out in front of Main Street Hotel to resounding hollers and shouts from the four men that arrived in town with him this afternoon—his current favorites among the company of nine that set off months ago from El Paso bound for the Kansas railheads. As I understand the rumors, Maddock's mama is an heiress to one of the largest ranches in the country, and after she and his daddy got fed up with dragging their darling son out of parties by his ear, they sent him out here to run the drive as a way to build his knowledge of the family business. Presumably, as a way to build his character, too.

To be honest, I'm not really sure how watching other people work hard is supposed to fix the fact that he's a complete shithead. Seems to me like a fault in the logic there. But I'm sure as hell not going to be the one to point it out.

Even the two men left behind this morning, the same ones currently at the bottom of Maddock's pecking order, knew better than to kick up much of a fuss. Likely recognizing that they're better off being stuck with the herd than ending up like the man stuck in a shallow grave after a disagreement got out of hand before we even cleared San Antonio.

They're also likely better off than me, since I still have no fucking clue what I'm doing here. Though I suspect I'm about to find out…

"*Aiden*," Maddock says with a smile as the others head inside, the kid happily tagging along at the back of the pack as I ride up to the front steps. The closer I get the easier it is to see our trail boss is already all shined back to his preferred luster. His brown hair slicked back, his thin beard shaved close, and his gray vest and slacks freshly pressed. "So good of you to come join us."

"Well, seeing as how you asked me so nicely," I respond, choosing to keep my seat until I have a better idea of what I'm in for here. Beneath me, the mustang shifts from side to side, seemingly as uneasy at being summoned as I am.

Around us, the town of Soldana is buzzing, using the very same cattle route we're on to grow busier by the month. Everywhere you look there's new construction. Houses and shops, a wealth of places to stay and places to eat for anyone passing on through or planning on settling. A bustling example of the new western frontier.

Too fuckin' crowded if you ask me. Especially now that it's past suppertime and people are out and about looking for entertainment. I direct the mustang a bit nearer to the hotel just to keep out of the way of the carriages, all of them going by at what feels like an unwise speed for a street full of pedestrians.

"Well?" I prompt Maddock after another loaded wagon passes by too close. Likely a bit too obvious with my irritation as I add, "You told me to be here, I'm here. Tell me what you want so I can be on my way."

My employer tilts his head, still looking amiable enough, but I can hear the warning in his words when he says, "You know, I can't seem to figure you out, Aiden. You're quite the puzzle."

I shrug, having no doubt that he's the kind of person who would happily force together any pieces that didn't seem to fit in his *puzzle*. Nor do I doubt that his bootlickers in the hotel would help him do it without so much as blinking an eye.

I should *never* have taken this job. I should have made my way back to Arizona. Would've been the smart thing…but given that there isn't really anything there needing me, it had *seemed* smart to take a contract that would keep me occupied for a while.

"Are you a betting man?" Maddock asks, pulling me out of my thoughts, and I almost laugh at the timeliness of his question.

"No," I tell him. "Can't say that I am."

"Really?" He appears genuinely surprised. "I would think, given your history, you'd love to test your luck."

"Don't believe in luck," I say, ignoring the comment about my past as I glance up and down the street, calculating the best path of escape should it come to it. However, I'm looking at Maddock again by the time I add, "Don't tend to trust things that can turn so easy."

His smile widens but it doesn't reach his eyes. "How pragmatic of you. All the more reason for you to help me over the course of this next week, yes?"

This next *week*? I reposition myself in the saddle, just to have an excuse to move as an anxious feeling crawls up my spine. "Don't you think that's a long time to be delayed? We're due in Kansas."

"*Months* from now," Maddock interjects, waving me off. "Plenty of time. In fact, we're ahead of schedule."

"We've been fortunate so far. But we won't be if we keep stopping at every town within spitting distance," I counter. "If we end up having to push the herd too hard later, we could lose more than a few head to injury. They're fine animals, but I've had some experience with this trail, and my advice is—"

"We're not following *your* advice," he snaps, civility abruptly gone. "*I* am in charge on this drive. My cattle. My authority. *My* decisions. Understood?"

"Your decisions," I repeat, silently tacking on a *May God help us all.*

"Excellent," he replies, all smiles again as he claps his hands. "Now, as I was saying, while you don't claim to be a gambler, given your *experience*, I know you'll understand how important it is to have the conditions weighed in your favor. How advantageous it can be?"

I don't reply, something he must interpret as a need for clarity rather than an indication that he should fuckin' steer clear of this topic. Something he always seems incapable of doing.

"Come now…" Maddock chuckles. "I'm giving you an opportunity to be a wealthy man. Well," he amends, frowning slightly as he looks at me, "wealthier than you are now. And all I'm asking is for you to use your considerable talents to help *me* in return."

My fingers tighten around the reins in my left hand, but I keep my right resting against the worn leather chaps that cover my thigh. "As we've already discussed many times, Maddock, you hired a cattleman. Not a gunman. If you're needing the former, then I'm happy to put my *talents* to use. However, if you're needing the latter, then you've got the wrong man. No matter if you've told the rest of the crew something different."

He laughs again in a way that makes me grind my teeth. *God, I really fuckin' hate him.*

"I didn't have to *tell* them anything," he says, when he's finally contained his amusement. "You do realize that your reputation spans more than one territory?" When I don't respond, he shakes his head. "Well, no matter. Cattleman. Gunman. Call yourself whatever you like, so long as you're at our table at the saloon every night by eight."

"I already told you I don't play."

"I don't need you to. What I need is for you to be there to prevent things from…getting out of hand." He frowns and I notice him covertly pressing the skin beneath his left eye with his fingertips. Undoubtedly remembering the shiner he came back with after his last trip into town.

Never did get a believable retelling on how he ended up with it, but given that his ego seemed to be just as bruised as his face, my guess is that it isn't a story he wants told. And that he likely gave instructions saying as much.

"I'm not finishing your fights for you, Maddock," I tell him in no uncertain terms. "And I'm sure as hell not starting them."

"Of course not." He holds up his hands in an attempt to placate me, though his tone remains unyielding. "However, *should* a situation arise, and as a condition of your ongoing employment, I will need to know that you can be trusted to do as I require to protect my interests. Is that understood?"

I squeeze my left leg against the mustang's side, guiding him to turn.

"*Stop*," Maddock immediately orders, stepping forward as if he intends to prevent me from leaving. "Where are you going?"

"To protect your interests," I tell him, continuing on while looking back over my shoulder at him. "Don't worry, if rustlers come for the cattle while you're gone, I'll let them know that any conclusions on how many they can steal will have to wait until you get back and decide."

"Damn it, Aiden. You will *stop*," Maddock calls after me, although his impending tantrum is blessedly interrupted when he is forced to step aside to avoid a man in a fine black coat and hat who is looking to get inside.

Place must be nice, I think, taking in the tall, well-tailored expanse of his disappearing back. *Really nice.*

"This opportunity will not come again. I'm offering you a potential windfall if you stay, a better quality of life. Better…lodgings," Maddock tempts, apparently believing I've now taken an interest in the building. "You'll get your cut of the earnings from the poker table. Same as the others."

I roll my eyes, immediately thinking back to the rest of the crew disappearing inside a few minutes ago. Of course, they've all got rooms here. Don't know better than to be spending money they don't have yet. And likely still won't after spending a whole week at the poker table. Awful hard to pay a hotel bill with empty pockets.

When I keep going, Maddock starts up again. "Fine. As part of our bargain, I'll give you that horse, too," he adds begrudgingly. "As a sign of my *immense* appreciation."

That actually does make me pause. Not only because the mustang is one of his preferred chips to play in our ongoing arrangement, but also because my biggest obstacle to simply getting gone is my lack of means to do so. I'd spent most of what I had just making it to this job, which means my allowance for practicing free will is alarmingly slim until I get paid more than promises at the end of this drive. However, if the mustang *were* mine, my options for new employment would improve significantly, as would my ability to cut loose and run without serious repercussions.

Skipping out and taking a loss on a bad job is one thing. Being branded a horse thief is another. And I'll be fuckin' damned if I end up on a wanted poster.

"I get the horse regardless of your performance at the table. Win or lose," I counter. "And I want it in writing."

"If that will make you feel more at ease." He smiles again, more believably this time since he's close to getting what he wants. "I'll draft it out on my personal stationary and give it to you tonight."

Personal stationary. Christ. The things people find to spend money on.

I must be silent for too long, thinking about the pointlessness of expensive paper, because Maddock lets out a huff and shoves his hands in his pockets. "Do we have a deal then?"

I consider one more time if I'm making a mistake here, if I'm allowing myself to be too swayed by the sudden surge of possibility. Or even more foolish, by the spark of hope that the very luck I just said I don't believe in might be about to change.

"All right, Maddock. We've got a deal."

CHAPTER 4
AIDEN

I leave the boss standing on the steps before he can add any additional stipulations, like requirements that I stay at the hotel, since not only the price but also the close quarters are far more than I am able to afford. Being stuck on the drive with this lot is bad enough.

Instead, I spend a few cents on a stall near the end of the aisle at the stable down the road, close to the back doors and big enough that I can comfortably set myself up in the corner with little fuss. The mustang doesn't seem to mind sharing. At least, not right now when he's got a full belly and a warm place to hunker down, and I can't say I feel much different once I have a chance to sit on a nearby bench with another meal assembled from my saddle bags. I'd be all too content to linger here versus heading back out a few hours later had it not been obligatory.

At least, I *think* it's about that long.

I'm fiddling with my broken watch again when I walk into the saloon, pausing once I'm through the slatted, wooden doors to slip it back in my front vest pocket and to brush the worst of the dirt off my clothes. Something I probably should've done outside based on the amount of trail dust that billows from my coat and hat.

I hadn't really bothered getting fancy. For one, I already cleaned up in the river this morning. For two, I'm already wearing one of my nicer dark red button-up shirts underneath my vest, along with my minimally-patched brown wool pants. It's the extent of effort on my part that this outing warrants and, regardless of the occasion, I'm not about to go around looking like some stuck-up snob when I ain't one.

"*Aiden.*" Maddock calls my name from a nearby table, raising his hand to beckon me over when I look in his direction, and I nod to show I've seen him so he won't say it again before I head his way.

"You have our agreement?" I ask as soon as I reach the table, and it's obvious he's not pleased with me being so curt by how he takes a quick look around to see if any of his other men heard. Can't be letting them get any ideas about the respect he's due.

"After," he mutters quietly before raising his volume and saying, "Glad to have you with us. Why don't you take a seat?"

"Now," I retort. "Or I'm gone."

I get more than a little bit of enjoyment seeing his whole face turn a deeper shade of crimson in his anger, a sharp reply most definitely on the tip of his tongue before I'm spared by the sound of chair legs scraping against the wood floor as someone else prepares to take their place in the game.

"Good evening, gentlemen," greets a smooth, low voice that would be enough to make me turn if I didn't know better than to put my back to Maddock right now. "You know, I don't think I've ever been so anxious for a game to begin." There's a smattering of laughs in response. "Nor so enthused by the players."

Their laughter shifts into encouragement as more than one man at the table starts calling for the owner of the voice to join them. The ruckus is enough that I almost *do* look to see who it is anyway before Maddock reclaims my attention by reaching inside his coat to take hold of a document that he then slaps against my chest.

I grab it from him, unfolding it to glance at the contents and confirm he's not completely full of it before I take the subsequently offered pen and lean over the table to add my signature below his.

"Everything to your satisfaction?" Maddock asks as I finish, clearly irked by my distrust as well as my disobedience. "You'll have a seat now?"

"Of course," I tell him, the corner of my mouth ticking up just to piss him off more as I stash the agreement in my pocketbook and sidestep him for the bar. Out of the corner of my eye, I see him almost think to go after me again like he did outside the hotel before he changes his mind, likely not wanting to draw attention to the fact that he's already losing.

One week, I tell myself after the bartender sets a tumbler of whiskey in front of me a few minutes later. I'll have to make the half-full glass last all night if I want an excuse to be taking up space, especially on a night when the noise around me is growing at the same pace as the crowd. *One week and then you're out.*

When I finally look back at Maddock's game, I wonder if his dissatisfaction has lessened given that his table is already full even without me there, each seat claimed by either him, his men, the dealer, or one of the other poor souls that they roped into playing with them.

If Maddock were as smart as he prefers to think he is, he'd spread his posse out a bit. Have a few different games going at once to improve their chances of making it big, but that might interfere with Maddock's desire to want to *feel* big by dominating the table. No matter how unnecessary that effort appears to be at first glance.

Of the three unfamiliar faces in the game, one is an older man who seems at ease enough I'd presume him to be local. Although it could also be that he simply isn't concerned about any money he might lose tonight since the cigar he's chewing probably cost more than some people make in a year.

The second is a grizzled cowhand, who very much looks like he's lived his entire life on the trail and is tough enough to still be here to talk about it. The calluses on his hands are so thick that the cards catch on them when he tries to shuffle them around, and something tells me that he won't throw away his survival streak on a bad hand.

All in all, a pair that is unlikely to cause Maddock, and therefore *me*, much trouble. Although, I'm not sure I can say the same about the last one...

He's harder to make out, yet I immediately identify him as the same man I caught a glimpse of walking into the hotel earlier, even though his face is still hidden from me beneath the brim of his pristine black hat that matches his coat, his vest, his pants, and...fuck's sake, his *shirt*. The man is head to toe in black, and I can't tell if it's because he's a preacher or a devil.

Suppose he could be both.

As if he can feel my attention on him, he looks up, his gaze connecting with mine just as the dealer passes a card his way, and I could swear the breath gets chased right out of my lungs.

It's his eyes. I'm sure that's what it is. Light blue in a way I've never seen before, but also calculating in a way that I definitely have. *Shit.*

Seeming equally caught off guard by me, his hand stalls over his new card for a few moments too long before he *grins*, then swings his focus back to the table as the players start placing their bets.

Maybe I imagined it. Or maybe I didn't…

No, I can *feel* it. Can *see* it in that half second between his losing hands, in that fleeting look of triumph that shouldn't be on his face but is when no one else is looking, in the way he *tap, tap, taps* his fingers on the table when Maddock is talking and he's feeling impatient.

No one seems to notice but me. Not remotely concerned enough to pick up on his tells when they don't believe they need to know them to win. However, the longer the game goes on, the more convinced I am that their faith is misplaced.

I'm also convinced he *knows* I'm watching, because every now and again, I catch him watching me, too. Those fucking *eyes.* Every time they turn in my direction, something crackles beneath my skin. An awareness. Christ, practically a fucking premonition that tells me to keep a wise distance.

"Well, it really has been thrilling, gentlemen, but I'm afraid I must depart." The man in black's voice carries over to me again after a few long hours have passed, the reach of his words helped by the fact that he's now standing, bracing himself over the table as he gathers the small amount he has left after finally winning the last hand. "My heart simply isn't at the table this evening."

I roll my eyes, shift in my seat, listen to the round of protests from the other men at the table, the pleas even from the old cowboy that he stay for one more game or, at the very least, join them again tomorrow. He kindly waves them off as he takes his coat from the back of his chair, making a good show of putting up a fight until he, of course, gives in and agrees.

"Whether it's heart or luck," Maddock says, standing too with a broad smile and extending his hand with a laugh. "For your sake, I hope you get your hands on at least one of them by tomorrow."

Without hesitating, the man clasps Maddock's palm in his, but his eyes flick my way once more, finding me and holding my gaze as he hesitates near the door. "You know," he says back, "I'm still hoping for both."

CHAPTER 5
AIDEN

I follow him.

Before I can stop myself, I'm out of my chair and walking out the back door of the saloon, planning to loop around to the street so that I can *keep* following without anyone—including him—being the wiser. As I round the corner into the side alley, my hand is already hovering over my gun, the pace of my steps picking up as I consider how far down the street he could have made it.

Not very far. As it turns out.

"Oh, I *really* do hope you're looking for me."

I jump at the disembodied voice, quickly drawing my pistol and pivoting to face the figure leaning against the wall at the mouth of the alley, the one who is almost impossible to see in the low light from the street's oil lamps.

I must have walked right past him without realizing it. All that damn black is certainly not helping, although the fact that he seems entirely unconcerned at having a gun drawn on him might be even more unsettling. He appears almost *amused* before he glances toward the street then back at me. His eyebrows rise as if to say, *You sure you want to do this here?*

In answer, I step back into the alley, drawing even with him as the shadows swallow me up. My vision adjusts in time for me to see him push off the wall and move toward me in return.

Now that he's closer, I note I have a couple inches on him, just enough that he has to tilt his head slightly to meet my gaze. Enough, too, for me to make out his features a little better than I could inside the saloon.

Mid-to-late-twenties like me, I'd guess. Dark hair beneath his hat and a tidy mustache on his face. Sharp jaw, sharp nose, and a cutting smile. Not to mention those fuckin' eyes that feel like they could slice right through a person.

A devil, for certain. *Although*, with that awareness simmering beneath my skin again, I can't say he isn't a good-lookin' one. Disarmingly so. Which I'll just bet comes in handy for him in more ways than one.

"Cypress." He offers his hand now as if I'm not still aiming to shoot him and looks genuinely disappointed when I don't take it, waiting a few moments longer just in case I might change my mind before he withdraws. "Not at the name stage yet, then?"

I narrow my eyes at him and he smiles again, same as he did when he first caught me looking, and it only confirms my suspicions that the expressions he aimed at the others inside were anything *but* genuine. That the ones I glimpsed when no one else was watching, the ones he *saw* me glimpse while he was busy watching me, were the true ones. And somehow just as beguiling as his eyes…

"I know what you're up to," I tell him, hoping to wipe the look from his face but his grin only broadens. "I know *you*," I add.

"Do you?" He sounds…pleased. Hopeful, even. "You know, I was feeling the same."

My stomach tightens, guilt and shame rearing up before I have a chance to reason with myself that, in this case, him knowing who I am is a *good* thing. "If you recognize me, then you should also recognize the position you're in."

"Yes. Not quite my favorite yet." He hums something that sounds like the beginning of a song. "I've been looking for you, too, you know."

"Why?" I snarl back. "You got a death wish?"

"Not today." He steps neatly to my left, out of the way of my gun until I move to follow. He starts to make a half circle, me turning with him, and any remaining ideas I had of him throwing up his hands in surrender once confronted completely dry up.

"You should've moved on," I tell him, and he shakes his head, smirking.

"So I've been told. But how fortunate, it's never really been my strong suit."

"It'll be the suit you're buried in if you don't do as I say." I keep my pistol aimed, thinking I should put some space between us even though I can't seem to get my feet to move. "I mean it. I know what you're doing. I know you're a fuckin' thief."

"A *thief*?" he repeats, pausing briefly in his path. "That is quite the accusation." His expression looks more curious than concerned. "What evidence do you have?"

"I had my eye on you tonight."

"I noticed." That grin again. "But that means you know I lost far more than I took. Wouldn't appear to make me a very good thief, would it?"

I shrug, undeterred. "Depends on what you're after."

"And what do you think that might be?" Instead of stepping sideways this time, he takes one step toward me and then another, continuing until he's standing right in front of me. The barrel of my gun presses into his chest, directly over his heart, so that all I'd have to do is pull the trigger.

But I don't.

He smiles again after a few moments pass with us remaining just like that, with him not taking his eyes off mine. At the last second, he finally shifts to walk past me, brushing his shoulder against my own as he goes. "I'll be seeing you, wolf."

Wolf? I turn to watch as he disappears into the night after one last lingering backwards glance, the slowly reemerging sounds of people on the street out front the only thing enough to finally make me drop my arm against my side. To make me drop against the same wall where he'd been waiting for me.

Who the fuck was that?

My heart is racing now that the moment is gone and I have a chance to think. Gut feelings aside, the truth—much as I hate to admit it—is that he's right. I have no evidence for the accusation I made. And if he *is* a thief, then he's a damn poor one since all he managed to do tonight was leave with his pockets lighter.

If he does come back tomorrow, I'll have to continue to keep my eye on him, as well as my distance. Because any man who worries so little about his own mortality is one best avoided unless strictly necessary.

And it isn't. It *isn't* necessary, because he *isn't* my responsibility either. I sigh, tilting my head back against the wall and catching enough of a glimpse of the star-filled sky that I wonder how late it is.

Out of habit, my free hand strays to my vest, reaching for my pocket watch only to find…nothing. I straighten, looking down and searching again as if it will suddenly appear before moving on to my pants pockets, and I must be more tired than I think because only when I've reholstered my gun and am *uselessly* patting myself down does it finally click.

"No…" I stride out to the street, searching up and down for someone who already moved on just as I told him to, his pockets no longer quite as light. "He fuckin' robbed me."

CHAPTER 6
CYPRESS

I think I might be in love. The feeling, however, does not appear to be mutual. Yet.

It does not appear to be mutual *yet*.

I feel like I at least managed to get under his skin a little? Left him wanting more? Even if it left me wanting more, too.

Seems only fair. I'd be lying if I said I wasn't disappointed that our first interaction was so brief, but this is still…something. And after all this time, if *something* is all I get, then I'll take it.

I rotate the pocket watch in my palm as I watch him from another concealed spot. Following the way he storms around the stable while muttering obscenities, and I really would prefer it if he'd be a bit louder so I could tell if he's more angry with me or with himself.

After all, by his own admission, he knew me to be a thief and I still lifted his watch from his pocket with minimal effort. Not exactly how I imagined getting my hands on him, but I'd been unable to resist provoking a little of the temper I'd seen simmering beneath the surface.

Likely *not* my best judgment, since he could very easily go back and tell his colleagues that I'm not to be trusted. Ruin a perfectly good town for me as well as a full night's worth of work. But I am almost certain he won't.

Wounded pride aside, he doesn't seem the type to ask for assistance based on the way he'd tracked me into that alley alone. Nor does he seem the type to admit a misstep to the company he's riding with.

He's very clearly the outsider of the bunch. The only one that does not appear to want to lead or be led. A lone wolf in every sense of the word.

At last. After *so* long waiting, I'd almost given up hope, and how lucky that I didn't, because while our moment in the alley was disappointingly brief, *he* is anything *but* disappointing. Handsome to the point of indecency. Hot-tempered to the point of recklessness. Perceptive to the point of being able to *see* me—which is arguably even more attractive than his looks. Plus, he's so damn *broody*, wound so tight that all I want to do is unravel him.

In truth, he is bigger than I thought he'd be. But it can never be said that I don't appreciate a challenge.

For now though, he's still rustling around, searching his belongings as if his lost possession will suddenly appear anywhere but in my hand, yanking at the ends of his hair every few minutes in what I suspect must be a sign that he's upset.

I frown and glance down at the pocket watch, already having noticed that it's more than a little… Well, it doesn't work, which seems like it would be a problem. He must be attached to it for other reasons, since its ability to accurately tell time certainly isn't the culprit.

Maybe it was a mistake to take it from him. Until tonight, it had actually been quite some time since I'd truly *stolen* anything. Years, by my recollection, although some might disagree with that view of things. Semantics and all that.

But there he was calling me a thief, and in the moment, I was willing to be just about anything he wanted.

I *could* walk over there right now and give it back. But I'm not sure I want to give him a chance to kill me twice in one day.

Why rush things?

I tuck the watch safely back in my pocket, catching a different pair of eyes on me as I do.

"What?" I whisper, looking back at Cerberus, the black Andalusian stallion who has served as one of my few constants ever since I won him in a game some years ago as a yearling. His past caretaker one of those who would argue *semantics* on that victory.

In what I can only assume to be an answer to my question, Cerberus continues to stare at me before letting out an extended exhale. *You know what.*

I chuckle quietly, reaching up to scratch behind his ear. "Come on now, we're overdue for a little excitement. Been a while since we've needed to really make a run for it. Besides, wouldn't you like a friend?"

Cerberus opts to change the subject, not so subtly nudging my pockets for treats before I acquiesce to his demands by giving him an apple from my coat, an offering he happily chews while I think about how I need to be getting back to the hotel.

If I don't go soon, I'll be missing out on my chance to take a quick peek inside the other rented but currently unoccupied rooms, therefore also missing an opportunity to take inventory of anything they might have of value, whether object or information. And I really do need—

I need to know about him, my thoughts argue, immediately reverting back to the surly cowboy in the stall at the other end of the aisle. *And he's* not *there.*

I had noticed the way he'd practically refused to come inside when he first arrived. Same way I'd noticed his name. *Aiden.*

A good name. A *strong* name. I think I'll really enjoy saying it. In all sorts of contexts. And I'll bet I can make him enjoy hearing it, too, far more than he does when that feckless man he has for an employer says it.

When I'd entered the hotel earlier, I'd purposefully lingered to overhear the conversation between the two of them once Aiden had undeniably and immediately drawn my interest, even going so far as to pretend to check my pocketbook just on the other side of the door of the front parlor. A dual-purpose activity, since it not only allowed me to continue to eavesdrop but also to *accidentally* let the men inside see how much money I had with me.

How fortunate it was *right* when they were discussing their plans for the poker table, too…and how nice of them to then nearly fall over themselves to make introductions once they were sure I was more than capable of buying in.

It's so *easy* sometimes. Barely worth my effort to conceal anything. Not when they are so quick to show me everything and anything I need to make them wish they'd never seen me at all.

I'd actually started to get bored.

But I'm not bored now.

This is going to be fun.

CHAPTER 7
AIDEN

When I wake up in the morning, there is a horse in the next stall. Coal-black coat and head tall enough to reach right over the wall separating his quarters from ours, which is exactly what he's doing when I crack my eyes open to the sound of the mustang stomping his hoof in a clear sign of irritation. To his credit, he's doing it at a safe enough distance from me that I don't end up with a horseshoe imprint somewhere on my body. Although it doesn't seem to be very effective, since his neighbor appears blissfully ignorant that he should entertain himself elsewhere.

I groan, sitting up on my bedroll before getting to my feet and stretching out after a nearly sleepless night spent on the hard ground. Far from comfortable, but seeing as how I've slept on and in worse, I can't really complain.

"You might want to stay to your own," I tell the new arrival, not wanting to seem like a turncoat by giving in to the urge to give him a pat on his great big nose. "At least until after breakfast. He's not real friendly until then." The mustang turns to look at me, his ears pinned with agitation, and I tack on, "Or really after."

The other horse whickers in my direction but remains where he is, so I decide to try and intervene in their oncoming dispute by getting a rope on the mustang and leading him away to a small pasture outside, one of only two that doesn't currently have other horses. Here at least he will be able to graze in peace, or so I think until a young stablehand emerges a few minutes later.

"You have to put him there?" I ask as he leads the newcomer into the other pen right next to us, my tone coming out more annoyed than the situation probably warrants, but that damn horse is starting to remind me of the man I met last night. Even if I can't imagine anyone so dramatic as to dress head to toe in black *and* to ride an all-black horse as if they were one of the four horsemen come to Soldana.

"Sorry?" the boy asks me, understandably confused by my question, and God, unlike Maddock's tagalong, this one really *is* a kid. No more than ten years old, and I wonder if he's got kin nearby to look after him. "Mister, I've been given specific instructions to—"

"Never mind," I mutter, waving him off with the hope that the horse will have far more pressing things to occupy his time than provoking my—*the* mustang once he's free to roam. Plus, there's other horses on his side of the pasture, so surely…

As soon as the stablehand slips the pricey-looking halter off his nose, the determined pest ambles right up to the adjoining fence and calls over to us as if we're good friends meeting up on a Sunday outing.

"Guess we've both got problems to deal with today," I tell the mustang, who appears as bewildered by this behavior as I am, opting to try to follow me back out of the pasture rather than to stay and make conversation.

"Try not to kill him," I suggest, giving the horse a consolatory pat after closing the gate on him. Before I go, I wrap his lead rope several times around the adjoining fence post, tying it off in a secure, tight knot. "I'll try to do the same."

CHAPTER 8
AIDEN

After debating most of the morning, I start with the shops. In part because they're the only places I can think to look besides the saloon, which is closed to me at this particular hour, and the hotel, which is closed to me at every hour.

The shops are also simply the most logical place for someone to go if they have something they are anxious to get rid of for a quick payout. Not that the watch will fetch him much in its current state. Still, the fact remains that it *is* mine, that he lifted it from *me*, and that I am *really* ticked off about it.

No one has gotten the upper hand on me like that in a long time, and it pisses me off all the more that it's my own damn fault. I'm the one who charged out there with some half-cocked plan to confront him. With no evidence, as he was so kind to point out, right before he gave me some by robbing me. It's fucking infuriating. Knowing he's out there. *Grinning* because I let him make a fool of me and walk away free.

I want—no, I *need* another shot at him. And tracking Cypress down now is probably the only one I'll get.

Cypress. Odd name for an odd sort, but I have to hand it to him, the name is as hard to forget as he is. The entirety of our interaction kept me up tossing and turning until the early hours of the morning wondering *why* I'd done what I'd done, as well as why he'd been so unafraid despite thinking he knows who I am…

To be frank, none of it makes any sense to me, including why I think I have a chance of finding him. Parting words aside, he'd have to be crazy not to have taken stock of things during our conversation, to realize he'd been caught regardless of if I had proof, and to skip town as soon as he turned the corner.

In all likelihood, he only took the watch to try to prevent the night from being a total loss. He has to already be gone…

A bell jingles merrily overhead as I push through the doors anyway to the small jeweler located not far from the hotel. The third establishment I've visited this morning since the general store and the haberdashery both came up empty. As soon as I cross the threshold, I'm greeted by a young woman with her long dark hair swept up into a bun at her nape and her light yellow dress buttoned all the way to her chin, which, I think, is the fashion these days.

"Welcome in," she says warmly, and even in my current mood, I'd have to be dead not to notice she's pretty. Even has freckles on her nose. Always have had a weak spot for freckles. "Can I help you find something?"

Preparing to answer her, I clear my throat as I step up to the counter, temporarily distracted by wondering how long it's even been since someone caught my gaze. Although, when a sharp jawline and a pair of blue eyes promptly spring unbidden to mind, I immediately scowl and push them right back out, muttering, "Absolutely fucking not."

"Excuse me?" the woman asks, drawing herself up with an aggravated frown, understandably thinking I was talking to her. "I assure you, I can help just as adequately as any of my counterparts. Why, only this morning—"

I hold up my hand. "No, miss, I—I'm sorry, I was thinking of somethin' and…" I trail off with an exasperated sigh. *What is wrong with me?* Has to be that I'm back in town. Always makes me jumpy. And apparently…an idiot.

"Wasn't meant for you. I'm sorry," I say again. "I would be grateful if you could help me. I've been looking for someone or, I guess, some*thing*."

She eases the severity in her expression a bit but the remaining purse to her lips tells me I'm not completely forgiven. "A gift, perhaps?"

"A gift?" I repeat, as if the concept is foreign to me.

She takes a deep breath, clearly praying for patience. "Maybe for someone special?"

I start to laugh, but then realize that isn't going to make her less irritated with me. "No, I—" My eyes dart to her bare left hand to confirm my earlier assumption before I put my foot in my mouth again. "Miss, I'm actually after a watch."

"I see." Her eyes brighten, the hint of a smile on her mouth now. "That is a popular request today."

"That so?" A rare burst of cautious optimism makes my eyebrows rise beneath my hat, reminding me that I'm still rudely wearing one before I quickly take it off. "Did someone come in and sell one?"

Just as quickly, my hope dims as her expression shifts back to a frown, her forehead scrunching. "No, afraid not. There was a man in to *buy* one, though. The most expensive we had in stock." She's suddenly teeming with excitement again. "A *gorgeous* piece."

"How nice," I mutter, having no doubt now why she's smiling when she thinks of that interaction versus this one. Payday is enough to improve anyone's mood.

"His *was* a gift," she continues, voice gone soft and dreamy. "Lucky soul. Whoever they are. Having someone like that."

"Right." I shift uncomfortably, feeling more ridiculous by the minute. "Well, sorry to bother you. If you do happen to have someone come in, then…"

Then what? I think. *Then come to the saloon tonight and let me know? Or better yet, come walk on down to the stall I'm sleeping in at the stable? Christ.*

"Never mind," I tell her, rather than offer either option as I move toward the door. "Thank you again."

"Wait," she calls after me, making me turn, and the way she studies my face when I do lets me know what's coming before she even gets the words out. "You look familiar to me… Have you been in here before?"

"No, miss, can't say I have," I reply, reflexively putting my hat back on and ducking to hide my face as I head for the door again. "You have a good rest of your day."

I really need to get out of town.

CHAPTER 9
AIDEN

I give up my search after that, walking back to the stable with my head still low and with every intention of going for a ride until I have to be back at the saloon tonight.

It'll help. Always does. If I can clear my mind for a bit, ride fast and pretend like I don't have to turn around, it'll help. Lessen how tight my chest feels as I round the barn for the pastures, unable to stop my hands from shaking even after I shove them in my pockets and pick up my pace.

It'll help. I only need to get out of here for a little while. I only need—

I stop dead in my tracks when I reach the gate of the pasture where I left the mustang this morning, staring at the rope securing it to the fence post like it's a rattler about to bite me.

The repurposed lead was altered while I've been gone, my hasty but sturdy (or so I thought) tie-off replaced with something that looks far less effective, but I'm relieved to see that the mustang is still here and currently plodding toward me. Unfortunately, for the second time today, my relief is short-lived.

I can't get the damn thing to budge. No matter how hard I tug at the knot or at either of the loose ends, the tie holds fast, well after the mustang has arrived to observe. And he's not the only one.

"Did you do this?" I ask the same boy I'd snapped at this morning, who's stopped to watch me struggle on his way to muck stalls. "Did you mess with this gate?"

"No, sir," he says with a shake of his head. "But I know there's a trick to it." The corner of his mouth lifts as he steps up to the gate and gestures at the piece of rope in my hand. "You have to take that end and put it back through the loop first." When I only stare at him, he offers, "You need me to do it for you?"

"I got it," I reply tersely, willing to follow the instruction as long as it gets the fuckin' gate open. "Now what?"

"Tug on the end." The continued skepticism must be obvious on my face, because he adds, "Just try it. You'll see."

I give the rope a sharp jerk, still expecting nothing to happen, even as it easily comes undone in my hand.

"Neat, right?" the boy asks. "I guess it's called a quick release? I've been practicing with it all morning."

"Then it can't be very quick, can it?" I glare at him in what I hope is a clear warning. "Don't be *practicing* on my gate."

"Oh, no, I wouldn't. I'm not the one who… Say…" I'm sized up for the second time this morning, although perhaps more efficiently, given the way he starts dancing from foot to foot. "Say, are you him?"

Really, *really* need to get out of town.

"No," I tell the kid as I yank the gate open. "I'm not."

"Oh," the kid says, disappointed. "You sure? You know who I mean, right? That famous shooter? My pa and I used to see stuff about him in the paper all the time." He sighs, scuffing his filthy boots in the dirt. "I want to be *just* like him when I get big."

It's *right* there, the tattered edge of a memory, those snippets of stories in papers, of another boy and his father reading them aloud. A different memory than the one that keeps me up most nights, so close that I feel as if I could grab it if I only reached out my hand for it.

But I know better than to try.

"You don't," I say as I take the now-free rope and loop it around the mustang's neck, leading him back toward the barn. "Trust me."

CHAPTER 10
AIDEN

I keep out of Soldana until I have no choice but to go back, leaving myself barely enough time to clean up and change my clothes before I head toward the center of town.

As I walk, I can't help noticing the weather warming up with the onset of spring, that and the briskness of my step more than enough to chase away what remains of the chill from stripping down at the river again. Not exactly enjoyable but *anything* has to be better than one of those bath houses. Paying a whole quarter just to sit in another person's dirty water? Doesn't seem worth it for a bit of warmth, especially since it's already stifling inside the saloon when I push through the doors.

It's even more crowded tonight than it was last night, but I still manage to find a spot at the bar after I see Maddock give me a curt nod that almost borders on acceptance. At the very least, he makes no attempt to call me over this time, which is good, since my attention is already elsewhere.

Pushing up my sleeves in an attempt to cool off, I search every face that walks in once I'm settled in the same place again with a whiskey, waiting for a glimpse of stark blue eyes, of a wicked smile, or the sound of that voice.

I'll be seeing you, wolf.

Why *wolf?* I've turned that part over and over in my mind as much as I have everything else, perhaps more so, because I can't escape feeling that there was a hint of familiarity in the way he said it. Not just for him but also for me.

Has someone called me that before?

Is it something people started calling me, and I'm only now noticing? Maybe his way of proving he did know who I was…

I've been looking for you, too.

What the hell had he meant by *that?* If he does really know my reputation, either because he recognized me or because Maddock told him during the game, he certainly doesn't act like it. Even before I had the gun on him, when he'd seen me watching him, there'd never been a trace of that reverential caution that so many aim at me from what they believe to be a safe distance.

Can't really be *safe*, though, if they truly think me to be capable of everything they hear, can they?

Doesn't matter. There's no way he actually appears. In fact, I'm certain he's halfway to hell by now. Except the doors choose that moment to swing open and—

Speak of the devil.

Rather than running for the hills, Cypress walks in as if he owns the place, shaking outstretched hands with a broad smile beneath his hat and calling everyone by name as he moves through the crowd. As he does, it's as if everything recenters around him, his long coat constantly sweeping out behind him every time he pivots to greet someone new until it, and him, finally settle at his destination.

"I'm here to try my chances again, gentlemen," he begins, standing at the head of Maddock's poker table, though his eyes flick my direction as he adds, "It would seem that I simply *cannot* stay away."

As if needling me is all simply a part of the game he's playing, he fucking *winks* at me then, and my temper gets up even faster than I do, the barstool I'd been sitting on nearly falling backwards in my wake. Fortunately, none of the other patrons appear to notice, but *he* does. Despite all the activity around him, his focus remains entirely on me, his mouth crooking into that sly grin that pairs so well with the challenge in his blue eyes.

I swear, it's as if he *wants* me to come after him, like it's the whole reason he's shown himself tonight at all, and I don't realize how close I am to taking him up on it until I hear Maddock call for him to take his chair. The tone, more than the demand itself, draws me up short from the step I'd been about to take.

The obvious contrast to the way Maddock always speaks to me versus the way he's speaking right now. The complete lack of condescension and disdain. Of anything beyond that he's delighted, *pleased* as can be that his new acquaintance has made his appearance. Just the same as everyone else is.

The longer Cypress and I hold this silent showdown, the more apparent the difference in our situations becomes. His offered chair quickly followed by offered drinks, by hearty backslaps, by a goddamn *toast* to his arrival. *Fuck's sake.* Was there really this much upheaval when he arrived yesterday? There must have been and I simply hadn't noticed, because how else would it be possible to become this well connected in the span of a day?

Even if I used my reputation, given that I have not similarly endeared myself, if I were to walk over there right now, Cypress likely wouldn't even have to lift a finger to have someone try to stop me. In fact, as the assumed leader of the welcome party, Maddock would probably have his own men toss me out on my ass. Ironic, considering the whole reason he wants me here in the first place is to protect him from such a character. And yet, there I'd be, down again without the means to get back up. And without a chance to get him back.

I let out a long exhale, my hand sweeping briefly through the still-damp strands of my hair under my hat. As if tracking the gesture, Cypress cocks his head, a frown flickering over his expression before he arches a brow at me. *Well, what'll it be?* he seems to say. *Your decision.*

My decision… My fingers twitch at my right side, a single second drawing out long enough to feel like hours, a single breath pulled in before I…I do the same thing I've been doing for the last several years.

I pull back. Take one step away, then another, each an unmistakable cue to him that the immediate threat has passed, no matter that I rest against the edge of the stool this time rather than fully reclaim the seat. I watch him while I do, expecting him to look relieved or, even worse, really fuckin' smug that he's gotten the upper hand on me not just once but twice now. Instead, I could swear he almost looks discouraged before he bends his head slightly and takes his seat himself, having no choice then but to break his gaze away and reach for the hand he's already been dealt.

Minutes tick by as he surveys his cards, shuffles the lot into some new order that he prefers, and calls the bet. All the while, the fingers of his left hand drum against the table. *Tap. Tap. Tap.* Not stilling until his eyes find mine again.

Just as the night before, few moments go by without his gaze flicking my way. Constantly watching, assessing, *searching*—for what, I don't fucking know.

But I do know I'm going to find out.

CHAPTER 11
CYPRESS

I draw everything out. Every deal. Every hand. Every decision I make to either raise the stakes or to let it all go.

I intentionally make the pace of the game so *agonizingly* slow that if the width of my pocketbook were not so tempting, I doubt a single person at the table would have been at all sad when I announce I am done for the night.

Really, they do an admirable job pretending they aren't ready to wring my neck. Truly a testament to what the human spirit can endure with the right motivation. And I have mine. Right where I want him.

Which, as it happens, is standing in front of me, slamming me up against the wall of the opposing building as soon as I'm within his reach. And now, *I* am right where I want to be, too. *Finally.*

I deserve more credit for my admirable patience as well, because I'd drawn this reunion out, too, delayed getting close until I was at my limit.

Even added an extra touch of suspense to the evening by meandering around out front with all the potential witnesses for a while before finally heading toward the alley. Fairly assured by then that he'd be waiting with his well of patience bone dry.

Should I feel bad for antagonizing him the way I am? Probably. But when the results are this satisfying…who could fault me?

"There—there you are, wolf," I say, the words coming out with somewhat of a wheeze due to the wind being knocked out of me. In part by the solid wooden boards connecting with my back and in part by the abrupt reminder of how large Aiden is as he puts me against those wooden boards without much difficulty.

He is so very handsome, his furious features illuminated by the lantern light from the nearby street. Warm amber eyes. Rich brown waves in his hair. A short, scruffy beard that would feel so nice scraping across skin. *Devastatingly* handsome, as they say. And I absolutely will be *devastated* if he doesn't turn out to be who I think he is. I'm already so attached.

"Now we're really…" I start, forced to try again after I look down to where he has his fists balled up in my coat. "*Really* getting closer."

"To what?" he scoffs, anger radiating off him. "Your untimely demise?"

I shake my head, managing a smile as I say, "My favorite position."

He searches my face momentarily before he catches my meaning, what appears to be color striking his cheekbones, and a thrill of excitement runs up my spine when I realize he is currently *blushing*.

Oh, this *is* going to be fun.

"Real cute," Aiden mutters, his tone telling me that he doesn't mean it in a complimentary way. Although I don't think it's *too* much of a weakness to hope he thinks I'm at least somewhat nice to look at.

"You're crazier than I thought," he continues, his voice menacingly low. "Here I was telling myself that you would have already left town."

I frown, genuinely confused. "Why would I do that?"

"Why?" he asks through gritted teeth. "You fuckin' *robbed* me."

"Ah, that." Despite the somewhat violent nature of our greeting, I've kept my hands raised throughout our conversation, nowhere near his pockets, and I glance at them to make sure he's noticed. "In my defense, you *did* call me a thief."

"And clearly, I was right to."

"But would I have robbed you if you *hadn't* called me a thief?" I ask, giving him the best shrug I can manage with my movements so constricted. "There is a question that will keep you up at night."

"Already have plenty of things to keep me up at night," he snarls back. "Not going to let you be one of them."

"We'll see." I cock my head. "But since we're on the subject, what *does* keep you up at night? Anyone I should be concerned about?"

He only stares at me in response, seemingly unable to comprehend why I would ask him that question. To be fair, I can't really comprehend it either beyond the fact that I have a burning desire to learn everything about any topic that centers around him.

"Too forward? Are we not at that stage yet either?"

Aiden grips my coat tighter, yanking me forward for a moment before shoving me back. I hit the wall again with a solid thud, and I hope whatever business is next to the saloon doesn't operate at night. Or at least has customers that know better than to stick their noses into the affairs of those that do. I'd hate to be interrupted.

Unfortunately, Aiden seems to have the same concern, and in a needless attempt to prevent my escape, he places the wide palm of his left hand against my chest to keep me pinned, his now-free right hand pulling a knife from his belt. The small blade glints in that same low lantern light as he brings it up close to me, and that's all it takes for him to no longer be the only thing keeping me trapped.

"You done?" he asks as my focus remains fixed on the knife, my hands instinctively gripping the arm he has keeping me in place, my fingertips pressing hard into the bare skin beneath his rolled-up sleeves. "You have it all out of your system?"

I shake my head, trying to pull my gaze away from the sharp edge before it can pull me away instead. To another place. To another time. To a dark, windowless room where I had never felt so alone. Until I wasn't. "Far from it."

"Figured as much," Aiden replies, and he presses the cool metal into the space just below my jaw. "How about now? How about, instead of running your mouth and wasting more of my time, you go ahead and tell me what you're up to? Why did you say you were looking for me?"

I wonder if he can feel it. How rapid my pulse has gotten. Can he feel it racing in my chest through my clothes, feel it racing in my throat through the blade? I have no choice but to believe he can.

"Come on, don't go quiet on me now," Aiden pushes, pressing the knife in a little more. A little more. A little more. Knocking the wind out of me again. "And don't bother trying to come up with some lie. I already know you're conning those men in there."

"And if I am?" My voice is shaking, though I try to hide it with a laugh. "Why would you care? You're not one of them."

I'm not sure if I say it for him or for me. I'm not sure who needs the reminder more. *He's not. He's not one of them.*

He's not going to hurt me.

"You're right. I'm not," he says, and I wonder if he can now feel my heart rate slowing with his acknowledgement. "I'm not like them." He leans closer, his voice dropping into an even lower register that seems to cozy up to every dangerous thought inside my head. "I'm way worse. Especially for you."

"Oh, I'm quite positive that's not the case."

"You really think it's smart to aggravate me right now? To insult me?" he asks, looming over me in an attempt at a threat, and it would probably be a very good one. On anyone else.

Rather than escalating my fear, my fingers loosen their grip around his forearm now that he's closer, and I must have been holding on tighter than I realized because even in the flickering light, I can see the blood-red indents my nails left in his skin.

Unlikely to be permanent, but judging by the way he doesn't even look at them, would he mind if they were? Would he mind the marks that are permanent on me?

"You think I'm insulting you?" I ask, repeating part of his question as my eyes remain locked on his. "While you've got a knife to my throat?"

He nods, still crowding into me, still pressing enough that one wrong move would have me bleeding. I grin. "Afraid only compliments come to mind."

Similar to earlier, the suggestion has the deeply satisfying effect of making him flustered, so much so that he actually steps back, and it requires all my remaining shreds of self-control not to chase him when he does.

"*Christ*," he mutters, eyeing me from the opposite side of the alley. "The fuck is wrong with you?"

"A combination of things," I say, doing my best to smooth out my rumpled clothes without having much success. "If you're going to try your fists next, you should know I tend to favor my left side. Gives me an advantage more often than you might think."

I look back up, only to see Aiden is now staring at the ground, shaking his head as he kneads the back of his neck with his hand. I could almost swear he's trying not to laugh.

"Are you some kind of punishment?" he asks finally, when he has composed himself. "Some sort of retribution?"

"Why?" I ask him, curious why this would be his assumption. "What have you done?"

He shakes his head once more. "Oh...*a combination of things.*"

I grin, hearing my words directed back at me, and my only intention is to extend this special moment following his threats against my life when I say, "I believe it." However, his shoulders fall, telling me he doesn't hear it the way I meant it. Hears it instead as a censure.

"Ah," I say, the realization dawning. "You're religious."

His head whips back up. "What?"

"You're religious. Makes sense."

His eyes narrow. "What makes sense?"

"You seem somewhat..." I take him in head to toe, thinking about the earlier blushing as well as how his entire body is currently coiled tight. "Repressed?" Unable to help myself, I also ask, "Catholic?" His jaw ticks as I seemingly strike his own vulnerability, similar to how he had unknowingly just struck mine. "I'll take that as a yes."

"You can take it however you want."

My eyebrows rise.

"*Look*," he says, really seeming ready to take a swing at me. "I'm not here to discuss morals with the man who robbed me in this same fucking alley last night."

"Aren't you supposed to, though?" I counter.

"Aren't I supposed to *what*?" he responds, fatigue and irritation warring in his voice.

"Aren't you supposed to try? To save my soul? Lead me down the path of righteousness? Bring me to my knees?" I offer, hoping that last option will appeal to him as much as it does to me. "Isn't that your calling? As a good Catholic?"

Aiden scoffs, folding his arms across his chest. "Afraid you're going to have to find God on your own."

"Ah." I watch closely for his reaction as I suggest, "But it's so much more enjoyable with a partner. Sometimes even more than one."

His mouth actually falls open a bit, and I have to bite the inside of my cheek to the point of bloodshed to keep my expression neutral. After a prolonged moment, Aiden starts to say something, thinks better of it, then closes his mouth before trying again. "Would you just give me my watch so I can leave? And, *God* willing, never see you again?"

"All right," I say easily even as his words sting, sticking my hands in my pockets and checking the contents as I walk closer. "I *am* sorry, by the way. About your watch. It was wrong of me to take it."

"You're sorry?" He stares at me, clearly surprised by my quick agreement and likely struggling to come up with anything to say back that would be appropriate for polite company. "All that and you're *sorry*?"

"Yes." I continue to watch him, weighing the two options in my pockets the closer I get. "Are you sentimental over it? The watch?"

"Am I *sentimental* over it?" he asks, repeating my words again, since he still seems to be at a loss for his own. "Don't you think it's a little late to be asking if I'm *sentimental* over something you took?"

"You really don't like to answer direct questions, do you?" I push, needing more to go on.

"Probably about as much as you like to provide direct answers."

"Oh, trust me, I would prefer nothing more than to be direct with you." I'm standing in front of him now, little more than a foot of space between us. "Does that watch mean something to you? Is that why you still had it even though it's broken?"

"Notice that, did you?" he asks, not bothering to put space between us once more. "Before or after you tried to sell it?"

"I didn't try to sell it," I correct, wanting us to understand each other on this front at least. "It was never my intention to profit off you."

"Sure," he says, disbelief evident and, frankly, unsurprising given the people he's riding with. Which is why I remind myself to be patient before opening my mouth to argue. I've waited this long. I can wait longer.

"Did someone give it to you?" I ask, a slight pain in my chest when I also suggest, "Perhaps a loved one?"

At the question, there's a sadness in his eyes that even the dark can't hide, but he covers it quickly. "Would it matter?"

"Yes," I say, suddenly desperate to know despite *just* telling myself to be patient. "If it holds special significance…if it's special to you—"

"I got it from a trader in Sante Fe two years ago," he interrupts, starting to turn away. "Wasn't worth what I paid for it then and it certainly isn't worth all this, so I tell you what, why don't you just keep it?"

"If it wasn't worth it," I ask, barely containing the urge to follow him as he gets closer to the street, "why buy it in the first place?"

"Because I wanted a watch like that."

"Why did you—"

"*To track the fuckin' time*," he snaps, pivoting to face me at the mouth of the alley. "I wanted a watch, and that's what I could afford." He lifts his hat, tugging at the strands, the same tell he had back in the saloon. In the stable. "Not all of us just take what we want. That *direct* enough for you?"

Before I am able to answer, he's already gone.

CHAPTER 12
AIDEN

I don't sleep again, still too busy mulling over everything that happened in the alley. Debating with myself *precisely* where I lost control of the conversation as well as the situation as a whole. It's better than the things that usually keep me awake, but even so…

There's something about Cypress that makes me feel off-kilter, and it's not simply his irritating tendency to share every stray thought that crosses through his head. It's also that he never responds in the way I think he will. It's that I've threatened him twice (with varying degrees of success) and in both standoffs, he's made no attempt to retaliate or to defend himself. Even with the watch…

But would I have robbed you if you hadn't *called me a thief? There is a question that will keep you up at night.*

I really *hate* that he gets to be right, because it fuckin' did. That question *had* kept me up last night, but not nearly as much as another one had.

Why was he so afraid of the knife?

My pistol he'd walked right up to, practically lined himself up in its sights for me, which is why I'd thought to try a different approach. But the knife—that *had* scared him. Enough to make him not just nervous but afraid. Really, truly afraid.

In those few moments when I first held my knife to his throat, I'd seen it in him. Sure, I'd felt it in his heartbeat thundering beneath my palm, in the crescent-moon cuts he left in my skin, but more than anything, I'd seen it in his eyes. I'd seen a man who not only knew of death but also knew precisely what he looked like when he came to collect.

I'd seen the weakness, and just like I'd been taught to do, just like I had taught *myself* to do, I'd exploited it. Or at least, I'd tried to. But the more I attempted to throw him, the more he'd dug into me.

Then he'd fucking *flirted* with me, and I'd jumped back as if he'd scalded me with a red-hot branding iron.

God, why does he keep doing that? Can't be normal, can he? Surely it's a sign of some severe imbalance to make advances at the person trying to kill you, regardless of if that person actually means them and regardless of how effective—

Not that his advances *are* effective. Entirely ineffective, I'd say. Goes without saying that Cypress is not the type of individual I would ever take an interest in. He's…well, he's a fucking thief, and that's more than enough reason.

It's been a while for me is all. That's what this is. It's been a while since I've had someone, and undeniably, he *is* attractive. Charismatic. Sharp-witted. Could even say funny…in a way that is *really* fuckin' irritating.

Anyone would react the same way. My reaction *is* normal, even if his isn't. I am fine. Even if he isn't. I am not the problem here, and there is—

There is a handkerchief that isn't mine on my bedroll. To be specific, there is a black, *silk* handkerchief tied up like wrapping for a goddamn Christmas present on my *goddamn* bedroll.

I close my eyes and take a deep breath, but when I open them, it's still fucking there. Somehow having appeared in the span of the five minutes I had just spent walking the mustang out to his paddock for the morning.

Rather than go right for the parcel, I first look over my shoulder, then peer up and down the aisle around the corner of the stall, expecting to see the only person who could be the owner of the abandoned fabric lurking in the darkened corners, as he is so very fond of doing. When he remains suspiciously absent, I direct my inquiry to the next best thing.

"I know that's his. And so are you," I say, pointing an accusatory finger at the black horse in the next stall, who is once again hanging his head over the wall to keep an eye on everything I'm doing and appearing decidedly morose now that I've led his reluctant companion away for a little while. "Of *course* you're his. Neither of you know how to keep a boundary, and *clearly*, he knows where I'm staying. *Christ*, he probably has that boy spyin—"

"You need something, mister?" calls a small voice from down the aisle. "Them knots giving you problems again?"

"*No,*" I shout back but hear his footsteps coming closer anyway. Without thinking, I reach down, grab the small parcel, and shove it in my coat pocket right as the boy pops up at the stall door.

"You sure you're okay? Thought I heard you talkin' to somebody."

"No. I was just…" I drag a hand down my face, preparing to ask a question that I'm not completely certain I want to hear the answer to. "You can be honest with me, all right? You're not in trouble. And you won't be if you tell me the truth."

The boy considers me for a moment, debating if I'm trustworthy before he eventually nods, and I continue, pointing once more at the black horse, "You took him out yesterday. Are you also the one who put him in that stall?"

He nods.

"Someone ask you to?"

Nod.

"A man?"

Nod.

"Wears a lot of black?"

Another nod.

"Fuck's sake." The boy's eyes widen. "Sorry." I grit my teeth, taking another steadying breath before I ask, "Did he tell you *why* he wanted him in that stall?"

The boy nods one more time, but seems to realize after a beat of silence that I'd like more of an answer. "He said that it'd be more, uh… what's the word he used? Oh, *covenant*?"

I stare at him. "Covenant? Or *convenient*?"

"Yeah, that's the one. Convenient."

I exhale. "He also tell you which paddock to put him in?"

"Yes, sir. The one next to whichever one you put your horse in." He scrunches his face in thought. "Say, what's that word mean? *Convenient*?"

"In this case?"

One more nod.

"A fuckin' problem."

"Oh." He frowns. "How come you say that? Isn't he a pal of yours?"

"No," I tell him, trying to keep the frustration out of my voice. "Did he tell you he was?"

"Guess not. I just figured since he wanted to be by you…" The boy frowns again. "There's this girl at my school named Sally, and I really like to be by her. But she *is* my friend. She's real smart. And pretty." He leans against the stall door, folding his arms. "Sometimes she makes me kinda nervous. But like in a nice way. You know how I mean?"

"No," I repeat without spending much time considering if I *do* know what he means. Can't say I do, but then, I'm not very good at talkin' to children. Didn't spend enough time being one, maybe.

"What else did he say?" I ask, attempting to quickly move us on from this change of topic. "Was there more than where he wants you to keep his horse?"

"Nothin' else," the boy says.

For some reason, the idea that Cypress could have had such a brief conversation is harder for me to swallow than the idea that he's been watching me more than I thought. "You swear?"

"Yes, sir."

I sigh, adjusting my hat after I drag my fingers through my hair, and the boy's expression lightens, perhaps sensing his testimony is over. "You sure you don't need help? I was thinkin', if you need to, you can use my targets."

"Your targets?" I ask, not following this second subject change any better than the first.

"Yeah, you know…to practice for your gunfights."

As usual, the reminder of who I'd been hits me like a punch in the gut, and my right fist clenches in my pocket, reminding me of the parcel. "I told you I'm not him."

"If you say so…" he says back, looking away and rolling his eyes before he tries something else. "Well, even if you ain't him, could you still give me some pointers?"

"Sure," I say, and he perks up right until I offer, "Stay out of trouble."

He rolls his eyes again, this time giving me an exasperated huff, too. "You sound like my ma," he mumbles.

"You ought to listen to her," I tell him, getting the words out even though my heart constricts in my chest. I reach into my other pocket to grab a few pennies, and apparently expecting the gesture, the boy holds out his hand for me to drop them in his palm. "If he says anything else, you'll tell me?"

To my surprise, he shrugs, but still pockets the money. "Might not. Now that I know you're not pals."

My brow furrows. I really don't know a damn thing about children. "What's that got to do with it?"

The boy shrugs again. "He pays better than you."

CHAPTER 13
AIDEN

I make it as far as two steps outside of the stable before I pull the little black bundle from my pocket, though I can't help checking over my shoulder a few more times for either Cypress or anyone else that might be on his payroll before I open it.

While it had been in my coat, I'd been able to feel the weight of it, note the hard smooth surface beneath the fabric to the extent that I already suspected what it is. But when I pull the cloth away, I have to lean against the outside of the stable to steady myself.

It *is* a pocket watch. But it is not *my* pocket watch.

This one is *beautiful,* a fine polished silver with delicate flowers and sweeping lines etched into its lid, the pattern almost appearing chaotic until you look at it close enough to make out the three distinct overlapping circles that act as its foundation. And inside—well, this one certainly functions, the three small silver hands ticking along over the simple clock face telling me how long I've been staring.

There's no question in my mind that this cost a fortune. Likely more than any other style in the shop that sold it. Just as she'd said it did.

About ten minutes later (I can't be precisely sure because for some reason continuing to use the watch feels like approval), I walk into the jeweler near the hotel for the second time. When I do, I find the same young woman behind the counter, who looks only slightly more enthused to see me now than she had the day before.

"Morning, miss." She's got a green dress on today instead of the yellow, and something about the color tugs at me in a way I can't place. "I'm afraid I need to bother you again."

"No bother," she tells me as she places the broach she'd been polishing back in its case, and I'd like to believe it. "How can I help you?"

"You told me yesterday that someone had come in and bought a watch."

"That's right," she confirms, watching me approach with a bit more interest. "A lovely piece."

I sigh, reaching into my pocket and pulling out the watch. I set it carefully on the counter in front of her before unwrapping it from the black fabric. "Would this be the one?"

Her eyes widen when she sees it, and she looks quickly between me and the item as if trying to understand how we could appear together. "It is." She places a hand on her chest, her expression turning worried. "Don't tell me…did something happen to Cypress?"

"Something's going to," I mutter, even more irritated that they seem to be on a first-name basis. "What did he tell you when he bought it?"

She frowns, crossing her arms. "I don't make a habit of freely giving out my customers' personal details. However it is that you came upon this watch, I suggest—"

"He gave it to me," I say, stopping her before she can finish telling me off. "He left it on my bed this morning."

She looks surprised, but then she smiles, her tone softening. "Oh. I see."

"*No.*" I hold up a hand to stop her again. "No, he's a—*we* are not—"

"Partners?" she suggests. "Why not? I'll bet you make an…" She looks me up and down and it dawns on me that I had done no more to my appearance this morning than pull on clothes to take the horse out. "An interesting pair." A quick glance at the hay on my shirt confirms that I am indeed not at my best, though she's kind enough to not explicitly point that out as she says, "Opposites can attract, you know."

I cough, nearly choking on the quick breath I pull in. "No, there is no…*attracting* going on here."

"I see." Her shoulders sag a little, but her disappointment is brief. "You must know each other well, though, for a gift this…extravagant. Would you happen to know if he is otherwise spoken for? I mean, is he available? Your friend?"

"Sure," I say, not bothering to correct her the way I did the boy. What would be the point? "Just save your commissions for bail."

She laughs, not believing for a second that I'm completely serious. "Well, perhaps when you see him, tell him…" She trails off, waving a hand and averting her eyes. "Never mind. Was there something else you needed?"

"Yes," I say, still irked. "How much did he pay for this?"

"Oh." Her mouth presses into a thin line. "It wouldn't be polite to say. After all, it was a gift." She looks once more at the watch, then at me. "Do you not like it? He was worried you might not, but he was hoping this one could serve as a replacement for the other. Although, I have to say, that one wasn't *near* the quality or—"

"He showed you the other watch?" I ask, knowing I'm being bad-mannered by continually interrupting but unable to prevent myself. "You told me no one came in to sell one."

"That's right," she tells me, her patience clearly just as thin as mine. "He didn't come in to sell one. He came in to have one *fixed*. Said he'd been all over town, but no one had been able to help. When I told him I couldn't either, he decided to buy another."

I think back to yesterday, to all the shops I had visited looking for him and my watch. I hadn't described Cypress to any of them, only asked if someone had been in to sell a watch. I'd gone to the right places. I'd just simply asked the wrong question.

"Did he tell you *why* he wanted it fixed?" I ask. "Why he was going to all the trouble?"

"He did," she replied, sounding dreamy again. "It was quite sweet, actually. He said he didn't think you deserved to have something broken."

"He…" I swallow, the words sticking in my throat as I try to make sense of it all. *He doesn't even know me*, I want to say. *He has no idea the kind of things I deserve.*

Instead, I only tip my hat as I turn away. "Thank you, miss. I'm grateful to you."

"Hold on a minute," she calls after me, and I think she's about to guess at who I am again before I see her carefully slide the watch and the silk wrapping back across the counter. "Don't you think you ought to take this with you?"

I don't. But I take it anyway.

CHAPTER 14
CYPRESS

I watch Aiden walk by the hotel through the front parlor window, knowing he just came from the direction of the jeweler, and I'm incredibly pleased to see a flash of black and silver still in his hand.

Judging by his expression, his mood is currently about as light as a storm cloud. Looks broody…*again*. Very likely cursing my name. The *things* I would do to hear it.

"Well, well, there he is," intrudes a grating voice to my right instead. "My Lord, he really is insufferable."

Before I can stop the reflex, my head snaps right to where Maddock is similarly surveying the comings and goings outside, and I see him smirk thinking he has just ensnared a captive audience. Which he has, but not for the reason he thinks.

"Truthfully, when I brought him on, I really thought he'd be more…" Maddock pauses, circling his hand in the air while he rests his shoulder against the tall window frame. "Awe-inspiring. All those stories you hear about him? Not sure if I believe any now."

I don't tell him that I think Aiden is plenty *awe-inspiring* to look at, frankly because I don't like the idea of Maddock looking at him at all. Nor do I like the way he's looking at me, even if it's the exact outcome I've tried to encourage.

This is always the aim, to have them look at me and see one of their own. Upper class. Influential. By all counts, an extremely advantageous acquaintance to make...otherwise described as a self-centered asshole who has no concept of their own inadequacy because the same laws of nature haven't applied to them.

At least, not until they meet me.

"You do know who he is, yes?" Maddock continues.

"Of course." I smile good-naturedly, shifting my stance so that we're facing each other, and adding the extra step of tilting my head slightly to make it clear that I have the option of looking down on him in more ways than one. "I'd know him anywhere."

Interestingly, Maddock's mouth falls into a frown, displeased with my response, and something tells me his vexation isn't only disappointment at not getting to be the first to share this information with me.

"If you ask me, the papers made too much of him," Maddock goes on, unconcerned that I've made no such inquiry. "Hard to believe he's some legendary gunman when I've never even seen him reach for his weapon."

Now that detail does catch my attention. Because I *certainly* have. Aiden aimed his pistol steady at me no more than two nights ago, not that I'll mention that to Maddock.

"Don't bother asking him about it," he prattles on. "I've tried many times, and he is strangely reluctant to talk about the whole thing."

I make a noncommittal sound, hoping my seeming lack of interest will be enough of a deterrent to halt this conversation. I don't want to hear about this from Maddock. Whatever Aiden's history, I want to hear it from him. Because he *wants* me to know it.

"A real misstep on his part that he won't," Maddock is still saying before he pauses to take a pull of the flask he keeps in his vest, evidently planning to celebrate last night's winning streak right up until he sits at the table again tonight. "As it happens, I'm more than a fair hand with a gun myself. Fastest in my county."

"Impressive," I say, wondering how fair the competition can be when you actually *own* the county. "I would ask you to demonstrate but I'm afraid my ego could not tolerate letting you outdraw me in more than one arena."

He laughs. So do I. Though I really hadn't meant it as a joke.

Maddock steps closer, leaning in enough to make us look like co-conspirators. "He's dirt poor, you know," he murmurs. "Barely has a cent to his name. God knows how he must have wasted his earnings. You'd think it would make it easier to get him to fall in line."

"To fall in line?"

There's a humming starting at the back of my skull, a white-hot rage flaring back to life in my spine. And however much I was planning to take from Maddock before, I decide it's not nearly enough.

"Talks back. Doesn't follow orders. Keeps to himself. He's hiding something if you ask me." Maddock makes an effort to shift his expression to one of sadness and regret, as if truly aggrieved at what he's about to say. "It's a shame, really. He's so intent on squandering his future when I could help him make a name for himself again. Only needs to see the potential. But, in his current state…let's simply say, he's not what I paid for. And I'm not in the charity business."

"No," I say, my restraint growing increasingly thin as he claps me on the back. "You wouldn't be."

He goes back to smiling as if I've paid him a compliment, then turns as the men he's been keeping at the poker table with him appear from the dining room.

"You ready to head out, boss?" asks the one named Arty, easily the greenest of the bunch and by far the most eager to belong. A combination that I can only hope doesn't bode nearly as ill for him as it once did for me. "Figure we should get going if—"

"Do I *seem* as if I'm ready?" Maddock replies coolly, not bothering to actually look at the young man. "Or do I seem as if I'm in the middle of a conversation?"

"Sorry, boss." Arty winces, immediately hanging his head as the others exchange amused glances. Similarly, Maddock sighs before giving me a small shake of his head.

"I apologize," he tells me. "Afraid there's not much sense in that one."

I wave him off, looking out the window once more to confirm Aiden's still headed in the same direction far down the road before I start heading for the door myself. "I *should* get going. Afraid I might lose sight of my priorities if I stand here much longer." I nod first at Maddock and then his men, and at the smallest bit of attention, Arty brightens again. "Until later."

"Wait now, where are you rushing off to?" Maddock asks, reaching out to grab my arm a little too forcefully to pass as casual. "Why don't you come into town with us? We're after seeing what trouble we can find."

"Afraid I've business elsewhere," I tell him, rolling my shoulder and moving to pull on the coat I had draped over my arm so he has no choice but to let go. "But I have every intention of continuing ours this evening. Rest assured."

"This evening," Maddock repeats, glancing out the window as I had just done before looking back in my direction. He takes another drink from his flask as he considers me. "Guess you probably do have *some* money left." He laughs, the tension of the moment slipping away but still hovering at the edges. "I'll be looking forward to it."

"That makes two of us," I say, mirroring his enthusiastic expression before again heading for the exit.

He pivots to face me as I go, laughing once more as I reach my hand out for the doorknob. "Never met a man so happy at the prospect of losing."

I shrug, giving the cool metal in my palm a twist. "Perhaps we're playing for different things." I tip my hat, smiling honestly now at the uncertainty on his face. Then I leave them to go find their fortunes while I go find mine.

CHAPTER 15
AIDEN

I take off for another ride not long after I get back to the stable, telling myself it's because someone should check the herd and on the men left behind, but I know I really just need to get some distance. In either case, at least the mustang gets in a good stretch of his legs, too.

I wasn't always as fond of riding or of horses as I am now. When I was young, tending to them was probably one of my least favorite chores. But years of necessity and close proximity can go a long way in helping two creatures understand each other, and I can safely say now that I prefer their company more than most people.

They're less confusing, for one. No hidden motives. No lies. A horse has something it's after? You'll know it. Likewise, a horse wants to kill you? You'll know that, too. Which is more than I can say for everyone I've encountered recently…

Why would Cypress give me that watch? Why would he think I

deserved it? No matter how far I've gone today and no matter how many hours I've spent thinking about it, I still can't figure out the answer.

Sure, he'd said he was sorry for taking my busted one. That he knew it was wrong, but in my experience, that rarely means much. People know things are wrong and do them anyway all the time. Rarely do the apologies they offer afterward actually mean anything. *Never* do they actually result in some sort of atonement that is worth more money than I'd ever see otherwise.

Even for a necessity, I simply cannot wrap my mind around the idea of spending that much in one go, and I consider once again that it has to reflect some level of imbalance on his part. Unless…

Maybe this is all an attempt at bribery, and I've been overthinking what is merely a way for him to continue pursuing whatever it is that brought him to Soldana by removing me as a potential risk.

That seems the most plausible explanation.

Or it *would*, except based on the prior evening alone, the likelihood of anyone turning on him before he gives them a personal reason to do so is extremely narrow. After all, even if I were to say what he'd done, there's no guarantee that their respect for my gun would translate to their respect for my word.

As much as it might chafe me to admit, the plain reality is that outside of a physical confrontation, I currently pose little threat to him—certainly not enough to necessitate something so extravagant as this peace offering. And he *must* know that. Not to mention, when it comes down to it, he doesn't seem to be that put off by getting *physical* with me either.

Though a memory pulled from last night's argument in the alley would have made the most sense for my mind to supply this train of thought, it chooses this moment to take an unexpected route. Briefly fixating on an entirely different type of activity that involves an entirely different type of closeness than me holding my knife to his throat.

"Fuck's *sake*," I mutter, immediately pushing the picture away and pulling the mustang out of his gallop as we get near to town once more. Not trusting myself to control a breakneck speed if I can't even control myself.

I should seek out some company soon. Or take myself to mass. Perhaps both, if I'm so overdue that I'm finding myself drifting into these types of considerations.

Not that I *am* considering it. I'm not considering him *at all* beyond figuring out why he seems so opposed to the idea of me having a moment of goddamn peace.

With hopes of finding one, I make the abrupt decision to divert toward the river before I return to the barn. Based on the way the sun is hanging over the horizon, I still have plenty of time before I need to head over to the saloon anyway. Plus, after riding all the way out to the herd, I'm not the only one who could use a cooldown.

It's no small mercy that everything looked to be going all right out there in our absence. Animals were good and the two men left behind were fine, if bored out of their minds. Can never remember their names… Tommy? Duke? Dutch? Put a gun to my head and I'm not sure I could tell you, though it seems far too late to ask 'em and they're hardly worth learning even if I did. Not like I'll be around long…

I dismount once I make it close to the bank, take off the mustang's tack, and turn him loose before I move to stand in the shade beneath a nearby oak tree, watching the water run by slowly while I just as slowly catch my breath. Still, my pulse picks right back up when I finally let myself reach for the piece of black fabric and its contents in my pocket.

What I *should* do is march right into town and sell it. Make myself enough money to cut loose. *Except…*

I look to where the mustang is grazing close by, and I know I can't just leave him behind. Not after he's refused to leave me more than once. And especially not when I know Maddock and his men would do nothing but make his life hard.

He doesn't deserve that. None of their animals do.

If I sold the watch, I *could* buy him outright. But then Maddock would wonder where I acquired the sudden influx of funds. Start asking questions that I wouldn't care to answer even if I could.

No, best thing is to finish out the week as planned, take the mustang and whatever portion (if any) of the winnings that Maddock ends up passing over. Then once I've put some distance between us, *then* I could sell it.

Examining it closer, I brush my thumb across the top of the three intricate rings of flowers in the polished silver, admiring the differences between the blooms, and frowning when I notice the smudge of dust that I accidentally leave behind. Without thinking twice about it, I move the pocket watch to my left palm before using the hem of my shirt to polish the dirt away with my right.

That's when I'm struck so violently by the recollection of my father doing the exact same thing that the force of it is strong enough to make me stumble back. To make me put out a hand to steady myself against the tree trunk as I close my eyes—not to chase away the memory, but to try to make it the only thing I can see.

Panic overcomes me when it disappears as quickly as it arrived, no matter how many times I repeat the motion. Again. Again. *Again.*

"Come on." Nothing happens. No matter how long I stand there and try, I can't get it back. "Come on, *please.*"

I open my eyes again. But there's still nothing. There's still no one.

No one but me. And all the consequences of the things I've done.

CHAPTER 16
CYPRESS

Aiden looks rattled. Far more so than he did this morning.

Watching him through the window earlier, he'd looked annoyed. Aggravated, even. But now…he seems *upset*. Spending almost the entirety of the evening staring at his clasped hands on the bar and not even pretending to reach for the whiskey in front of him.

When he does glance up, it's always in my direction, a deep crease in his brow as he studies me before he notices me watching him back. Then he returns to trying to pull apart the wood grain beneath his fingers through sheer concentration alone.

I think I preferred when he looked like he wanted to lunge for my throat. No, I *definitely* did. That was far, far better than this.

Did I overstep with the pocket watch? What if I ruined things? I still have the other one if he wants it. He can have it back this instant. I only thought—

"Cypress, are you in this game or not?" someone asks, and I momentarily pull my attention back to the table and my cards, smiling a bit at my three of a kind before putting my hand down to a series of groans from around the table.

"Having a rough go tonight, aren't you, son?" asks the older man to my left, the pile of cash and coins in front of him a good indication that his luck is treating him as well tonight as it does on plenty of other occasions.

According to Clayton himself, he was barely getting by before he struck gold out in California a few years ago, enough that he got to come back to Texas as a newly minted heir to the aristocracy. Although not enough to have men like Maddock want to count him among their ranks.

New money, I've heard Maddock sneer to his men more than once. An apparent insult that they all nod along with as if they themselves are displaced members of the elite rather than working men and women's sons with barely any money of their own. Thanks in large part *to* the elite. New and old.

Only more proof that misplaced loyalty can be as dangerous as calculated hostility.

Not that I need more.

"You are playing even worse tonight than you did last night," agrees Maddock, almost managing to look sympathetic as he rearranges his cards. "Didn't actually think you meant it when you said you were looking forward to losing earlier." He chuckles before tossing a few more bills in. "Did your business today at least go as you wanted?"

"Still too early to tell," I say, even though, as a matter of fact, *no*, it had not gone as I wanted. I had *wanted* to talk to Aiden, had even headed down to the stable after leaving the hotel with the intention of doing so, though I hadn't been entirely sure what I was going to say when I got there. An unusual predicament for me, but I had kept walking because… because what I'd *really* wanted was simply to see him in the daylight.

No quick glances. No shadows to hide in. I'd have liked to see him clearly, at least once. Just in case. Even if the idea of him seeing me the same way made my stomach turn.

I sneak another glance at Aiden, broad shoulders hunched up to his ears, and think about how I'd instead arrived this morning right in time to see him flying off on his mustang and had forced myself to fight off the impulse to follow him. Knowing after my conversation with Maddock that I needed to make a few preparations elsewhere while I still had the option to do so.

I'm too invested in this game due to the players. Less able to keep a clear head and therefore less able to keep up the mirage I've constructed. Something that I have a feeling Maddock has noticed, even if he can't exactly put his finger on it yet.

He's not quite as ignorant as some of them are, I'll grant him that. But the greater risk is that he is *far* more entitled. And, like so many men who fancy themselves as gods, far more likely to interpret any disagreement as dissent. And to resort to violence when he does.

"Remind me what line of business you are in again?" Maddock asks, smiling at me as the hand progresses around the table. "Can't recall how you said you made your living."

"Transportation," I reply, easily returning his insincere smile with one of my own. "Trains mainly."

"Lucrative, is it?"

"Depends."

"On what?"

"Who is aboard."

"Right," he says, nodding as the corners of his mouth turn down into a frown. "Hate to see the wrong sort crowding in. Sure, they want things more accessible, but at what cost? I have a friend back in El Paso in the stagecoach business. Similar occupation to yours. And I've told him time and time again, he needs to just stop offering third-class tickets, but then he always asks who would get out and push the coach when it gets stuck!" Maddock laughs, looking at his men who quickly laugh, too. Once again, at their own expense.

"Suppose he's got me cornered there," he continues. As if struck by a sudden surge of brilliance, he snaps his fingers, then points one in my direction. "You know, you really ought to get in on those luxury trains. Have you seen those? I've heard they're really something fine. Wouldn't have to worry about them getting stuck, would you? No need then to be dealing with—"

"You not plannin' to play either, Maddock?" cuts in a gravelly voice, and given the way I'd been thinking of how satisfying it would be to slam Maddock's head into the table, it's a toss-up whether I or he is more narrowly spared when Charley, the oldest cowboy at our table and the only one not employed by Maddock, goes on to tell him that if he *is* planning to play he'd "better hurry up and fuckin' do something other than make mindless chatter."

Maddock's face scrunches, intensely offended by the interruption, but he does stop talking long enough to look at his cards and raise his wager. Wisely, I suppress my smile before I let my gaze and my awareness recenter on the one and only cowboy it has any sort of appetite for.

"He makes me nervous, too," mutters a voice to my right as the game moves to the next man at the table, and I reluctantly turn my head from Aiden to Arty. The young man is also already out on this hand, playing even more terribly than I am tonight.

"Who? That one?" I ask, nodding my head in Charley's direction as I keep my voice low so as not to embarrass him further. "I think his bark is worse than his bite, but better to be safe than—"

"No," Arty says, his eyes flicking toward the bar. "That one."

I barely manage to keep myself from tensing, not needing to look for myself to realize he must mean Aiden. I must have already done plenty of that this evening for *Arty* to have picked up on it.

Apparently, I'm bluffing even worse than I thought. And certainly not by design.

"The last time I said a word to him he pulled a knife on me," the young man continues and I frown, more bothered than I should be that I'm not the only one to have had that particular experience, even with the temporary distress. Typically, I'm not the jealous type, but I *did* think—

"Guess it's better than him pulling his gun though," Arty says, and I don't bother disagreeing given that he's already glancing around before lowering his voice. "I've heard he's killed *twenty-one* men."

My eyebrows rise. "So few?"

Rather than respond, Arty's mouth drops open slightly, and I berate myself for the comment, knowing he's easily spooked as it is. "Simply surprised people don't say he's killed more. Tall tales and all that."

"Oh." Arty looks visibly relieved. "Yeah, I suppose, but don't you think—"

"Pretty sure I told you that you should be trying to learn something for the rest of the hand," Maddock cuts in, the disapproval clearly meant for Arty though he still doesn't deign to look at him. "You need to be watching, not talking."

"Sorry, boss," Arty mutters, staring down at the table with his posture remarkably similar to how Aiden's currently is. "Won't happen again."

Maddock's lip curls with satisfaction, and before he even starts talking again, I know he's not done with his process of public humiliation. No matter that he's scolding Arty for the same exact thing he had just been reprimanded for doing himself. What better way to recover his pride, as well as his position at the table, than at someone else's expense? Especially the one least likely to put up a fight in return.

"All your prattling is probably the reason Cypress is so off his form tonight," Maddock suggests, knowing as well as I do that he has nothing to do with it. "You've been distracting him." He smiles. "Apologize."

Arty looks at me out of the corner of his eye, his head still low. "I'm sorry if—"

I shake my head to stop him. "No need. My troubles are my own."

A hesitant smile begins to appear on his face, but it vanishes as soon as Maddock adds, "Kind of you to say." He pauses briefly to play his turn, his voice cool and casual as he raises the bet again. "Although, for all you know, he could be counting on your kindness to try to cheat you."

"To—to *cheat*? No, boss, I wouldn't do somethin' like that," Arty stammers, his distress growing as he looks around the table to the other men in his group for support. But no one is brave enough to offer any. "We really were just talkin'—"

"Oh?" Maddock smirks, apparently still finding the torture of the young man to be incredibly amusing. "What is there to even discuss?

What could you possibly have in common?"

"Nothing really," Arty says, his hands beginning to twist in his lap. "Was nothin'."

"Always is when it comes to you," Maddock sneers. "Not sure cards are the thing you need to be learning after all. Would be far better off learning your place before—"

"That's *enough*, Maddock," I bite out, unable to listen to it anymore, and I see the brief flash of anger on my opponent's face at the lapse in my loyalties. Before I can cover for it, Arty diverts him with a misfired shot of his own.

"Was about him," he blurts, also having reached the limit for what he can endure as he gestures toward the bar. "Was about Aiden is all. We were talking about if it was all true. What they say about him."

"I see." Maddock's eyes shift from Arty to me, an attempt at a smile back on his face. "Seems to be a particular interest for you today, Cypress. My apologies that this seems to be taking up so much of your focus."

"If I recall correctly," I say, identifying the test as it's given and tilting my head as if carefully considering my response, "the topic was by your introduction this morning."

"Suppose it was." He's staring at me, and though I'm rarely an advocate for dishonesty, I really wouldn't mind right now if Arty took up the practice. "Still, you'll have to let me know if you want me to make introductions."

I smile. "That won't be necessary."

"Who is it we're talking about now?" Clayton asks, kindly inserting himself into the conversation while grabbing another cigar. "Feel I've missed something."

Instead of answering, Arty wavers between the miner and a severely irritated Maddock, unsure of what to do. Unfortunately, the dart of his eyes toward the bar proves to be plenty.

Poor young man. It's a wonder he's survived more than a day out here.

"Is that…" Clayton starts to say, his eyebrows shooting into his hairline as he follows Arty's gaze precisely to where I'd prefer it not to go. "God, it looks like him, doesn't it?"

"Could we get back to the damn game?" Charley asks, as bristly as I feel. "Barely going to make it through two rounds at this rate."

"Great idea," I say, turning to my left. "Clayton, my friend, I think it's your—"

He's already up, stubbing out the cigar he just lit in the ashtray before brushing his hands over his suit. "Never thought I'd… Why, the man's a damn hero."

Maddock scoffs. "A hero? Not sure I would—"

"I would," Clayton argues, a firm set to his expression as he becomes the third person at the table to give Maddock's ego a well-deserved kick tonight. "What he did for the McHenrys…" Clayton clears his throat. "Excuse me."

With that, he's off, and I at least have the cover of not being the only one staring as I watch the proceedings, though I'd wager I feel the worst about it when I see Aiden startle at the sound of his name. He quickly looks in my direction as if to confirm I haven't moved before he stands and shakes the hand of the man who has appeared in front of him.

Whatever Clayton tells him next, he tries to keep it between them, his head bent as he mutters something that has Aiden glaring at the floor this time instead of the bartop. The exchange looking so tense I nearly get up when Clayton grabs him by the shoulder, squeezing as he finishes saying his piece while Aiden shakes his head as if to disagree. Only when Clayton seems unwilling to take no for an answer does Aiden finally nod, receiving a hearty backslap from the older man before he leaves and allows him to retake his seat.

"Imagine that," Clayton is muttering as he returns to the table and reclaims his own chair. "Seeing him here of all places. I wonder what brings him."

"Employment," Maddock responds, pretending to sound politely disinterested when it's obvious to anyone who's paying attention that he's actually enraged. "He's one of mine."

Not yours, I think, still watching Aiden as he goes back to staring at his hands, although I'd swear he first took something black and silver out of his left pocket.

Beside me, Clayton picks up his cigar again, relighting it with a match from his vest and a few deep puffs. "An honor for you, then. Few finer men in my book."

"An honor? Him?" Maddock sneers, making an attempt at a laugh as he reaches for his drink. "He's practically worthless now. Your book must be missing a few pages."

"Must be," I agree, pleased to see Maddock looking smug before I say, "Need to save a few for…what was it? The fastest man in town?"

As soon as the words are out of my mouth, I know I've pushed too far. I also don't particularly care. *Too invested*, I think again. *Far, far too invested.*

"The *county*," Maddock corrects, staring me down. "Fastest draw. Likely in the whole state. If you'd care to test—"

"Sure as fuck can't tell by the way you play cards," Charley cuts in again, the old man sounding like he's about to draw a pistol himself. "Can we please get back to the goddamn game? Can't even remember whose turn it is with all this talkin'."

There's a sudden fluster of activity, one of Maddock's men having enough self-preservation to quickly get the hand going again while I continue to bide my time until the next one. Even Maddock's seething glare eventually moves on as well. Beside me, Arty's shoulders finally relax.

"Sorry," he mutters to me after making sure his employer has refocused on the game, so quiet that I almost miss it. In return, I give him the barest hint of a nod to show him there's no ill feelings. At least, not where he is concerned.

Across from me, Maddock knocks back the remaining contents of his drink and chases it down with a pull from his flask before he looks away from the table, and even if I hadn't been looking the same direction all night, I would feel no qualms about going all in on where his glare lands. As well as on how all this is going to play out in the end. If I let it.

"How about another, boys?" Clayton asks, pulling his pile of winnings toward him after he takes the hand with a two pair. "Night still has plenty of life in her."

"I'm in if Maddock is," I say, giving him what I hope is a contrite smile. "Or maybe he's grown tired of taking my money."

Maddock looks at me, a little wary at first, but just as I suspect, even that small appeasement of his ego does wonders in terms of turning his mood around.

"Not nearly," he says, nodding at the dealer for him to continue before he holds up a hand for another drink. "Although, you never know, perhaps you'll surprise us all and actually put up a fight."

"Careful what you wish for, Maddock," I say, taking my cards when they're offered. "You might just get it."

I lose spectacularly for the rest of the evening.

CHAPTER 17
AIDEN

It's past midnight by the time they finally call it a night, and Cypress once again closes the evening with less than he started. Substantially less, by my estimate. His accumulated debt seeming even worse than the night prior since he stayed far longer.

"Beginning to worry I may be out of my depth," he's telling Maddock and the others as the table gets to their feet, shaking his head with a sheepish expression while they try to reassure him otherwise. "Perhaps I ought to excuse myself from tomorrow's game?"

"You really are having one hell of a bad luck streak. Those last few hands…you have my sympathies," Maddock says, both his words and his steps swaying slightly with the influence of drink as he rounds the table toward Cypress. "Or you would, if your misfortune wasn't working so much in my favor."

"Well," Cypress replies, continuing to do a good job of looking both innocent and amiable as Maddock laughs at his own joke. "Most important thing is that you're enjoying yourself."

From what I'd observed earlier this evening, things had seemed somewhat strained between them for a time, Cypress's fingers drumming away at the top of the table whenever he didn't have a hold of cards. But it seems to be water under the bridge now, Maddock still laughing as he says, "Remind me to never ride one of your trains. Given what I've seen of you, I'm not sure I'd make it to my final destination."

"I'd ensure it personally," Cypress replies, standing impressively firm when Maddock claps his hand hard against his shoulder.

I cover my own laugh behind my hand, positive there's a double meaning in there, but Maddock doesn't seem to notice any more than he does that Cypress is letting him win.

Certainly *is* a curious thing for the thief to do, unless it's his goal to go broke, but I don't think that's the case simply based on the way he likes to dress and the company he likes to keep. Nor am I of the opinion that he comes from such an endless supply of money that there's no risk he might run out.

Haven't met many wealthy people who know how to pick pockets that well. Never consider it a skill they need to bother with when they are plenty comfortable stealing right in front of you. Key difference being that they can afford the consequences of getting caught. If there even are any.

"You're being too hard on yourself," Maddock says, draping an arm around Cypress's shoulders as they start for the door, practically giving the thief an open invitation to rob him blind, and I suppose I ought to try to stop him if I'm to hold up my end of the deal.

With a sigh, I straighten from my barstool, the shift in my position immediately recapturing Cypress's attention. He turns his head to look at me, and the quickness of his response is enough to get Maddock looking, too. Upon seeing me, he withdraws his arm from around Cypress, his face screwing up.

"Ah, of course, the legend himself," my employer says. "Practically the second coming, according to some." Maddock directs this at the older man who favors cigars, the same one who came up to me earlier talking about things I'd rather forget.

"Think you've probably had enough for the night, Maddock," he says, shaking his head at him. "Maybe should've called it when Charley did."

"I'm far better off than that old bastard," Maddock snaps back, the end of his sentence slurring in unintentional disagreement. "Besides, *I* say when we're done." He turns again, squinting in my direction as if to see me better from across the saloon, and some of the other patrons still left in here promptly part ways to clear his path. "Isn't that right?"

"Sure, boss," I say, doing a quick count of the twenty remaining souls in the room, including the bartender and the shotgun he has stashed under the bar, before planting my hands on my hips as I stare right back. "Whatever you say goes."

Maddock smiles. "Look at that. Suddenly, so quick to obey." He glances back at Cypress. "And we're supposed to believe he's some great fighter?"

My jaw tenses, teeth grinding together as I bite back a retort before I catch Cypress's gaze flicking to me. His own smile stays easy enough, though the way he's *tap, tap, tapping* again with his thumb against his thigh says it's all for show. *Does he even know he does that?*

"Prudent fighter knows which fights to take on," Cypress says, voice low as his eyes stay on mine. "And which to leave."

There's a warning in there, I'm positive. One he's hoping I'll heed, because I suspect he has as little interest as I do in this taking a turn. Him because he's yet to have earned his money back, plus whatever amount he planned to add to it. Me because I have no interest in observing firsthand how Maddock or one of his crews ended up leaving a man dead outside of San Antonio.

I'd been out with the herd when it happened. I'd been doing what I thought I ought to be doing that time, but maybe it still counts against me regardless.

"How right you are. Always best to be prudent," Maddock replies to Cypress, his agreement pulling my gaze back to him. "That how you killed so many, Aiden? Knowing how to be *prudent* about your battles?"

The saloon goes quiet as one conversation dies away, then another and then another, as more people catch wind of what's going on. Although, honestly, it's hard for me to hear the silence over the rushing in my ears.

"That's enough," the older man cuts in again, and I really wish he wouldn't. He doesn't need to out of some misguided sense of duty. "If you're implying—"

"I'm not *implying* anything," Maddock replies with a shrug. "Just curious how many of those famous duels were against men who actually knew their way around a weapon. Maybe if he'd had some real competition…perhaps the papers would have read different? Not so *complimentary* after all."

Maddock steps toward me, and Cypress casts another warning glance my way before calmly saying to him, "I think we need—"

"What we *need* is a demonstration. Otherwise, how do we even know he is who he says he is?" Maddock asks, and I think the older man cuts in with another warning, one that I mostly miss because I'm too busy watching Cypress move to put himself more firmly between me and my employer.

"Maddock, whatever it is you're hoping to prove—"

"Won't need to prove anything. Not after everyone sees," Maddock counters, pushing past Cypress and weaving closer to me through the tables. "This is about twenty paces, isn't it? Maybe not quite."

"Maddock," I say, my left hand up as my right hovers near my holster, which conveniently hides the fact my fingers are shaking. "Let's take this outside."

"Why?" He laughs. "Are you telling me you're *actually* going to grab for that gun?" He nods at the pistol in my belt. "Never seen you so much as look at it."

"Haven't had a reason to," I reply, keeping an eye on Maddock while also trying to keep his men in my periphery. All of them look ready to reach for a weapon themselves—well, all of them except the kid, who is white as a sheet as he lingers near the front door. "You going to give me one?"

"I want to see what all the fuss is about," Maddock continues. "And I'm sure I can't be the only one."

The man who approached me earlier also seems to have noticed the kid's quick escape path because he's shifted quietly his way, bending to whisper something in his ear before the kid nods and slips out the door.

"I think I just need to see it for myself," Maddock says. "Have my own chance to weigh in on the myth." He smirks. "You know, I've been told I'm pretty fast. Pretty *damn* fast."

"Outside," I offer again, doing an obvious look around the room this time as a reminder of the others present. "We don't want someone getting hurt."

He looks around too, as if this has only now occurred to him, but instead of innocent bystanders, he merely sees an audience. "We won't really shoot. We'll just see…" Maddock's hand starts to stray toward his own belt beneath his coat. "We'll see who's really the better man after all. On the count of four?"

Fuck, is he actually…

"One." Maddock smiles, then widens his stance as if he's bracing for the rush of a bull rather than a bullet. Something that might have been funny if it didn't also let me know there's a fairly good chance that even if he doesn't intend to shoot me, he still might out of sheer ignorance.

"Two." I wonder how many of Maddock's men will shoot at me if I take their boss down. No matter if I only aim to wound. My gaze lands on each of them in a rapid assessment, stopping when I reach Cypress. The only one who meets my eyes.

"Three." Almost imperceptibly, he shakes his head. Expression pleading with me to trust him, but there's no reason for me to. Not one that makes any sense. *None* of this makes any sense.

"Four." Maddock reaches, and I…I don't. *Fuck*, I—

"The *hell* is my gun?" Maddock's outburst brings my attention to him in time to see him staring blankly at his empty holster. "Who took it?"

It takes everything in my power not to look right at Cypress again, even after he's turning toward the table as if helping to search. "Are you sure you had it with you? Perhaps you left it back at the hotel this evening?"

"Who do you take me for?" Maddock protests, sounding more like an angry child. "I never leave without my—"

"What's going on in here?" a new voice cracks in, booming from the front door. A burly-looking man more than twice my age strides in without waiting for an answer, rifle already in hand and a shiny sheriff's badge on his chest. "No one had better be starting something in my town."

"No, sir," Maddock says, perfectly pleasant again as he turns, and I wonder if he's also seen the kid sneaking back in behind the law. "We were just heading out for the evening."

"That right?" the sheriff asks, highly suspicious as he switches from glaring at Maddock and me to looking elsewhere for confirmation. "Everything good here, Clay?"

The man with the cigar nods, solidifying my belief that he is a local. "S'alright I think now, Ben. Appreciate you coming down in the middle of the night."

The sheriff nods, but then turns again to Maddock. "Well, if you are heading out, then I suggest you get movin'." He jerks his head toward the door. "Now."

"You got it, Sheriff." Maddock holds up his hands, still smiling as he makes for the street out front with his entourage on his heels, including Cypress, who gives me one last once-over.

"You have a good evening," he tells the sheriff before disappearing out the door.

In return, the sheriff tips his hat, then faces me once more. Fortunately, I need no further prodding, already digging a few coins out of my pocket to leave on the bartop for the trouble before exiting in the opposite direction out the back.

CHAPTER 18
AIDEN

I don't linger in the alley tonight once I'm out the door. Nor anywhere else for that matter. Not until the rain chases me back inside long after I'm sure everyone has either passed out in the street or in their beds.

While I never would have considered us to be on friendly terms, I still hadn't expected Maddock to actually attempt to pull a gun on me. Even with liquor serving as his second, I'd thought he would know better, but my reputation must not be offering me the same protection it once did.

All the more reason to cut ties at the end of the week. If I make it that long. Christ, I might not have made it through the night if Cypress hadn't gotten involved. And I have no doubt that's exactly what he did.

What does he even want with me? What purpose is it serving him to try to gain my good graces? To risk his own safety in an attempt to protect mine? Is he really so desperate to have me in his debt? So worried I could thwart his plans?

How much is he planning to take?

The mustang greets me with a low whicker when he sees me coming down the stable aisle, his head bobbing up and down as if he's excited to see me, and I have to admit, it's kind of nice that someone is.

"Take it easy," I say in reply, reaching out to give him a good scratch behind the ear before stripping off my drenched coat and hat and hanging them to dry outside the stall. "You been stayin' clear of trouble?"

As if in answer, the dark stallion in the next stall also peeks his head over his door, bold enough to reach out his nose and inspect my pockets when I step closer. Chuckling, I take the intrusion more kindly than the mustang does, his ears immediately flattening as he glowers at his neighbor, but the fact that he doesn't try to also bite a chunk out of him tells me that at least some progress is being made.

I give the mustang a nudge to get out of the way before I go for the knot securing his latch, my fingers moving to pull apart the rope before I have a chance to notice it's once again not the same one I tied this morning.

"Damn it," I mutter, trying to remember how I'm supposed to get the knot to slip apart. "Told him not to be messin'—"

"Pass the end through the loop first."

As if the rope scalded me, I jump back with a curse, pulling my gun and aiming it high and to my right where the sound came from. In response, all I see is a grin. "Hello, wolf."

"Fuck's *sake*." I reholster my gun, but keep my glare locked on Cypress where he's just swung himself up on the back of his horse so he can be seen over the wall, looking so right up there that I can't believe I ever let myself believe that the horse wasn't his. "The hell are you doing in here?"

"Needed a change of scenery for a while," he says, making himself comfortable by flopping down and resting his head on the horse's haunches. "Hotel was feeling a bit…confining."

"Confining," I mutter, taking a quick glance around our current close quarters to confirm we're alone before I ask in a low voice, "Maddock happen to locate his gun?"

"In his room," Cypress says easily while staring up at the rafters. "Where he appears to have left it."

"Right," I reply, knowing for a fact Maddock had it on him when he walked into the saloon, my tendency to count weapons coming in and out of a room a remnant from my old life that I haven't bothered to shake. "You didn't have to do that back there. That was…" I clear my throat once, twice. "Thank you."

He turns his head to look at me, appearing amused by my struggle, though he doesn't say so directly. "It was the least I could do."

I roll my eyes. "You gonna tell me what it is that you want?"

"What I want?"

"What you're after here? What's your goal?"

"Is it not obvious?" he asks, frowning. "I feel like I'm making it obvious. Within the limits of my pride, of course. And general laws of decency."

"Christ," I say, huffing out a breath and choosing to ignore that last part before it can distract me like he wants. "I'm not going to tell him about the watch, if that's what you're so worried about. Or that you're letting him win."

He arches an eyebrow at me. "Am I?"

"Yes."

"What makes you—"

"You've got a tell. A few of them."

Both eyebrows shoot up now, and I feel no small amount of satisfaction that I seem to have caught him unaware given how many times he's done the same to me. "And they are…?"

"Not sure I should tell you."

He barks out a laugh, and I find myself suppressing a smile as he asks, "Why not?"

"Might need that information for later."

"For later," he repeats, and I don't think I'm imagining the implication in his voice when he adds, "Sounds promising."

I clear my throat again and look away, focusing once more on the knot that won't budge instead of the fact that my skin suddenly feels too hot.

Absolutely fucking not. I'm not—*no*. It's just been a long day is all. I'm tired. Excess nerves. And he's fuckin' *irritating*. And this fuckin' rope has me at the end of mine.

"The loop," he says, being helpful again. "Pass the tail through the loop."

"I got it," I snap, trying two other routes before doing as he suggested. As I had no doubt it would, the knot immediately comes loose with one sharp tug, just as I'm sure the identical one would do on his own horse's stall.

"The knot is you, too?" I say, phrasing it as a question even though it really isn't one.

"They're an…*interest* of mine." He shrugs, but something in his eyes tells me there's more to it. "That quick release has all sorts of uses. Can come in handy if—"

"Yeah, I'll bet," I shoot back, finally letting myself into the stall so I can set about cleaning up for the night. "Why are you messing with my things anyway?" I ask as I grab a rake. "You always pester everyone like this or am I just the unfortunate exception?"

"You are most certainly the exception."

"I'm afraid to ask why."

"I'm afraid to tell you."

For a moment, I go still, my rake hovering over the bedding I'd been about to turn over as I glance his direction. "That why you replaced my watch? I scare you?"

He sighs. "You don't scare me, wolf."

"Wasn't so sure after last night," I say, alluding to our exchange in the alley, half in an attempt to provoke some truth out of him and half due simply to curiosity. "You want to tell me why you're more afraid of a knife than you are a gun?"

He's quiet for a while, long enough that I wonder if he's going to ignore me until he finally says, "More personal."

I frown, not sure why I suddenly feel a wash of guilt. "Suppose it is." I go back to mucking out the stall, more hastily than I normally would with him there watching. God knows he probably had one of the stablehands do his, the extra expense likely not even registering if he can lose as much as he's been at the poker table.

"You didn't need to replace it," I say, doing my best to move around the mustang while looking squarely at the fresh straw I'm putting down instead of at Cypress. "The pocket watch."

"Least I could do," he says again. "Besides, the other one was broken, and I thought—"

"I would've managed," I tell him. "I don't need your pity."

"Never said you did."

"Good. Just so we're clear."

There's a long pause, interrupted only occasionally by the soft sound of straw brushing across the stable floor, the crackling hum of the lanterns, the distinct patter of rain falling on the tin roof.

"I do still have the old one," Cypress says at last, apparently unable to take the silence any longer. "If you want it."

I should tell him to hand it over. Give him the other one when he does, no matter how much it's worth. Have that, at the very least, stricken from whatever ledger he's been keeping between us. But when I go to reach for it in my pocket…I can't. Not after what happened earlier by the water.

It's been so long since I've been able to remember anything but the end.

Besides, given how things went tonight, I'd be even more foolish to throw away a potential lifeline for pride. If nothing else, it's an insurance policy should things go sour once again. Holding onto it is simply the sensible thing to do.

"You keep that one," I tell him, purposefully not bringing up its replacement and putting my back to him as I toss down some more fresh straw. "Perhaps you can convince some poor sap that it's worth thousands if you ever get bored with pulling cards. Or, sorry, what was it again…trains? That one of the lies I heard you tell Maddock? That you own a railroad?"

"*First*," Cypress says, sounding so offended that I can't help but turn my head again, "I did not lie. I told him I made my fortune with trains. Which is true. As for owning a railroad or cars or whatever else, he added that bit of flourish on his own. They always do."

"Who is *they*?"

"Second," he continues as if I hadn't interrupted, "I only take advantage of people who already have far too many advantages to speak of. Far more than they deserve."

The sudden coldness in his voice is enough to stop me from what I'm doing, and I let the rake rest as I study him. "And how do you determine that?"

"Apparently the same way you do," he says, the darkness in his expression fading as quickly as it came. "I see their tells. The ones they never think to hide." His eyes narrow, assessing. "Are you really not going to divulge mine, Aiden?"

I roll my eyes, hopefully covering the way my pulse skipped when he said my name, but I catch that grin of his before I get back to work, walking to grab a few big bales of hay from the aisle so I'm not sleeping on the wet floor if it floods with the rain. "Considering those tells might be my *only* advantage, no, I still don't think I will."

"Oh, I don't know." He sighs, continuing to watch me as I carry a large bale with each hand back into the stall. "I can make out at least a few other *advantages* from where I sit."

"Then sit somewhere else," I snap at him, wondering when he's going to leave so I can get some sleep, but given how comfortable he seems sprawled out on his horse's back, I suspect he has no intention of moving anytime soon. "And don't be saying my name like that."

"Like what?"

"Like we know each other. Just because Maddock gave it to you—"

"Maddock didn't give it to me. Well, not knowingly."

"Says the thief," I mutter in reply to his half-answer.

He smiles again before continuing, "I overheard him say it when you arrived in town. Outside the hotel."

"Thought that was you," I say, glaring at him when he appears delighted for some reason. "Why'd you ask me for it then if you already knew it? In the alley?"

"Seemed polite."

"Polite," I repeat. "Funny thing to worry about when you have a habit of picking up things that don't belong to you. Anything else you manage to lift?"

"Yes," he replies with zero hesitation. "You have a deal with Maddock. That's the paper he gave you at the saloon."

"Christ." I let the bale drop against the wall, raising a hand to lift my hat only to remember it's not there. A distracted slip-up that seems to amuse him more.

"If it helps, I don't know all the terms," he reassures me. "Sadly, the walls of the hotel are only so thin." He waits. "But if you'd like to tell me—"

"Why the *hell* would I tell you?"

"Well, perhaps, *if* you told me," he says slowly, "I could help…"

"I don't need your—"

"Pity, I know." His mouth presses into a tight line as he thinks over his oncoming argument. "But if we were to have, say, aligned interests…"

"We don't."

"We might."

"We do not have aligned *anything*," I say, more forcefully this time, and I could almost swear that I see him flinch. "Whatever you're up to, I want no part in it. All I want is to make it through the end of this week, get paid my share, and get gone."

"I see," he says, voice quiet again. "And where exactly are you and…" He gestures toward the mustang who has at last hunkered down in the corner of the stall, clearly having decided to ignore us. "Apologies, I don't know his name."

"He doesn't have one," I say, tone clipped.

"Why?"

"Hasn't been given one."

"You haven't named your horse?"

"No."

"Why not?"

You know, maybe Maddock shooting me earlier would have been kinder. "*Because*…" I say through gritted teeth. "He's not *my* horse."

"Ah," he says, still frowning. "He's one of Maddock's?"

"Yes," I reply, then because I know he'll likely ask anyway, I tack on, "Until the end of the week at least."

"I see. So you agreed to work for Maddock until the end of the week, and in exchange, he will give you No Name there along with your *share* of whatever money he takes at the table. Do I have all that right?" he asks, continuing without really giving me a chance to deny it. "And you are to do…what? Act as an enforcer for him? That why you jumped me that first night in the alley?"

"Not entirely," I say, irritated that my initial refusal to tell him the details of my agreement were, apparently, completely futile. "That was mainly for me."

His crystalline eyes practically sparkle in response. "*Really?*"

"Christ, not like *that*," I reply, not sure if I'm more exasperated with him for taking the opening or with myself for giving it to him. "I went after you because I knew you were a thief, not because you're…"

He arches an eyebrow again. "Not because I'm…*what?*"

"Look," I say, quickly changing the topic. "There's no love lost between me and Maddock. *Clearly.* But I need our deal to get out of here, and I'd appreciate it if you didn't fuck things up with whatever it is you're doing."

"Where will you go?" he asks, holding my gaze for a moment too long before looking away and toward the roof. "When the deal is done?"

I exhale, not entirely sure myself. "Home, I guess?"

"And home is…?"

"Somewhere you will never be invited."

He doesn't reply for some time, and I start to wonder again if I've actually wounded him before he shrugs. "Your loss. I'm a wonderful house guest. You'd hardly know I'm there."

"Somehow, I doubt that," I mutter, certain that there would be no way of knowing he *wasn't* there in my small cabin. I clear my throat. "What about you? You going home whenever you finish causing chaos here?"

"Trying to." He sighs. "In your deal, what happens if Maddock loses it all by the end of the week?"

"I still get the horse," I tell him, dropping to sit on one of the hay bales, not seeing much of a point in hiding that detail from him when he's already pieced together everything else. "Well, that is unless he figures out I knowingly let him get played. I take it that is your intention? That he *does* lose it all by the end of the week?"

"It was initially. My priorities have shifted somewhat," he replies, frowning as he thinks. "You said in the alley that you knew me, and just now you said you saw me at the hotel. Who did you…what made you notice me?"

"Hard to miss you," I say without thinking, clearing my throat again when I realize how that might sound. "You're always dressed like a well-moneyed undertaker."

Cypress blinks in my direction, then laughs deeply, repeating the words between attempts to stop. "A—well-moneyed—*undertaker?*"

"*Yes,*" I say, now also struggling with a smile. "Fuck's sake, even your damn horse is black. Guarantee all your tack is, too."

"You would be right." Cypress grins in further confirmation. "But come now, wolf, I thought you were a cowboy. Surely you know the importance of a distinctive brand."

Wolf. There's that same nickname, but I'm too busy huffing out a laugh in spite of myself to ask him about it. "Afraid of someone claiming you, are you?"

The lightness in his gaze shifts to something heavier, to something that makes my blood thrum as his gaze does a slow sweep up and down my body, his eyes locking on mine again as he murmurs, "Not at all. In fact, I think I'd rather enjoy it."

The space we're in is suddenly feeling far too small, even as I wonder what would happen if I got to my feet and closed what distance there was. "Don't you think you ought to be heading to the hotel? It's…it's getting late."

Cypress shrugs, his head lifting slightly before he drops it back down and stares once more at the roof. His horse barely seems to notice the change as he continues to nose around his feed bucket, not at all bothered by his rider treating him like a feather bed. Thief or not, he must, at least, take good care of the horse for him to be so trusting.

"It's raining," Cypress finally says in answer to my question, making it sound more like an observation than an explanation for why he hasn't left. "You hear it?"

"Course I can," I reply, glancing up too as I listen to the raindrops pinging against the roof. "What's wrong? You afraid a little water won't agree with the fancy clothes?"

"Can't see it on the clothes," he replies, sounding strangely far away as his thumb starts to once again tap out his tell against his thigh. *Tap. Tap. Tap.* Over and over. "Can't see it. But it makes it hard to sleep…"

"Cypress." His hand stills at the sound of his name, those blue eyes finding mine in the dim light. "You really should…" I lean against the stall wall as the tiredness from the day begins to set in. "You should really know if you keep me up snoring, I'll have to kill you."

He smiles, softer this time. "You know, wolf, I think I'd let you."

CHAPTER 19
CYPRESS

I'm waiting in the front parlor for him when he finally comes down the stairs in the very late morning, a nearly frigid cup of coffee in my left hand and a newspaper in my right. I pretend I don't see him, but I know he sees me and, by the looks of it, has half a mind to turn back around before he decides to descend the last few stairs.

Based on the bags under his eyes and the several nicks on his chin from his morning shave, I'm guessing he could have used a few more hours of sleep. And, honestly, I would be happy to help him sleep forever if it weren't for the fact that he's still needed. Apparently.

"Good morning," I say cheerily as Maddock approaches. My mood lighter without me even having to pretend, because last night, unlike him, I had one of the best night's sleep I've had in a very long while. "You want some coffee? It's strong stuff."

"No," he says, still looking a bit green under the collar. "Think I'll wait."

"Perhaps a seat then?" I offer, gesturing toward the extremely uncomfortable-looking wingback chair across from me. "To catch your breath?"

Maddock frowns, but he sits, though I suspect it's mainly because he's not sure he can keep his feet. "Appreciate you…" he starts, then takes a deep inhale through his nose. "Appreciate you helping me to my room last night. I think…I think the bartender might have been pouring a bit too liberally there toward the end."

I shake my head, clicking my tongue in sympathy, even though we both know the most liberal pours last night came directly from the flask inside his coat. "Sore head?"

"Like you wouldn't believe." Maddock closes his eyes, but opens them again to see my expression as he adds, "Can hardly remember a thing from the last few hands."

"Ah, well," I say with a shrug, not at all surprised he's choosing to plead his ignorance rather than admit his responsibility. "Might be a blessing. I'm not sure there is much you'd *want* to recall."

There it is. That twitch of his eye. That tiny little indication that he very much *does* recall.

"Had me wondering if we were going to make the papers," I continue with a laugh. "Can see the headlines now…" I raise a hand, pretending to place the letters in the air. "*The Bad Draw: How Maddock Douglas Was—*"

"Would've been fine," Maddock interrupts, abandoning his amnesia alibi with alarming speed. "Wasn't planning on actually shooting."

"I know," I say, making my voice soothing. "*I* know your character, but some people *do* tend to jump to conclusions. Especially when weapons get involved. And add a famous gunslinger to the mix?" I shake my head. "I believe you were right, though. Plenty of people in the bar probably would've liked to see him in action."

"Of course they would," he says, brushing off his pants while he sits as though he can brush the thought away, too. However, I know I successfully baited him when he says, "Especially when it would be one of the only times he actually had a fitting opponent. Someone to truly test him shot for shot."

"Of course," I say, repeating his words back to him, because in the end, that's all he really wants. "Not that you were actually planning to shoot…"

"No, no. Not then," Maddock agrees, and I don't miss the way he doesn't deny the scenario so much as the timing. "But as you said, people get overexcited over nothing. Clayton calling for the sheriff…I won't forget it, I'll tell you that much."

"Did he?" I ask, playing ignorant while knowing that even if Clayton had given the directive, Arty had been the one to make a go for the jail. He'd divulged as much to me after Maddock was back in his room, wondering if he should come clean. I'd told him that he should take it to his grave and that I'd make sure Clayton did the same. And I will, though I doubt I'll have to do much convincing. Seems a good man…

"There's one thing I can't figure out though," Maddock continues. "No matter how many times I think about it."

"Oh?" I ask, taking another sip of cold coffee and immediately regretting it, though I'm careful not to let it show on my face. "And what might that be?"

"My gun," he says, frowning and staring down at his folded hands in his lap before he looks back at me. "I'm certain I had it on me when I walked in. But then all of a sudden…it's nowhere to be found."

"Was in your room, wasn't it?" I supply, reacquainting myself with the familiar sensation of trying to balance on an exceptionally narrow line. "Last night when you got back, you found it on your desk. Or don't you remember?"

"I remember all right," he says simply. "I remember having it on me in the saloon."

"How strange." I lean back in my chair, hands resting over my chest as I mirror his posture. "But surely you don't think someone took it, do you? Would be extremely polite of them to then leave it in your room for you if they did."

His forehead creases in frustrated thought. "Suppose it would. But I think I'll ask Arty about it in any case."

The genuine surprise must show on my face, because he rolls his eyes and chuckles. "Beginning to think you must have been the one to overindulge last night. You didn't notice that either? That he disappeared right before my gun did?"

Damn. I'd been so focused on shielding Arty from blame for the sheriff that it hadn't even occurred to me that Maddock would think to blame him for the missing pistol.

"Arty isn't exactly…he doesn't exactly seem like a seasoned criminal," I start to say, hoping to let what Maddock has witnessed with his own eyes speak for what he didn't. "Do you really think he'd be able to? To steal it without being noticed? From *you* of all people?"

Maddock's chest puffs up at the purposefully implied compliment, and the inflated egos of less-than-mediocre men should truly be studied. "Ordinarily, I would say there'd be no chance. That kid can barely tack his horse, but I'd been hard on him earlier to try to help him learn. Then after, I'd been so focused on making sure Aiden didn't do anything rash, that he didn't hurt someone."

"That *Aiden* didn't?" I repeat, and likely not with the tone I should have used as I try to keep up with the history that Maddock is rewriting even from the beginning of this conversation. I blend my indignation into something that more resembles curious intrigue. "He seemed opposed to the idea of the *demonstration*, no?"

"It's all a show," Maddock replies, rolling his eyes. "Didn't want me calling him out is what it is. Wants to keep everyone fooled. But he won't me. I'm more discerning than most."

"How tragically true," I reply, sighing deeply. "You're *that* certain, though, that the claims about him are exaggerated?" I ask, setting my coffee down on the table so that I can rest my left hand on my thigh. "That the papers made too much of him?"

"Course they did." He shrugs. "Makes a good story, doesn't it? A poor boy playing vigilante? Fills headlines and sells papers. Meanwhile, those of us who are really worthy, who are moving this country forward, are left to toil in obscurity. Paving the way for industry with nothing to show for it."

"Except a fortune," I say, wondering how deluded he must be to believe any of this, and I have little doubt that he does—with the type of true devotion you'd be pressed to find in most cathedrals. "Surely the large piles of money must ease the sting a little?"

Maddock smirks. "It does help. Although my parents…let's just say we have very different ideals on how that fortune could be best put to use."

"How frustrating for you," I say, contemplating picking my coffee back up to have something else to focus on but not entirely trusting myself *not* to hurl the mug at him if I did. "To have parents that cannot see your vision."

"Yes, that's *precisely* it," Maddock says, clapping his hand against his leg. "They can't see the possibilities that I can. Nothing exists for them outside of our land and our cattle, but me? I can see it. I see the opportunity, and I have the conviction and the resilience to make it happen. The courage to make the tough choices when it comes to the obstacles in our country's way."

"I'll bet you do," I say, afraid to ask just how many of those *obstacles* are actually human lives. "Tell me, have you considered a career in politics? Your mentality seems perfectly suited for it."

"I have," Maddock says, smiling proudly before he frowns. "Another area of disagreement between my family and me, as it happens, but they'll come around eventually. It's partially why…" He pauses, considering whether to press on until the temptation of a willing listener once again proves to be too much for him. "It's partially why I originally brought the gunslinger on. I figured with him at my side…"

I think back to what Maddock said yesterday morning about helping Aiden make a name for himself again, the true reason now revealing itself. "You figured you could make some headlines," I guess. "Ones that might help launch a campaign?"

Maddock nods, eagerly leaning forward. "You saw how Clayton practically tripped over himself last night simply to shake his hand. People…people like Clayton…the *little* people—"

I laugh, picturing the towering older man. "Is that how you would deem him?"

"You know what I mean," Maddock hedges. "He's not like us. He doesn't come from the same…he made his money quick. What's to say he won't lose it just as quickly? Not that I wouldn't take a donation all the same."

"Of course not."

"But these people, they look at Aiden and see a hero. Practically a king."

"A god."

"*Yes*, and who can blame them when they've so little to look toward? But still…a powerful weapon in the right hands. The kind that could make real change."

"As interesting a picture it is that you're painting, Maddock, I don't see him agreeing to be your *weapon*."

"He is already. The whole reason he's in town at all is by my request. By my order."

"And what will your next order be?" I ask, wondering how much Maddock knows about Aiden's plans to leave, the ones he'd told me about last night.

"When we reach the next town? Same as it was here." He sits back in his chair, looking deeply satisfied with himself. "I told you I don't believe in letting opportunities pass by, and this trip we're taking up to Kansas—"

"The cattle drive?"

He rolls his eyes again. "Yes, the drive. Why not treat it as the beginning of my campaign trail? Why not have it be the start of something that actually matters?"

"I see," I say, understanding more why he and his parents might be having some differences of opinion if he's treating their business and their animals as little more than a ticket to get from town to town. "Well, certainly a packed agenda that you've laid out for yourself, which reminds me, I should—"

"You should be getting in on this," Maddock says, shooting forward to grab my arm when I begin to stand. "You're like me. You're someone with vision."

"Oh, I most certainly have a vision," I reply, glancing down at my arm. "Though perhaps I'll have to get my own gunslinger by my side to execute it."

Maddock laughs, letting go of me as I get to my feet and reclining with a smile. "Let me know if you find a better one than what I have. Or at least one more agreeable." He tips his head back against the chair, closing his eyes. "Although, you know, he doesn't really *have* to be on your side. Not if you play things right."

I pause, studying him closely. "Oh? Do tell."

He shrugs. "All you really need is the name. Hardly matters if they're standing next to you or…across from you."

"Across from you? As in…you do plan to fight him?" I ask, needing to make sure I have it right. "I thought you said that people looked to him as a hero? A king? What would that make you then?"

"Something new. After all, what better way for a new king to rise than by exposing a false one?" He surveys me, and I know I need to say something, do something. To react in *some* way, but there's a rare thread of panic wrapping around me, holding me in place.

"As I told you, Cypress," Maddock says, hopefully mistaking my speechlessness as consideration. "The courage to remove obstacles. Also," he continues, with a half-laugh, "wouldn't mind not having to look at his self-righteous face anymore, you know what I mean?" He shakes his head, pleased with his own humor. "Well, I suppose I've kept you long enough. Thank you again for your help last night and for your conversation this morning. It's not often I find someone who truly understands."

"Oh, I understand," I reassure him. "Have no doubt about that." I grab my coat from the back of my chair. "Until tonight then."

"Until tonight," he says when I'm already halfway to the door. "I can hardly wait."

And neither can I, it would seem. *I'm running out of time.*

CHAPTER 20
AIDEN

I don't think I dreamed last night.

I mean, I must have, but…I didn't have *the* dream. And it's almost disorienting waking up not because of the things waiting in the dark but instead because of the sunlight streaming in.

What is waiting, however, is the mustang. Who must decide he's been patient long enough as soon as he sees me stirring, and who decides to help by tugging at the blanket over me and blowing a big puff of warm air into my face when that doesn't seem to get me up off the hay bales faster.

"All right," I tell him, lightly shoving his soft nose. "Give me a minute."

He grunts in reply, although the shrill whinny piercing the air a moment later from the next stall over is a good indication that apparently, everyone is getting a late start today, and that some of us wake more happy than others. *Christ…others.*

I sit up, getting to my feet so fast I nearly get tangled up in the blanket that I belatedly realize isn't mine. An *all-black* blanket. *For fuck's sake.*

"*Hey*," I hiss in the direction of the other stall while both horses look at me like I've lost my mind. Honestly, it's really starting to feel like I have. "You over there?"

No response.

I sigh, take a glance around as I listen for the sounds of someone else in the stable, then try again. "*Cypress*, you over there?"

There's still no response, and a quick check over the wall does indeed reveal that he has already left to…to do whatever it is that he does during the day.

I let out a relieved breath, glad to have a moment to get my bearings and to brush off the large amount of hay that has fixed itself to my person over the course of the night. I must have looked a mess when he left earlier, although I'm not sure *why* I give a damn about what I would have looked like when he saw me.

However, this is also the moment I see the note fastened to the stall wall not two feet from where I'm standing. Right beside the mustang's feed bucket so I couldn't help but see it, but also right where no one who was simply passing by would spy it.

I grab the folded-up piece of fancy stationary that has my name on the outside. Almost surprised the paper isn't black too, but then I suppose that would make the ink hard to see. At least he has *some* degree of practicality even if, when I open the note, I *am* surprised to find the writing so brief given its author.

When you're awake, find Simon.

"Simon?" I mutter, turning the paper over and then flipping it back when no additional context is revealed. "Who the fuck is Simon?"

"I'm Simon," replies a small voice, the stablehand suddenly appearing in the aisle as if summoned. "Was comin' to make sure you weren't dead. Kinda disappointed you aren't. Never seen a dead body before."

I arch an eyebrow at him. "Appreciate the concern."

"Your friend—er, your man—"

"Not my man."

"Right, but you know who I mean?"

"The one that pays better than me?"

"That's the one. He told me to give you a message." The boy pulls himself up on the stall wall, swinging a leg over to sit on the edge like a bold mouse. "Said I should make sure you get it. That it's important, but he didn't want to wake you."

"Okay, and it is…?" I prompt, hoping to God it's not something inappropriate.

"He said to tell you that you ought to start riding No Name down to the saloon."

I frown, not having expected that to be the message he deemed so important that he'd leave a note and send the boy. "He say why?"

"No, he just said he was going to ride Cerberus down there and you should do the same with your horse. Just in case."

"Just in case of—wait, did you say *Cerberus*?"

The boy nods, the black horse also whickering in what I can only assume to be an acknowledgement as he hangs his head over the stall door and starts nudging the boy's hand in hope of treats.

"Is that…" The name sounds familiar, but I come up empty when

I search my brain for information, for any bits of education from the orphanage that I've shoved aside because I hadn't needed it to survive. Until now, possibly. "He named for something?"

The boy shrugs. "I dunno. Neat though, huh?"

"Certainly distinctive."

"What's that mean?"

"Hard to ignore." I drag a hand down my face. "So, that's all he said? That I ought to ride my horse to the saloon? He didn't say *why?*"

"Not really," the boy says, his face screwing up as he thinks hard. "Just that you should, too, cause then you could ride together after."

I shake my head as I stare at the ground, regretting letting Cypress stay since it's apparently given him new ideas. I need to put an end to this. Now. Whatever *this* is. "Listen, you tell him if you see him that he can do what he wants, but I'm fine walkin'."

"You sure?" the boy asks. "He really seemed to think it'd be a good idea."

"I'll bet he did," I say, reaching over the stall door for the latch, only to find it once again secured with the quick knot. I roll my eyes before slipping the tail end through the loop and tugging it loose.

"Hey," the boy says, seeming genuinely excited. "You got the hang of it."

I let out a laugh, even while discovering my coat and hat to still be damp after hanging out overnight. "Suppose I'm not as dumb as I look."

"Suppose not."

Little shit. I turn to the boy, who is currently eye level with me up on his perch. "There something else you need?"

"I'm just waiting for you to take your horse out."

I sigh. "Because?"

"Because I need to know where to put Cerberus," he says, looking at me like *I'm* the one asking stupid questions. "He really wants them to get to know each other."

I open my mouth to reply, then close it, only willing to try again when I'm sure that the words that come out of it will be suitable for a child's ears.

"Look, uh—"

"Simon."

"Right, how much is he paying you?"

"A lot."

"How much is a lot?"

"He gave me a whole dollar for bringing the message."

"He gave you—"

"So you tell him I did it, okay? When you see him? Please?"

I chuckle. "Why? You afraid of losing your employer if I don't?"

"Nah." The boy shrugs. "I mean, I like the money, but he's also…"

"What?"

"Nice," he says. "I'd hate to let him down."

I frown, considering that. "Nice, huh?"

"Yeah," he replies, but then seems to second-guess himself. "I mean, not that you ain't…well, not that you are either. Main thing is I like him better."

"Thanks for your honesty."

"But maybe if you taught me how to shoo—"

"No."

"*Fine.*" He lets out a truly aggrieved sigh. "If you ain't gonna be dead and you ain't gonna teach me to shoot, then can you at least move your horse? I want to go get Sally somethin' with my dollar, but I can't until I'm done with my chores."

"Sure, I'll move him," I say, reaching for Cypress's slip of paper along with a pencil from the pocket of my coat. "On one condition."

CHAPTER 21
CYPRESS

Alley. After.
P.S. You owe the boy another dollar.

I bite the inside of my cheek, battling a ridiculous grin as I look down and again read over the note I have hidden in my hand beneath the table.

I'd never expected him to write back and I'm so distracted trying to figure out what it means that I almost miss my turn to play when it comes around the table, quickly covering by tossing a few bills in the middle though I'm not sure if I've even really looked at my cards. And I really *should* because…

It's a good sign, right? He's *asking* to see me. *Wants* me to be in the alley after tonight's game, although, of course I will be. Where else would I want to be?

"Cypress?" Clayton gives me a friendly nudge. "You all right?"

"Fantastic," I say, a bit too enthusiastically, because now that I actually do check my hand, it contains very little that deserves it. "Fantastic night, that is. Good weather. No rain." I clear my throat, shocked at how truly terrible that explanation was. "Are we…who is…"

I trail off as Clayton starts laughing. "Find yourself a pretty distraction while you're here?" He tips his head in the direction of the note, and I quickly tuck it out of sight in my pocket before giving him nothing more than a wry smile. He nods, then lowers his voice conspiratorially. "Who is she? I'll bet you anything that I know her."

"Not like I do," I say, refusing to let my eyes drift toward the bar. To that broody cowboy, who unlike me is absent his usual hat tonight and had looked very unenthused about it when he'd placed it on the back of his chair along with his coat. Though I have to say, that full head of soft brown waves on display is also not making it very easy to focus.

"You won't even give me a hint?" Clayton asks.

I shake my head. "Not a one."

Clayton raises an eyebrow. "Married?"

"Not yet."

"A secret?"

"For now."

"And you're in love?"

I sigh. "In a way that is life-altering."

Clayton lets out another laugh. "The two of you had better slip out of town and run for it then before anyone can convince you otherwise."

I eye the wedding band on his left hand. "That what you did?"

"What I wish I'd done," he says, looking momentarily sad before giving me a wink. "Don't look back when you do."

For the second time today, I'm reminded of how much I like Clayton, the first being when I caught him out on the street to talk before the game. As I had a feeling he would, he'd immediately agreed to keep Arty's involvement with the sheriff a secret, even expressed regret at making him go in the first place.

"I was worried if I left, it might be Aiden on his own," he had told me, frowning deeply, while the very idea of it also made me drift toward rage. "I know you were doing your best to put a stop to things as well. Seemed the easiest solution in the moment."

"It was," I reassured him. "But Maddock is the type to—"

"I know exactly the type he is," Clayton replied, his look of guilt turning to one of disdain. "Which is why I'm back tonight. Needs addressing. I've already spoken to the bartender about watering down Maddock's whiskey."

"He'll still do his best to make your night miserable. Sober or not," I told him, while giving him a grateful smile. "You sure you're not just a glutton for punishment?"

"For *his* punishment? Yes," Clayton replied, now sounding angry, too. "I've known too many like him. Many during a time when I did not have the power to make their lives more difficult. If you get my meaning."

"Very well," I'd admitted, even more honest than I normally would be, in part because talking about Aiden made me almost as anxious as the note had to get inside quickly. "You don't have to explain it to me."

"No," he said, openly considering me. "Had a feeling I might not. You're ready then?"

"Of course." I was already heading for the door and wondering how long it would be until I came back out to the alley. "Been waiting."

Thinking about it now, the exchange should have left me more uneasy than it did. If Clayton has been able to work out that I am not entirely as I appear, then it means others could have, too. And given that I have already slipped more than once in front of Maddock…

Across the table, the man in question stares at his cards, the fact that he's playing fairly well meaning he hasn't bore much malice toward anyone else at the table so far. Still, the night is young.

"Fold," he says, tossing down his cards like a child tosses down a toy that no longer pleases them, and the couple of his men that were still in the game quickly follow suit. Likely regardless of if they had a hand that could have kept them in.

Can't win if the boss doesn't.

"What about you, Cypress?" Charley asks, still in it along with Clayton and me. "You actually going to play at some point this week or are you just going to keep sitting there all moony-eyed?"

Damn. Really isn't just Clayton that's noticed then.

I smile, leaning forward with my elbows on the table and my hands clasped in front of me. "Can you blame me, Charley? When I have your sparkling blue eyes to stare at?"

"They're green, you horse's ass," he replies, though I catch a grin hiding in the wrinkles on his face. "You're lucky my wife isn't here. Saying stuff like that."

"Why? Wouldn't she agree?"

"She would," he says, smile broadening. "Which is why you're lucky."

Almost everyone at the table laughs, except Maddock, who has the type of dismal expression on his face that makes him look even worse than he had this morning. "Are you all going to finish the hand or not?" he asks, sitting with his arms folded across his chest. "Barely worth it if we can't make it through more than a few rounds."

I suppress the urge to roll my eyes before setting my cards face down on the table, still not entirely sure what I even have in hand because Aiden's just stood to stretch and I'm too busy sneaking glances at the long expanse of his back as he leans against the bar. At the way his shoulders and biceps pull the fabric of his dark shirt taut. At the way he drags a hand across the whiskers on his jaw and— "Fold."

There's another short round of laughter, their heads shaking at my expense before Clayton claps me on the back in sympathy and leans in to mutter, "You sure you're ready to do this?"

"Without question," I say, pulling my gaze away from Aiden as something about the seriousness in his tone in contrast to the lightness I feel finally catches me. "Wait, ready to—"

"You might as well go ahead and start simply making donations at this point," Maddock says before I can get my question out, unable to resist making a comment about my loss if it'll make his own smart less. "If you're going to play, at least try to make it interesting."

"Well, that's not a bad idea, Maddock," Clayton replies for me, setting down a straight flush and smiling when Charley promptly swears and drops his own cards. "We *could* make things more interesting."

I glance sideways at him, and his subtle nod tells me he thinks we're on the same page. Only, I don't even know what book we're reading. Apparently I should have let Clayton explain it to me after all. *Damn it. What have I agreed to?*

"You have something in mind?" Maddock is asking, nearly echoing my silent question, and I do my best to keep my face neutral but interested as I get ready to pivot my plans. "Higher limit?"

"How about *no* limit?" Clayton responds, gathering up the healthy stack of new additions to his winnings. "We go as high as that dwindling pocketbook of yours will allow."

No, I think, finally understanding what he's doing and answering his question far too late. Ordinarily, I'd take the opportunity being presented to me. Take *everything*. But I can't. Not now… *I'm not ready.*

"Oh, I wouldn't worry about my pocketbook," Maddock counters, rising to the challenge as expected. "Yours will run dry long before mine does."

I risk another glance in the direction of the bar, only to find Aiden looking back this time, and my face must not be nearly as neutral as I thought because his brow furrows. *Shit.* I'm playing this whole thing worse than I ever have and the stakes could not be any higher than they are right now.

Except, apparently they can be.

Clayton shrugs, tilting his head from side to side in thought before pulling a fresh cigar out of his coat. "How about property? You got something you can stand to lose?"

I can't do this now. I haven't explained things to Aiden. I'd been counting on the ride tonight, on our time in the alley to try. He won't know. And, if I start playing to win and end up having to run, I don't know if I'll be able to turn around.

I might not be able to get back to him. Again.

"Pretty sure you're the only one here with property nearby," Maddock is saying to Clayton, tone dismissive. "Not all of us are so *familiar* in this town."

Clayton chuckles, not remotely concerned about Maddock hinting that he's unhappy with him calling for the sheriff the night before. Although, to my right, I feel Arty tense, and I do what I hope is a very inconspicuous shake of my head. Only one of us needs to be giving themselves away tonight.

"You have cattle, don't you?" Clayton raises. "A significant number not far outside town from what I hear. Wager a few head."

Maddock's jaw clenches, and I suspect he couldn't bet them even if he wanted to. They don't belong to him. Not really. Not until his family decides to pass the reins or die. And from what I've seen so far, I'm inclined to believe it'll probably be the latter.

"What would you even want with cattle?" Maddock asks, laughing, but there's no humor to it. "You even know how to make a living doing something other than digging in the dirt?"

"Likely better than you do," Clayton says easily, still calmly counting his winnings while also coming to the same conclusion I did. "You know how to make a living doing something other than what your mama says?"

One of Maddock's men snorts out a laugh, then promptly regrets it as the clear fury on Maddock's face from Clayton's perfectly aimed insult changes targets.

"Sorry, boss," he says, eyes wide. "Wasn't laughin' at you. Was just— was only—"

"No limits," Maddock agrees, stopping the man's rambling before looking back at Clayton. "And we can wager horses. When your money runs out."

Horses. Immediately, I remember what Aiden said last night, about his deal with Maddock, that he'd get that horse he won't name at the end of the week. That he was counting on it so he could cut himself loose from the group, because as of right now, the poor animal still belongs to Maddock. And based on the looks of the other men at the table, I'm certain he's not the only one in that predicament, though I'm surprised by the one who actually speaks up.

"Boss," Arty says, so near to a whisper that I'm amazed I can hear him, let alone anyone else. "We need them horses, don't we? To work the cattle?"

"What we need is for you to keep your *goddamn* mouth *shut*," Maddock snaps, jamming a finger in Arty's direction. "You hear me?"

"Yes, sir. I was only thinkin'—"

"*Don't*," Maddock says, voice cold. "Do us all a favor and *don't* think." He rounds back to Clayton. "We're agreed?"

Clayton frowns, gaze flicking between Arty and Maddock with an increasingly determined set to his expression. "Agreed."

Out of the corner of my eye, I see him then glance to me, waiting, expectant, but I'm already staring at Aiden. At the way his frown deepens before his eyes drop to the table in front of me, to where my fingers are tapping against the surface. *Tap. Tap. Tap.*

I force myself to stop and reply, "Agreed."

"Not me," Charley says, already getting to his feet. "I'm too old for this foolishness. And so is my horse." He puts his hat on, giving Clayton and me each a pat on the shoulder as he walks by, even lingering to give Arty one, too. "I'd tell all you boys that you ought to go to bed, but I know you won't listen. So I'll only say that I'll be seeing you. Hopefully."

Maddock rolls his eyes, not letting him get more than a few paces away before he points at each of his men and says, "You're all playing."

Each of them, except Arty—who is still staring at his lap—blink at him in confusion. "But, boss," starts the same one who had laughed before. "We don't—"

"I'm not asking," Maddock barks, then to the dealer says, "Deal 'em in."

I don't have to play to win. I can still lose. After all these years, I've become really good at losing until the time is right. And I can continue to do so, no matter how much it'll cost me to stay at this table all night. If it will simply buy me time, it will be worth it.

It doesn't have to be me that teaches Maddock a lesson. I can let it be Clayton. I don't mind Maddock's money going to him. I can be at peace with that. Don't mind the horses going to him either…

Well, except one.

And wouldn't you know, it's the same one Maddock bets without hesitation not three deals later. Deals be damned.

And that's when I realize maybe I'm not as good at losing as I think I am.

CHAPTER 22
AIDEN

Something has gone wrong. *Really* fucking wrong.

Maddock is standing from the table, cards thrown down so he can point a finger at the man who remains seated across from him. His usual all-black ensemble partially hidden by the frankly obscene pile of money now in front of him.

"You're a fucking *cheat*," Maddock snaps, enraged. "How the *hell* did you pull that card?"

"You sure like to make a lot of wild accusations, Maddock," the older man from the night before says, stamping out his cigar before getting to his feet himself. "I saw the whole thing, and you lost fair. You shouldn't play unless—"

"*Fair?*" Maddock replies, disbelief clear. "All week he's barely been playing well enough to keep his shirt and now all of a sudden he can't lose? It's *bullshit*, and you know it."

The conversations around the bar are growing progressively quieter as their table gets louder, similar to last night, only this time I'm not caught in the middle. Still feel like I am, though, even before I find myself up from my barstool and inching closer.

"Maddock," the older man tries again, calm as he holds up a hand for order. "You understood the stakes and you agreed. It's no one's fault but yours if—"

"You can't tell me you're really buying this," Maddock says, starting to sound a little frantic now. "You can't be planning to accept this when he's—*you've* lost almost as much as me. Nearly half the money in that pile is yours."

"It is," he replies, still appearing more amused than upset. "However, it would seem that your pocketbook apparently does run out before mine. You're done, Maddock. Time to call it a night and get to moving on."

My boss stares back at him, purposefully not looking at his men, who I suspect are far more shocked than I am that we've arrived at this conclusion, all their hopes for a share of the week's profits now dead because of a man who really does look more than ready to preside over the funeral.

And who is…still remarkably quiet.

"I'm not leaving without my money. I can't—" Maddock clears his throat, but his voice remains as unsteady as the hand he lowers to hover over the pistol that is most definitely at his belt tonight. "I won't stand for being cheated."

At long last, Cypress sighs, his head tilting up from where he had been looking down at the table, and neatly compiling his winnings. Now that I can see his face again, the unaffected demeanor he has somehow appears far more menacing on him than I think it would on anyone else. "I've not cheated you tonight, Maddock. Although, even if I had, I do not think you ought to be talking about dishonesty." His eyes flick in my direction, but only for a moment, and I wonder what it means before he continues, "You can lick your wounds all you like, but don't for a second pretend you are not the one who inflicted them."

"You *will* give me back—"

Maddock's sentence cuts off as Cypress pushes away from the table, tucking all the money into his vest before drawing himself up to his full height. He smirks as his opponent unconsciously takes a step back.

Can't say I blame Maddock. Because suddenly, there's not a trace of the charming aristocrat who has been sitting at the poker table with him for half the week, the disguise wholly abandoned to reveal the captivating thief I keep meeting in the shadows. The one who walks right up to a gun without flinching. The one I've known all this time.

"Believe I'm done here," Cypress says, turning his head in the older man's direction just enough that he'll know he's talking to him even if he never takes his eyes off my employer. "You'll mind my other winnings, won't you? All except—"

I know Maddock is going to do it. Maybe before he even knows it himself. I see the way his fingers twitch, see the way he widens his stance too far again like a goddamn idiot, making it all too easy for me to draw my gun before Maddock even reaches for his.

Around us, the previously silent room erupts into exclamations of panic as pistols are pulled and aimed. Tables and chairs scrape loudly against the wood floor as people hurry to take cover beneath them. And,

God, I can't say I fault them this time, because I'm almost as shocked as they are.

Maddock hadn't outdrawn me. Not by a long shot. But Cypress sure as hell had.

"Gentlemen." He calmly aims the gun in his left hand at Maddock while the one in his right moves to each of his men in turn. All except the kid, who has joined most of the other bar patrons in hiding beneath the table. "Being a poor loser really is so…*unattractive*. And as you already have so few redeeming qualities, I'd recommend not adding it to the list."

Twin pistols. He has *two* shining silver pistols, though I would have sworn he only had one. Drawn faster than I've seen perhaps anyone else do so from a shoulder holster beneath his coat. Anyone but me when I'd been at my best, and since I'm certainly not right now, he would've had me had he been aiming my way.

But he isn't. And he hasn't been. Several times now we've been alone, and he clearly could've killed me during any one of them without me seeing it coming. He *could've*, but he didn't. He hasn't even tried to hurt me. Not even when I hurt him.

As if he can hear me thinking, his focus switches momentarily to me, and in that brief second, I see him take in not only my raised weapon but precisely *where* it is I'm aiming. He grins, those blue eyes of his practically dancing, and I know exactly the reason why.

Because I'm also not aiming at Cypress. I'm aiming at Maddock.

Or at least, I am, until I see the distinct outline of a shotgun appear to my right.

"That's enough," the bartender says, pointing the barrel past me toward the table, although with far less accuracy of target. "I'm not having this. All of you need to take this out of here. Now."

At the order, I glance in his direction without changing my aim, and I'm surprised to find him to be around my age, even though I'm certain I've ordered a drink from him every night this week. "Not sure that's such a good idea," I say, quietly. "It goes into the street and there's likely to be bloodshed."

"Better there than in here," he says with a shrug. "Don't really care if they end up killing each other, so long as I don't have to clean it up."

"Right," I say back, able to see his point, though I'm not sure I share the same indifference on whether or not they keep breathing. Well, at least one of them.

It'll really eat at me if Cypress dies without me having a chance to figure him out first, to at the very least understand his motives even if I likely won't have a prayer of ever really understanding *him*.

Although, maybe this *is* his motive. Maybe all of it was just to get us right here. So that when this very thing happened, I'd be the fool pointing at Maddock instead of at him.

My arm starts to drop, the pistol moving from aiming at my employer to aiming at the floor, so that by the time Maddock pivots toward the bartender while leaving his gun on Cypress, it looks like he's far more ready to shoot than I am.

"I mean it," the bartender says while I keep my eyes on Cypress, feeling guilty for some reason for the way his smile falls with uncertainty as he watches me finish lowering my weapon. "I'll call for the law."

"A fine idea," Maddock agrees, the brightness in his tone undercut by the desperation in his eyes. "Let him come and arrest the criminal."

"You really think anyone will agree with you on that charge?" the older man argues from near Cypress. "Everyone here saw him play a fair game. Just as they saw you lose."

"They will," Maddock says, glancing and nodding at his men for the first time since he stood from the table. "That's the word of five—" He seems to remember again that I'm here. "No, six men. Against the word of two."

"No judge is going to take the word of men you're paying as gospel."

"That right?" Maddock replies, gesturing with the gun between Cypress and him. "And what's he paying you? How much did he offer you to go along with this? Once a servant, always a servant, hm?"

For a moment, I worry if Maddock might be on to something, if perhaps I'm not the only one who received an attempt at a bribe. I'm not sure why it bothers me. A lot more than it fucking should.

"There are worse things…" the man mutters, giving Maddock a glare that would be enough to kill if there were any real justice in the world. "Far worse."

Maddock sneers back at him, then turns to the bartender. "Go on. Call the sheriff. He'll have an opportunity to weigh the evidence, same as everyone else in here." He looks around, meeting the eyes of more than a few men who are still barricaded behind tables and likely prepared to reach for their own pistols if they need to. "Everyone can determine if they want to be on the right side of this. If they're going to allow some pathetic thief to rob a Douglas right in front of their eyes. If they're ready for the type of *retribution* that might come about as a result."

All around us, I can see a few people exchanging looks at the name, and the power, it holds in this state. Even the older man, who has been so outspoken up until now, seems to falter as the tide of the room shifts. But Cypress? He only laughs, shaking his head before he replies, "If your only hope here is calling on your daddy's name, then I'm not sure *I'm* the one they're going to find pathetic."

In confirmation, there are a few low chuckles, but they fall silent as soon as Maddock's lip curls. He cocks his gun, still aimed right at Cypress's chest, and it's all the provocation Cypress should need to pull the trigger. But he doesn't. He only stares at me. And though his guns are raised, I see that expression in his eyes again. The one he'd worn in the alley when I'd put a knife to his throat. Like it's not really death he's afraid of, because there's something else he fears more.

I shouldn't care. I've seen plenty of men afraid. I've seen plenty killed. *Innocent* men killed for far less, and I doubt there is a single definition of the word that would apply to Cypress.

All week he's been playing these men. Letting them win, tricking them into thinking he's not a threat, only to finally turn the tables on them now. This is his game, and he ought to have planned for when it would end.

He *is* a thief, and I…

My left hand strays to my coat pocket, to the watch that's still there wrapped in black fabric, to the bribe that I still haven't bothered to give back because…maybe we both have things we fear more than death.

"Any last words?" I hear Maddock ask, and even though Cypress says nothing, I hear him in my head.

I'll have to kill you.

You know, wolf, I think I'd let you.

Is he really…is he really not going to put up a fight? I glance around for something that will prevent this, for *someone*, but of course, not one of them moves. Not one of the people that were cheering and lifting their drinks to him only the night prior lifts a finger for him now. No one speaks for him. He has no one.

No one else he's looking to but me. *Goddammit.*

"Maddock," I bark, stepping forward without fully knowing what I intend to do beyond carefully studying my employer for any ideas he might have about turning his gun on me.

He warily watches me approach, and I wait until we are side by side and I've turned my back on Cypress before I drop my voice and say the only thing I can think of that might get Maddock to hold. "You'll never get your money back if you shoot him. Not right away. The law *will* get involved. And when they do, you'll wind up stuck here until things are resolved."

He regards me with contempt. "You can't be suggesting that I let him—"

"What I'm *suggesting* is you take this out of here like the man said. And that you let me handle it when you do."

"You?" he asks as his eyebrows rise, clearly not expecting the offer but also interested by it. "Why? You decide to finally do your job?"

I bite my tongue, nearly in two, but I get the next words out. The ones I'm sure he needs to hear. "I protect your *interests*. That was our deal, right?"

Maddock barely removes his gaze from Cypress for more than a second, but I still see it when he flicks his eyes to the floor, appearing slightly nervous before he shakes it off and nods. "It was. You planning on holding up your end of it?"

"Outside." I turn, choosing not to acknowledge that last part before letting myself brave Cypress, letting him search my face in that all-seeing way he seems to have. "We take this discussion outside."

There's no real reason for him to agree. He's better off in here where there are witnesses, even if none of them appear ready to come to his defense. But I trusted him last night when he silently told me to stand down. And I'm hoping that might be enough to convince him to at least consider—

Both of Cypress's arms drop without hesitation, both guns returning to their holsters as he nods in my direction, then waits for his former opponent to do the same.

"Don't," I tell Maddock again when he hesitates, his finger still hovering near the trigger. "You'll get your chance. But not here."

A minute that feels like an hour passes before he finally nods, too. His arm falls in much the same way Cypress's had, though far slower, and even if he doesn't reholster his pistol, I feel like I'm able to start breathing once more.

"He goes out first," Maddock says, gesturing toward Cypress and then his men. "You follow him. And you…" He addresses the older man. "You best stay out of it this time if you know what's good for you."

The man opens his mouth as if to reply, but thankfully looks to me before he does, sees me shake my head, and falls silent right as Maddock steps forward. On reflex, I grab his arm before he can get far, and when I do, his eyebrows shoot up again, this time in anger as well as shock, but I don't care. "Don't do anything until I get there."

"And *where* are you—"

"Need to check my weapon over." I say, not entirely having to lie about the excuse. "Before."

"Really are *prudent*, aren't you?" Maddock rolls his eyes, jerking his arm away. "Fine. Do whatever it is you need to do so long as *he* gets what he deserves. This is your chance to prove yourself, you understand?"

"I do," I assure him, looking past his shoulder just in time to see Cypress hesitate by the door, his eyes finding mine as they'd done that first night I'd seen him. Before the first time I'd followed him.

How fitting for him to do it again before the last.

CHAPTER 23
AIDEN

I'm grabbing my coat and hat and moving before the door has a chance to fully swing closed behind Maddock, gesturing for the older man to follow me as I take the shortest path toward the back of the saloon.

"You're not…" he starts to say, practically having to jog to catch up. "You're not going to leave him out there with them?"

"*No,*" I say, the word coming out a bit sharper than I intended. "And neither are you." Quickly, I look back over my shoulder, pointing at the bartender so he understands my next order is for him. "You stand by the front door and you don't let anyone in here. Otherwise you really will have a mess, you understand?"

He nods and goes to take his place as the older man asks, "What can I do?"

"You can go get your buddy," I tell him as we arrive at the door to the alley, pausing before reaching for the handle. "When we step outside, you go left until you're far enough away that you're not going to be seen. Then, when you get to the sheriff, tell him he needs to bring backup with him. More than a couple people."

I glance to my right, catching the eye of the closest armed citizen inside the saloon. "*You*. Take this door when we leave and don't let anyone back in if you want to remain alive. Got it?"

The man's eyes widen, but he gets up to do as I say. Redeeming himself, albeit only slightly. When he assumes his position, I turn to the older man while I start checking my gun, just as I said I would.

"Tell me honestly," I say, counting out the six rounds in the chamber. "He cheat?"

"No," he replies, confidently. "Seems to me he only started actually playing."

I nod. "That's what I figured, but wanted to be sure."

"What will you do?" he asks, expression shifting to concern. "You'll go out there? On your own?"

"Not entirely on my own. I'd like to believe Cypress might participate in his own rescue." I pause, noticing the way the older man is suddenly studying me. "What?"

"Didn't realize the two of you were on a first-name basis." The corner of his mouth twitches upward. "How'd that come about?"

"Must have..." I clear my throat, glancing around the room and wondering how long the men in here will actually have good sense to stay put despite the guards I've placed. "Must have overheard it."

"Interesting," the older man says. "Then you know mine, too? Since I gave it to you directly."

"Sure I do. It's..." My mind remains completely blank, though I know he *did* give it to me, and I sigh with exasperation before replying, "It's *hurry the fuck up and go get some help when I open this door.*"

He chuckles. "I wish you two the best of luck. And, if you make it out of this, a long life tog—"

"Oh, for fuck's sake," I mutter, abruptly shoving the door open and stepping out into the lantern-lit alley. Pleased for more than one reason when he slips out behind me without another word and takes off in the opposite direction.

Last thing I fucking need right now—yet *another* person in this town getting some idea about what Cypress and I are to each other. Which is nothing. Apart from a growing source of agitation. And a likely death sentence.

No sooner have I taken a couple steps toward the side of the building than I'm able to make out their voices, the echoes of their threats, the cruelty of their laughter that gets louder the closer I get. I don't even need to hear the exact words to know exactly what they're saying, to understand that they've already trapped him in the few minutes that have passed.

A quick check around the darkened corner reveals there are indeed seven of us total in this alley, more than enough to make it plenty crowded, and I take stock of each man's exact location before proceeding. Fortunately, Maddock is closest to me, a consequence of him standing where he is at the least risk of being seen while he's got the kid standing closest to the street playing lookout—even though he seems to want to do anything but look at what's happening. At what he thinks is *about* to happen.

"Well, well, here he is," Maddock says when I come into view. "You really are a man of your word after all."

"Try to be," I reply, my gun raised and aimed behind him. "We'll see how the next few minutes go."

As I already knew, Maddock's other three men are in the middle of the alley, two of them with their guns out and hanging uselessly at their sides while the other has blood on his raised fist, its intended mark the last man counted and the only one not currently standing. At least, not on his own.

"Fuckin' *told* you to wait," I snap, adjusting my aim slightly. "Let him go. Now."

Maddock's head tilts in confusion as he looks at me then behind him, pausing the straightening of his suit after whatever scuffle had occurred before I got here. He sighs, waving a hand at his man. "Do as he says," Maddock tells him, laughing slightly. "Suppose he at least wants it to *appear* to be self-defense."

I realize I don't remember this man's name either. Not that it really matters, since he might as well be another of Maddock's limbs for how easily he bends to his boss's every whim. Although right now, he *is* hesitating. "You sure? We turn him loose and—"

"*Now*," I repeat, cocking my gun to help him along. "Let him go."

Far quicker this time, he relaxes the hold he has on his captive's neck, and I get my first true glimpse of Cypress as he sags against the wall, then takes a jagged breath in.

Alive. At least he's still alive. And, somehow, still smiling.

"There…" He wheezes, brushing the blood from a busted lip with his thumb. "There you are, wolf. Thought maybe you were going to miss our appointment."

"Really *not* the time, Cypress," I reply, watching as the understanding of where my allegiance currently lies ripples through the rest of the crew. Something I confirm for them when I decisively turn my gun on Maddock, my finger hovering near the trigger. "You lost. Make your peace with it, and let him be on his way."

"You must be joking," he says, eyes widening as he glances first at Cypress then between my face and the gun. "You—you work for me. You said it yourself in there, we have a *deal*."

"And I told you when we made it that I wouldn't be finishing your fights for you. You knew that when you sat down at the table."

"He cheated," Maddock argues. "All week I've been winning against him until tonight when he—"

"When he stopped letting you," I finish for him, getting impatient. "He's been *letting* you win all week."

"*No*," Maddock argues again, even more adamantly this time, regardless of this being the one argument he could actually claim in his favor. "He hasn't *let* me do a goddamn thing."

I glance at Cypress, and from the widening grin on his face, I can tell Maddock is acting exactly as he knew he would, as he's seen others like him do before.

Pretty smart, the way he lets them box themselves in. Playing it straight on the one game they'll swear he cheated on, then cheating at every game they'll swear he played straight. In the end, he probably doesn't even need to cheat them. Their own pride beats them worse than he does.

"Tonight," Maddock is still saying. "He manipulated the deck. He had cards stashed. Something."

"Witnesses say otherwise," I counter, wondering how close the older man is to reaching the sheriff's office. He didn't have far to go, but it'll take them time to round up reinforcements. Time I'm not sure I have. "There's local folk who will swear to it. You need to stand down."

"We had an agreement," Maddock reiterates. "In *writing*, by your own request might I add, that you look after my interests."

"I *am* lookin' after your interests," I try to reason. "You do this and you're not making it to Kansas with the herd."

"Won't if we don't either," mutters the man who had Cypress against the wall, though he falls silent again as soon as Maddock gives him and everyone else in the alley a warning look. 'Course, not everyone heeds it.

"He bet the horses," Cypress explains, by no means cowed even though he's still wheezing slightly as he straightens. "Lost every one of them along with every dollar in his pocket." His head tilts, regarding Maddock with an expression that's once more bordering on delighted. "Which, might *I* add, makes that deal completely void."

It takes me longer than it should to click into place, although in my defense I have a few things on my mind right now, like how Maddock is twitching toward his gun again. Before he does something stupid, I step forward, placing the barrel of my gun against his skull.

"I wouldn't," I warn, pleased when he puts his hands up. "Glad we're finally listening." I survey the other men in the alley, all of whom are now also acting a bit twitchy for my liking. "Toss your weapons."

"Do it," Maddock orders with a jerky nod, and fortunately, they all obey, except the kid, who picks this moment to finally make a run for it. I let him go. One less to worry about.

"All right," I say, my hand perfectly steady as I hold my weapon in place. "Now, we're all going to have a nice, calm chat. Nobody needs to lose their life tonight."

"If you really think I'm going to let you—" Maddock starts, the words breaking off in a satisfying yelp when I pull back the hammer on my gun.

"Have had enough from you for a bit," I tell him, finding the silence to be tremendously satisfying even if there's something I want to hear more. "Cypress, can you repeat what you were saying? So I'm sure I understand."

He grins again, and I decide that however much I might be starting to enjoy this, I have nothing on him. "Got a little overzealous at the table with his wagers tonight toward the end," Cypress supplies. "He bet the horses. Including Helios."

I blink at him. "Who?"

"The mustang," Cypress clarifies. "I've been thinking of names for you, since you told me he didn't have one. Thought Helios would be good since…" He trails off, perhaps due to the look on my face. "We can talk about it later."

"Yeah, let's," I say, pointedly glancing around at the other men present. "You going to help me out here or…?"

"Oh, yes." He finally starts moving, collecting the guns from where they landed and frowning at each of them in turn before chucking them in a nearby empty barrel. "None of them really appear to be worth keeping."

"Well, no, they wouldn't. Considering they're not *yours*."

"Of course," he says, pulling out his own weapons now. "Sorry, old habits and all that."

I roll my eyes, then press my gun harder into Maddock's head so he knows I'm talking to him. "You bet and lost the mustang?" I ask, thinking of the now useless piece of paper in my pocketbook. "The one you agreed to give me in exchange for protecting those interests of yours?"

He laughs bitterly. "However much good that seemed to do me."

"Well it certainly doesn't do you good now," I mutter, angling my head toward Cypress and wondering how I keep finding myself further entangled with him at every turn. "You won him? He's yours?"

He shakes his head, pistols momentarily dipping. "Yours. I wouldn't—"

"Ah, I see now," Maddock says, tone seething. "You're working together. He runs the scam, and you make sure he gets away. Then you split it. That how it works?"

"*No*," I say, right as Cypress says, "*Sure.*"

I look at him again, dumbfounded. "What the fuck are you saying *sure* for?"

"Well," he replies, shrugging, "it's not a terrible idea."

"The *hell* it isn't. We are not—"

A single shot rings out in the alley, the bullet ricocheting off the wall, everyone suddenly going for cover in the resulting chaos, and my first thought is that it must be the calvary coming in. That is, before I have a chance to look toward the mouth of the alley. To see the one lone shooter, shaking like a leaf.

So much for one less to worry about.

CHAPTER 24
AIDEN

Everything that happens next seems to happen all at once.

The second shot aimed too high, the shouting from Maddock and his men, the brush of Cypress's shoulder against mine as he turns to fire back...

In the initial scramble, we'd ended up closer to one another, both choosing the same old stack of barrels and crates to duck behind, which makes it easier for me to intervene, my arm coming down on top of his to force him into a crouch and to force both of his pistols toward the ground. "*Don't.*"

He looks at me, clearly surprised. "Don't what?"

"The kid," I snap, having to bend closer to be heard over the noise. "Don't shoot him."

"I wasn't going to *shoot* Arty. Just scare him a bit," Cypress replies, appearing slightly hurt. "Although, I might point out, he is trying to shoot *us.*"

"Yeah, well…" I back up against the alley wall as I wait for the next shot. "He's doing a piss poor job of it."

"True," Cypress concedes, but then he leans forward and takes a peek around one of the crates. "They might do better, though."

I don't need to ask who. The shot that splinters the crate a moment later, no more than an inch from where Cypress's head had just been, lets let me know that Maddock and the rest of his men have made good use of the distraction to reclaim their weapons.

"*Fuck*," I mutter. "Where the fuck are those deputies?"

Cypress laughs. "Home. With their feet up."

"I sent the old guy to go get them," I say, counting shots as another series hits the containers beside us. "The one with the cigars."

"Clayton?" Cypress asks, and I wonder again how he seems to know everyone and why he seems to *want* to. "I'm sure he'll try, but…at this point, I have more faith in divine intervention than I do lawful. If they arrive, it likely won't be to help us."

"Don't need them to help us," I reply, not needing him to explain this to me. "I just need them to inconvenience Maddock enough that he might decide you're not worth killin'."

"Not sure that's going to happen." He ducks down lower as another bullet flies over our heads. "But I admire your sudden bend toward optimism."

I roll my eyes, count off four more shots. "They're all shootin' at once. In a second, they're going to have to reload. Run when they do. Got it?"

Cypress nods, looking toward the back alley behind the buildings. "We can both swing right, head west. I can draw them after me while you go get our horses out front."

I curse, thinking of the message he'd made that boy at the stable bring me. "Is *this* why you had him tell me to ride my horse down here? You knew this was gonna happen?"

"Wasn't thinking it would tonight, but always a possibility. So best to be prepared. Which is why I should've—" Cypress stops himself, barely audible over another round of shots and yelling when he starts again. "Wait, why did you think I wanted you to—"

"God only fucking knows," I reply, not sure why I suddenly feel embarrassed in addition to everything else. "All right, wait two more shots, then you run for your horse."

"What about you?"

"Let me worry about me."

"Aiden—"

"*Now.*"

I break from my position, Cypress right next to me as we both sprint for the alley and somehow manage to turn the corner without either of us being gunned down. Certainly a mark of success, but I'm far from letting it make me cocky, considering I can hear them right behind us.

"Go," I order, pointing toward the next side alley as we come up on it fast. "That way."

He shakes his head, matching me stride for stride. "We'll be separated. I'll go with you."

"*No*," I reply, not wanting to waste the air in my lungs on talking. "Go."

"But—"

"Cypress. *Go.*"

He looks like he wants to argue again, hesitating long enough for my eyes to meet his, for my gait to falter a bit, too, as I realize this might be the last time I see him. That there's a part of me that doesn't want it to be.

"We'll find each other," I tell him, a bit softer this time. At last, he nods, cutting down the other alley before I can say anything else, my moment of relief fading fast when I hear Maddock and his men emerge into the alley behind me.

The first shot that rings out from their newly reloaded guns strikes the building next to me, the wood siding splintering as I dash down a different street.

The second strikes the ground, scattering the dirt near my feet once I break for the other side of the road.

The third strikes truest to its mark, singeing a streak along my left arm before it cracks through storefront glass.

I don't think it's deep, but even if it is, the blood loss will take me a lot slower than another bullet might. The stable is a few more blocks away. I only need to get there.

"*Stop!*" There are new voices behind me now, people that had been out on the street, and I don't know if they're yelling at me or the men chasing me, but I'm pretty sure if I do stop to look, I'll be dead before I figure it out.

"*Stop!*"

I'm so close. If I can just get to the barn. If I can—

There's hoofbeats now, too. Falling like a drum beat, growing louder and louder and louder until—

A dark streak flies by me at full speed. A demon on a black horse, neither of his hands on the reins because they're too busy firing behind him. I don't stop to look this time either, not just because I'm afraid to die but also because I'm afraid to know how many names I'll have to put on my ledger if I live.

Close on Cypress's heels, three men tear after him on horseback, straight for Soldana's border, and I wonder how far he'll get before they catch him. If we really will get the chance to find each other again like I said.

My lungs are burning by the time I reach the stable, a metallic taste in my mouth, another bullet connecting with one of the barn slats as I race inside and tuck myself behind the open door. My chest rapidly rises and falls as I try to catch my breath, my eyes doing a quick count of the now eight men outside. "*Fuck*, where is the fucking law—"

"Told ya you should have brought your horse."

My head jerks up at the small voice intruding from the direction of the hayloft, and I see the stable boy peering back down at me. *Fuck. Fuck. Fuck.*

"Get out of here," I snap at him. "You're gonna get yourself killed."

"Not if you get out of here first," he argues, listening to the sounds of a few more shots hitting the stable. "They seem awful mad. What'd you do?"

"I got involved," I mutter back, glancing out the door and stepping forward just slightly to let the men out there see me and my pistol. Fortunately, rather than receiving a bullet, I'm rewarded by the sight of them scampering back a bit.

"Hey," I shout toward the boy. "Sid, I need you to—"

"*Simon*," he replies, rolling his eyes at me.

"Right, Simon, you know how to tack a horse fast?"

"Sure do," he says. "For the right price."

"Little extortionist," I grumble. "How about this? You tack up the mustang, and I'll give you some *very* quick pointers on how to fight."

"I don't know…" he says, still lolling about in the hayloft while a few more shots go off. "You don't seem to be doing too great with that right now."

I glare at him, then show myself once more to the men outside to a similar effect as before. Doubt it'll last much longer, though. Not without a casualty. My hand starts to shake.

"You can have whatever is left in my wallet," I offer instead, starting to get desperate. "How about that?"

"Deal," he replies, and I think maybe it's worth it when I hear him start running away up there, dropping down in the aisle a safe distance back near the mustang's stall.

"Tell me when you're ready," I shout his way, and sure enough, I do have to resort to firing a shot in the air a few moments later when the men outside start getting close enough for adrenaline and instinct to kick in.

"You want the saddlebags, too?" asks Simon, when the sound of the shot fades. "Or you leavin' em here?"

I stare at him briefly before returning my attention outside. "Why would I leave—"

"I'm only askin'." I fire another shot in the air. "But I suppose you aren't coming back anytime soon."

"Suppose not," I reply, having no choice but to aim a shot at the dirt in front of Maddock when he doesn't retreat as far as I would have liked after the last round. "Not willingly."

"All right," the boy shouts. "Ready!"

I nod, shoot once more to scare, then I turn and run for the stall, thinking to take the mustang out the back until I realize that will likely bring them into the barn and right past the boy. Instead, I whistle for the mustang right as I reach the knot still keeping his door closed, and I have to admit, it does come loose fast in a pinch.

"Stay out of trouble," I tell the boy, unintentionally brushing against the watch in my pocket before grabbing my entire pocketbook and throwing it his way. The mustang bursts through the opening stall door a moment later, as if he knows he's charging into battle, kicking into full speed down the aisle past several other startled horses as soon as I grab his mane, swing myself up, and land on his back.

For the first time in a long time as we thunder toward the front doors, I remember what it feels like…that suspended weightless moment, where you're still able to experience the frantic hope of evading an unavoidable fate. Only this time…

"*Aiden*." A shout from my left immediately once we're out under the night sky draws me toward a black horse and its rider racing to my side, a rifle now in his hands as we turn and head straight for the dark expanse laid out before us without slowing. Without a single shot managing to eclipse our escape.

As I start to let myself believe we're actually going to get away with this, an elated laugh escapes me. The short-lived sound drowning out whatever it is that Maddock is screaming, even if it can't drown out the quickly dawning realization of what I've just done while I turn to watch him grow farther and farther away over my shoulder.

"*Wolf*," Cypress calls to me again, and I look at him in time to see his grin before we reach the end of the stable's lantern light. "Don't look back."

CHAPTER 25
CYPRESS

The sun is coming up by the time we finally stop, drawing our spent horses into a pocket of trees and waiting to see if we really had managed to give them the slip. The more hours that have passed, the more unsaid things have piled up in the silence, until when we both agree that we're in the clear, I'm not sure which of them to address first.

"Aiden," I start to say right before he turns, dismounts, and begins walking with his mustang deeper into the woods, headed toward the valley on the other side and hopefully a continuation of the stream we caught a glimpse of a ways back. "Aiden," I say again, getting down too before moving to catch up. "We should—"

He rounds on me so fast that Cerberus startles with a snort from where he'd been plodding along behind me, a noise that Aiden's horse greets with pinned-back ears—a perfect extension of the look his owner is aiming at me.

"Let's get one thing real fucking straight," Aiden says, pointing a finger in my direction. "There is no *we*. There is you and there is me. That's it. You understand?"

No, I want to say. *No, I don't understand. You left with me. You chose me.*

Hadn't he?

"Wolf," I try again. "Maybe if we—"

"Jesus Christ." He shakes his head before turning his back on me. "You really don't get it, do you?"

"No," I do say this time. "I'm sorry if—"

"You're *sorry*?" he repeats, pivoting to face me once more without letting me get a full sentence out, without letting me even try to explain. "For which part? For running your little con? For making us fucking *fugitives*?" He steps nearer with each question until we're only a couple feet apart, close enough for me to see the absolute fury in his eyes. "We very easily could've died back there. You sorry for that?"

I frown, noticing for the first time the tear in his clothing along his arm and the blood seeping from beneath. "It wasn't my intention. Although it might not have been such a close call if you'd ridden your horse down to the saloon."

In response, he only stares at me for a long moment before he starts to walk away again. "You're fucking unbelievable," I think I hear him mutter. "Of all the fucking…"

"I'll fix it," I offer quickly, jogging to catch up. "I'll sort it all out. And when I do, it'll be better for you than it was before."

"*How?*" he scoffs. "How could this be better?"

"You wanted to be free of Maddock," I remind him. "And now you are."

He shakes his head, not turning toward me this time, and somehow, the fact that he doesn't is so much worse. "We'll see how *free* I am when we're both sitting in a cell waiting on the noose."

"It won't come to that," I assure him. "I promise."

"Don't," he warns me. "Don't do that."

"What?"

"Make promises you can't keep. Don't lie to me."

"I'm not. We'll sort it out."

"There's that *we* again."

"Well," I say, wishing he would simply stop and listen. "You have to admit, *we* were great together. A few hiccups, sure, but you...*you* were spectacular. When you stepped into that alley? You were better than I even hoped you'd be. And to think, I had..."

He finally does stop. So abruptly that I almost bump into him, and the sense of victory I feel is perhaps part of the reason why I don't see the real collision coming.

Aiden's fist *slams* into my jaw.

"*Motherfu—*" The swear word cuts off as the rest of him quickly follows, his shoulder barreling into my chest and sending both of us crashing to the ground in a complicated heap that serves as a nice distraction from the fresh, blinding pain in my face.

"I fucking *knew* it," he's saying, going for another right hook as he looms over me, one that I manage to redirect into my left side more than I manage to block. While not the most ideal, it does at least throw him off balance enough that I can get my feet beneath me, pushing myself up into him. I roll us across the ground until our positions are reversed.

"*Aiden*, wait—" I get out, trying to pin his arms down as I straddle his legs. "Hold on, please stop trying to kill me. Let's talk for a minute first. What is it you think you know?"

"The alley," he grits out, eyes narrowed as he stares up at me, then breaks free of my hold and fists his hands in the front of my shirt. "The *watch*. All of it *was* a fucking bribe because you wanted me to work for you."

"*What?* No, it wasn't—" He yanks me down right before his damn hard head connects with the bridge of my nose. Fortunately, not *quite* hard enough to break it, but I do see stars before they're extinguished by Aiden putting me on my back again. Fuck, he really is big…

No, not the time.

"Wasn't like that," I manage to get out, scrambling for purchase beneath him. "That's not what I wanted."

"Oh, yeah?" he asks, his thighs on either side of my legs now in much the same position I'd just had over him, although he's now using his grip on my shirt to pull me up so that I'm inches from that perfect face of his. From those dark brown eyes and that strong jaw and that full mouth that is questioning, "Then what *did* you want?"

"*You*," I admit, figuring I have nothing to lose at this point. "I only wanted you."

His brow furrows, confusion clear on his face, but at least he temporarily stops trying to finish the job Maddock started. "Why me?"

"Because…" I try to catch my breath, holding onto his forearms as he continues to hold me up. "Because I knew who you were the moment I saw you."

His expression tenses, his eyes going even darker than they were before. "I don't do that anymore. I'm not a—"

"A gunslinger, I know," I finish for him as I lightly pat his arm, a gesture that's meant to be comforting, although the way his jaw clenches tells me that maybe it's not. "I know you aren't. That's not… I don't need you to be that. Not for me."

His eyes are still wary, but he releases me, dropping me against the ground before he lets out a deep breath, rolls himself off me, and flops down beside me. "What is it you want, Cypress?" he asks after both of us have had a chance to recover. "Spell it out, because I'm not looking for another damn employer right now."

"Why?" I ask, staring up at the lightening sky. "Trouble with references?"

It almost sounds like he laughs, and I do consider it progress even if he follows it up with a "Fuck you."

"I don't want to be your boss," I tell him, trying to think of how to put it in words that he will not only understand but believe—until I get a chance to tell him the words I really want to later. "At least, not all the time."

Out of the corner of my eyes, I see him roll his, but since he stays where he is, I continue, "I'm not trying to offer you a position. I'm trying to offer you a partnership."

"A partnership?" he asks. "In what?"

In everything, I think. *In sickness and in health. In this life. In the next.*

"In…in wherever the road leads us," I say instead. "Fifty-fifty split."

"For which I would be doing what, exactly?"

I honestly don't care, I want to say. I'd offer the same if all he was going to do was sit there and continue to look devastating. Chest and shoulders heaving. Disheveled waves on display again since he'd lost his hat in the tussle. Eyes wild… *Focus.*

"For which…" I begin to reply, trying to come up with something that is not a lie but is also a truth he will believe. "You could keep things from going…sideways."

He's quiet, and since I can tell it's because he's thinking, I try to be patient again. I really, really do, even though my pulse is skipping more now than it had been when he'd pinned me.

"It's not my first time," I say not a minute later, unsure if that will tempt him more or less. "Having things go sideways."

"You don't say," he replies dryly. "I find that so hard to believe."

"Thought you might."

He lets out a long deep breath. "You actually want to do what Maddock accused us of? You want to run scams and have me help you get away with it?"

"Oh." I risk a smile even though it smarts my split lip. Pretty sure my nose is bleeding, too. "I want far more than that."

"Fuck's sake, you really are a fucking demon," he mutters, rolling his eyes again and sitting up so that he can rest an elbow on his knee as he stares out in front of us. I attempt to do the same until doing so results in a resurgence of pain in both my battered head and my bruised abdomen. Something he also appears to notice, likely because of my grunt of pain right before I give up.

He shakes his head, but reaches over to grab my hand to help me until I'm sitting up next to him. Off in the distance in the valley, I can make out the horses, who finally found some common ground by both deciding that the water and grass were much more enticing than watching Aiden and me have a spat.

"Sorry about your ribs," he says after a while longer has passed.

"And about your jaw. And your nose."

"It's all right," I say, doing my best to keep my tone light. "I've certainly had worse."

Aiden turns his head to look at me, his eyes studying my face, and it's only then that I realize he's no longer the only one without a hat.

"Suppose you have," he says, and I know he's seen the scars on my face before I have a chance to reach for my hat where it lies a few feet away. Clearing my throat to cover another sound of discomfort at the movement, I put it back on my head without bothering to dust it off.

"Cypress," he says, a hint of something in his voice that lands harder than any punch he could throw. "Why is it you never fight back?"

"I fought back," I tell him. "Did you not see me as we were riding—"

"I saw you," he affirms, and I really try not to read too much into his tone. "You fought them, but you don't…you don't fight me."

I only glance at him, still feeling too exposed to fully look his way. "Sure I do. See, we're disagreeing right now."

"I'm not talkin' about a disagreement," he corrects, and while he may not like answering direct questions, he certainly doesn't seem to mind posing them. "Since we met, I've threatened to shoot you, to stab you. I've clocked you in the face."

"Twice."

"Twice," he amends. "You never try to hit me back. Why is that?"

For a few seconds, I contemplate giving him a far more complicated answer, something that will keep him stewing over it whenever we finally get to sleep, but since I don't think either of us have the energy for that, I ultimately decide on the simple truth. "I don't want to."

"Why? I've given you plenty reason to."

"You've also given me plenty reason not to."

"Not from where I sit."

"Then sit somewhere else," I say, repeating his words from only an evening ago, though it feels like much longer. "I don't want to hurt you, wolf. So I don't."

Despite my best efforts, this still appears to give him something to mull over, because he's quiet again for a while, and I find I'm starting to mind it less. The quiet. When he's here in it with me.

"There are others you do want to hurt though," he says at last. Not an accusation this time, only a statement of fact. "People like the ones we had chasing us. People like Maddock."

"Yes," I say. "And I do. Hurt them, I mean."

"Seems silly to ask why…"

"You still can."

He frowns as he stares down at the ground. "Another time."

"There going to be one?"

He faces me again, and this time, I let him, because however much it would kill me to have him look at me and leave now, I suspect it will only hurt more later.

"Probably makes good sense. To stick together for a while," he finally says, dragging a hand through his hair and tugging at the ends while at the same time sending my heart into such a frenzy that I almost feel compelled to start humming so he won't hear it. "At least until we figure out what sort of hell Maddock is going to bring down on us."

I nod, not trusting myself with much more than that.

"Cypress."

"Hm?"

"This partnership you're suggesting…I won't kill anyone for you," he says, quieter than his usual tone. "I can't."

"I wouldn't ask you to."

His mouth presses into a firm line but then he nods, too. "Then we're agreed. For now."

"For now," I repeat, knowing I'd be grateful whether *now* lasted five minutes or five years. And knowing I'd still want more either way.

"Should probably find a place to lie low," he continues, mercifully interrupting my thoughts again. "You got any ideas?"

"As a matter of fact, I do." I stare up at the clear morning sky, finally giving into my body's insistent request that I lie back down in the patchy grass. "Think we ought to go see an old friend."

PART TWO

GUNSLINGER

CHAPTER 26
AIDEN
SIXTEEN YEARS OLD
NEW YORK

I have been looking for him for *so* long.

So long I can't think of a time when I wasn't anymore. So long I'd be lying if I said it wasn't the lion's share of what keeps me going.

I can't fucking remember. I can't remember my life before this. Before *him*.

I can't remember what it was like not to feel this unending, all-consuming determination. This single-minded, relentless pursuit of the *one* thing I believe might bring me peace.

Hell, that might just let me sleep.

This *has* to be what helps me breathe again. It *has* to, because I don't know what I'll do if it doesn't. I don't have anything else.

If I do this, will the other stuff come back? The good things? It'll probably hurt if they do. But I'm already hurtin', so what does it matter?

I can hear his voice from here. I thought he would sound different. Bigger. Tougher. Meaner. I thought he would sound like my nightmares.

He's asking for another drink but the bartender is shaking his head while my hands are shaking beneath the bar, my own drink untouched because I want to be clear-headed. Because I *want* to remember this.

He asks again but the bartender waves him off before turning his back on him, and I watch as the thief waits less than a minute before pinching the bottle from behind the counter and heading toward the door with a sway in his step.

I thought he would *look* different, too. Bigger. Tougher. Meaner. I thought he would look like the devil. But he doesn't.

He's just a man.

"You know who I am?" I ask him, still trembling as I aim my gun at him. He sits against the decaying wall of the deserted building I followed him into, and I hate the sound of the door clicking closed behind me, wondering if I'll make it back out. Wondering if I want to. "You remember what you did?"

He laughs, a hollow and whiskey-soaked sound. "Out past your bedtime, ain't you, son?" He takes another swig as he eyes my weapon. "Put that thing away and go on home. Your mama's probably calling."

It's like a punch to the gut. A twist of a blade that I only drive deeper as I step forward, my hand no longer shaking. "She isn't."

CHAPTER 27
AIDEN
TWENTY-SIX YEARS OLD
NORTH TEXAS

"That's far enough. You stop right there."

I follow orders, putting my hands up at the sight of the second shotgun in two weeks that's come far closer to me than I would prefer. Although, even as close as we are standing, I have my suspicions that the person holding the gun can't actually see us.

"Ma'am," I say to the woman who makes *old friend* seem like a vast understatement. She stands in the front doorway of her two-story farmhouse in the early evening light, a floor-length blue dress on beneath her apron and her gray hair in long braids that shift over her shoulder as she adjusts her ancient grip on the gun that's nearly as big as she is. "If you would be kind enough to put that down, I think we—"

"Afraid this is not a *kind* house for trespassers." Her dark brown eyes narrow as she tries to peer past me. "Who is that you have with you?"

"Told you I should have gone first," Cypress mutters, and I sigh as he sidesteps out from where I'd put him behind me. "How you been keeping, Dolly?"

Had I not seen the transformation myself, I would never have believed the woman threatening to gun me down a moment ago was the same one that smiles radiantly as soon as Cypress makes his appearance and starts confidently walking up to the house. Nor would I have believed she could move as fast as she does, exchanging the shotgun for a cane before hustling to the weathered porch railing.

"*Cypress*, as I live and breathe," she says, pulling him in for a hug when he meets her at the bottom of the stairs. "How have *you* been keeping? That's the real question." She frowns, studying his face, including the faintly visible bruising still around his eyes. "You look like you got caught up in something."

"Might be putting it lightly," he replies. "I want you to meet Aiden."

He pivots to the side so that I'm in her view again, though as soon as he does, her happy expression fades to something far more critical. "Aiden, hm?" she asks, still eyeing me warily even after I've stepped forward and given her hand what I hope is a gentle squeeze.

"Handshake needs work," she says in return, refusing to let go of as she uses the end of the cane in her other one to push up the brim of my hat and get a better look. "You know, your face is liable to get stuck in that scowl if you aren't careful."

Beside me, Cypress snickers, and I shoot a glare his way, wondering if we're going to break what has been our longest stretch to date without some sort of dispute. Only because this is also the longest stretch of time where he hasn't insisted on talking my ear off, since I had insisted he keep his mouth shut while we approached the house, unsure what he was getting us into this time.

Otherwise, he *never* stops talking. From the moment he gets up in the morning to the moment he finally falls asleep on the other side of the campfire, his mouth is runnin'. Half the time, I'm not even sure what he's going on about. Books he's read, songs he likes…which fuckin' *stars* are his favorite.

And then after every time, he looks at me like he wants me to tell him the same, and the truth is, I don't have a single fuckin' clue. Never really thought to read for leisure. Never really thought to look at the stars except to use them to find my way. And as for the songs…there's one in particular he keeps humming, one I feel like I know but can't place.

Rational thing would be to simply ask him what it is, but then he might take that as encouragement, and God knows that is the *last* thing he needs.

"Wondering if you might have room for us for a bit, Dolly?" Cypress is asking, leaning against the porch as if he doesn't have a care in the world. "Found ourselves in a bit of trouble over in Soldana."

"Should've known that was you," she says, and I detect more amusement in her tone than disapproval. "Was sure it was, but then the rumors said there were *two* involved." She glances back at me, openly taking me in from head to foot. "Where'd you find him?"

"He robbed my employer," I say, past done with being talked about like I'm not here.

"I see." One of her thin eyebrows rises. "With your help?"

"*No*," I snap. "Wasn't part of that. I only—"

"You only came here with him," she counters. "Rather than staying with your—I would assume now—*former* employer."

"He saved my life," Cypress explains before I can, a touch of something in his voice that makes me shift my weight from foot to foot. "Was all very heroic."

I roll my eyes, but the corner of the old woman's mouth is tipping up now. "So to be sure I understand, *he* robbed your employer, and rather than prevent it from happening, *you* helped him get away? Likely putting your own life on the line in the process? That about cover it?"

"Feels like we're leaving out a few details there," I mutter, grinding a pebble beneath the toe of my boot into the dirt. "Important ones."

"Undoubtedly," she says, and I catch her eyes flicking back and forth between Cypress and me, and… *Christ. Not again.*

"Ma'am," I start to say, "whatever it is you're thinking—"

"Right now, I'm thinking you boys could use a warm meal. And a bed," she says, turning away and walking back up the stairs with her cane thudding along on each step. "I'll let you pick which one. Cypress, you remember where everything is."

"I'll take my usual," he replies, jogging up the stairs so he can open the door for her. "Aiden will want to sleep on the ground floor. Back bedroom will do. We'll go get the horses settled and then we'll be in." The old woman nods and disappears into the house before he looks back at me, finding me staring while frozen at the bottom of the stairs. "What? No good?"

"Fine," I say, frowning. "How did you know I'd want to sleep on the ground floor?"

"Closest to an exit," he says with a shrug. "Easiest escape."

"Right," I say, folding my arms across my chest. "But wouldn't you prefer the same?"

The corner of his mouth twitches. "Are you suggesting we share?"

"*No.*" I take my hat off to run a hand through my hair. "I'm *suggesting* that it might also be the room you'd prefer, and I don't want to impose. You're clearly more familiar here and—fuck's sake, I'm trying to have… some fucking *manners*. You familiar with the idea?"

"Why?" He saunters to the edge of the porch, looking down at me with that fucking smirk. "Would it help if I said *please*?"

I could kill him. I really could. After two weeks in constant close proximity, it would be so goddamn easy to charge up these stairs, get my hands on him, push him up against the side of the house, and…*and…*

I clear my throat, taking a few cautious steps back while grasping my hat in front of me with both hands, and I'd swear he almost looks disappointed again. Like when he'd come to stand at Maddock's table and I hadn't gone after him, knowing it wouldn't end well if I did.

This wouldn't either. And all his teasing aside, he *must* realize how bad of an idea it would be to let this veer off course any more than it has already—not that there's *anything* to veer into. At least not on my side. Probably not on his either. Not really.

It'd be dangerous to blur lines with each other—to allow something that could end up being a distraction. We can't afford that. Not now. Not ever.

"Listen," I say at last, letting out a sigh. "You want that room for yourself or not?"

He frowns, shaking his head. "It's not my preference."

"What is?" I ask, certain that I should know this detail about him if he knows it about me. "Where you prefer to sleep?"

"Outside," he says as he comes down the stairs. "When the sky is clear."

"Then why the fuck are we here?" I ask, gesturing toward the house. "This was your idea. We could have kept moving."

I still could…if I decide I'm better off on my own, which is indisputably the case.

"Didn't come for the bed," Cypress explains, calm as can be, which somehow irritates me further. "As I said, we're here to see my friend."

"I thought you meant someone who could actually be of…" I start to say, then pause, taking a deep breath before continuing. "Please tell me that we did not ride for two weeks for a damn *social call.*"

"We didn't," he says quickly, but then glances away. "Not *entirely.*"

I take a step toward him, still expecting for some reason that he will take a step back when I do. Like anyone else would. But of course, he doesn't. Never does. So instead, all we end up doing is standing far too close as I ask, "*Cypress*, what are we doing here?"

"Seeking counsel," he says simply, as if that's all the explanation needed. "On *what?*"

"Our next move," he replies, though his gaze drops to my mouth as he says it. Something I choose to ignore for the sake of my own fucking sanity. "I have a few…in mind."

I grab the front of his shirt, yanking him closer and erasing what little space there was between us. "Speak. Plainly."

He gives me a look, both of his hands gripping my forearms, and the touch shouldn't feel as familiar as it does. "Well, we are currently fugitives."

"I'm aware," I bite out. "Which is why we need to put as much distance as possible between us and them."

"*Running* is not a strategy."

I roll my eyes. "And playing house is?"

"Depends on the house."

"*Christ.*" I let go of him, turning away in an attempt to get some air. Doesn't work, though, since he stays right by me, hovering near my elbow. "How the fuck did I get myself into this?"

Out of the corner of my eye, I see him frown. "I said I'd fix it. I'll get it straightened out."

"How?" I ask him, not really expecting him to have a response even when I expand on the question. "How exactly do you plan to fix this?"

"The usual way."

"The *usual* way," I repeat, closing my eyes and hanging my head as I take another breath that doesn't do a goddamn thing for me. "The fact that you even have a *usual* way…" I turn, angling my body toward his again as I inform him, "I told you I'm not killing, just because you got us into this mess."

"And I told you I wouldn't ask you to." He frowns, eyes searching mine. "If you would just give me a *fraction* of your trust—"

"*Why* would I—"

"If you two are going to argue in my front yard, can you at least speak up?" interrupts a voice from the front doorway. "I can't hear you from the kitchen."

I bite my tongue, glancing between the old woman and the man in front of me. "Are you kin?" I ask him. "Related?"

Cypress shakes his head, about to speak before she replies for him. "We're not blood, but I do consider him one of mine." She arches an eyebrow at me. "You'll remember that if you have any sense."

"Not sure I do," I mutter, turning my attention back to the man in question, who is now trying hard to suppress another grin despite our most recent disagreement. "I'll take care of the horses. You go inside and catch up."

"No, I'll come," he continues to argue as I whistle for them and start heading toward the barn. "I should at least show you—"

"I can figure it out," I say confidently when he starts to follow. "Might figure out *I* prefer to sleep out here, too, while I'm at it."

I hear his footsteps falter, the frown in his voice when he asks after me, "Why?"

"Closest to an exit," I repeat back to him without turning around. "Easiest escape."

CHAPTER 28
CYPRESS

I'm beginning to think he's avoiding me. Actually, I'm fairly certain of it at this point.

Apart from dinner last night, which he consumed largely in stoic silence and one-word answers, I've barely been able to locate Aiden all day, much less hold a conversation. Somehow, I had an easier time keeping track of him in a town with hundreds of souls than I am in a house and property with only three.

Around noon, I arrived at the barn right in time to see him leave it, flying off on... I still haven't confirmed if Aiden is in agreement with us calling the mustang Helios, since the one time I tried to bring it up again ended in Aiden telling me I could call him whatever I pleased since he belonged to me.

But he doesn't. I've told him that, too. Multiple times, each as unsuccessful as the last. But given that he seems to view any assistance as pity, it's not hard to guess why.

What we need is a chance to actually work together, for him to see how good things could be, how good *we* could be as partners. Maybe then he'd understand it's not only the horse that's his. That when I'd said a fifty-fifty split, what I'd really meant was that he could take everything, and I wouldn't care.

"Dolly," I call out, taking my hat off as I walk back in following an unsuccessful venture out with Cerberus. Fortunately, I don't have to go far, finding her in her usual chair by the window in the kitchen. "What are your thoughts on us riding in with you later? When you head over to your place?"

I tried my very best to make the inquiry sound casual, but the look on her face when she puts down her sewing to consider me tells me she's onto me. "My thoughts? On which part?"

"Too big of a risk?" I ask her, knowing she rode into town this morning and would have listened to the locals. "Would we…cause a stir?"

She laughs. "Isn't that always your aim?"

"Not in this case," I tell her, not sure why I'm bothering to reassure her and myself when the one person I need to convince isn't here. "Thought we could keep things…"

"Boring?" she offers, and I feel the corner of my mouth quirk.

"Contained," I say.

She tilts her head, her fingers going back to the needle and dress fabric. "I'm still waiting to hear back from my contact near Soldana, but what I can tell you is there's already posters hanging at the station."

"Maddock's got a friend in the stagecoach business," I supply. "I'm sure he's the one printing them for him. Would keep him from having to go through the law."

"Wouldn't be uncommon," Dolly agrees. "Means word will have spread though."

"So you think it would be better to not? To not risk it, that is?"

"Didn't say that." Dolly shrugs. "You know how things are at my place. We handle our own. We take care of our own."

I nod, glancing out the window. "And you'll include Aiden in that?"

"If you do," she replies. "That what he is to you? Your own?"

I nod again.

"He know that?"

"He will."

"When?"

I sigh. "When I think he might actually want to hear it."

"And until then?"

I start to answer before a flash of movement outside catches my eye, prompting me to look out the window again as Aiden comes racing into view, pulling the mustang to a stop in the side yard. He dismounts, using the front end of his untucked shirt to wipe sweat from his brow as he catches his breath, and exposing no small amount of toned stomach in the process. "Well…" I say, swallowing since my mouth has gone dry. "A significant bit of yearning, if I were to guess."

CHAPTER 29
AIDEN

As soon as I come in for dinner, I begin the process of removing my hat and boots, knowing better than to bring either into Dolly's home. The obscene number of books stacked on every surface don't take away from the fact that it is also neat as a pin.

"I appreciate it, but don't bother," she tells me before I manage to work my left boot off, walking toward the door with what appears to be a long winter coat even though the majority of the mid-spring day heat is still clinging outside. "We are on our way out."

"Oh?" I repeat, wondering where it is they are headed and if Cypress will wind up getting himself into another calamity in the process. "You taking a walk?"

"A ride," she informs me. "Cypress is bringing the horses out front, so we can go over there together."

"Over *where* together?"

"My bar," she replies, and she must see how enthused I am about the destination because she also adds, "It was my idea, so don't go grousing at him."

"Doesn't seem like a particularly *good* idea," I point out, understanding more and more why she and Cypress are friends. "If someone spots him—"

"Then they'll be wise to keep it to themselves," she says. "Trust me on that."

I roll my eyes. "Everyone talks if you pay 'em enough."

"Not if they want to keep living." She reaches for a pair of gloves in her pocket, pulling them on along with her coat before grabbing the shotgun resting by the door. "Hard to spend money when you're six feet under."

"Suppose it is," I say, granting her that before I let out a resigned sigh. "And I suppose if Cypress is going, then I'm going too."

This appears to pique her interest. "That so?"

"We have an agreement," I inform her, crossing my arms over my chest in preparation for an argument. "I'm meant to be keeping him alive. And I can't do that if I don't know where he is."

"Haven't seemed concerned about that most of the day today," she points out. "Barely seen hide or hair of you."

"Figured it was your turn to watch him," I mutter back, not wanting to get into the real reason I'd been making myself scarce. Which was that I *had* spent all goddamn night wondering where he was while I was lying in that back bedroom, trying to convince myself to sleep.

After my discussion with him yesterday, I really had thought to stay in the barn, but in the end, the promise of a bed had been too tempting to ignore, and I'd swallowed my pride long enough to carry my bag inside and change before supper.

God, I hadn't been able to remember the last time I'd sat down for a meal in someone's home. Years at least, maybe not since…before. Some of the families I took jobs for used to insist on it when the work was done, but I never wanted to linger longer than I had to, never wanted to take up a place at a table that wasn't mine, never wanted to hear them talk to me as if I were someone they would have if things had been different for them.

Here though, sitting down for supper with Cypress and Dolly had been…well, it had been nice. It'd been nice listening to them chatter, even if some of the stories Cypress told made me think my hair was going to turn as white as Dolly's. It'd been nice having something in my stomach that was warm from a stove instead of cold from a saddlebag, even if Dolly kept loading up my plate with more meat and greens than I could ever possibly eat. And as the evening had worn on and everyone continued to sit around the table and keep company, it'd been nice…to watch Cypress with someone he loved, even if I wasn't part of it.

Because it was clear he did. He cared for Dolly in a way that was impossible to doubt was genuine, in ways she never had to even ask for. Getting a blanket for her when she was cold, putting the kettle on when her tea ran out, grabbing her book for her, helping her out of her chair when her bones had grown as tired as she was by the end of the night.

Was hard not to think I was getting a glimpse of who he really was beneath all of it—all the careful games and clever words. Beneath all that damn black he insists on wearing to every occasion.

The more I watched him, the more I realized coming here really hadn't just been a social call. It'd been…it'd been that he was in trouble and the first place he wanted to go was home.

And that was something I understood. Something that made me understand him a little better, too, just as I thought I'd wanted. But it was also the reason why, when he'd come back to the table from helping her to her room, I hadn't wanted to still be sitting there.

This is a job. A business agreement. One that has come about as a result of necessity. And I need to remember that. Because lying in a bed at night that isn't mine, staring at a watch that isn't mine, and thinking about a person that sure as hell isn't mine is not going to do me any good.

"You know, you are kinda funny," Dolly says, pulling me back from the night prior to this afternoon, both of us still standing in her front parlor. "Mainly when you don't mean to be."

I frown, struggling to remember what I'd last said before it comes to me. "What?" I ask her. "You don't think he needs watching?"

"He does," she replies. "What's funny is you thinking you have to tail after him to keep him out of trouble."

"Oh?" I ask, doing my best to intercept the annoyance that wants to creep into my tone while she's armed, the mean hook at the end of her cane looking as if it could do even more damage than the shotgun. "And what is it I need to do instead?"

"Likely?" she says, moving past me now toward the door. "Just walk the other direction." She stops as she's about to reach for the doorknob, and any explanation I was about to ask for gets cut off by her continuing on. "You should know before we get to my place…" She eyes me, then sighs. "Actually, never mind, I don't think I need to threaten you. Seem to do a fine job making yourself skittish on your own."

I scowl at the old woman. "I'm not—"

"There he is now."

I pivot quickly, looking back out the front window for Cypress and the horses until I hear a low chuckle behind me. "You see?" she says, gesturing at me when I glance at her over my shoulder. "Skittish. Come on now, we can wait outside."

I roll my eyes, but follow her, pulling the door closed behind us once we're on the porch. "You have a nice spot here close to the river," I say, an attempt at making conversation since I haven't had much else to offer as a guest. "Always liked the water myself. Peaceful."

"It is peaceful. Although I find myself hearing them trains in the distance more and more. Yard they've got a ways from here gets busier every year, and I'm not sure how much longer I can keep them at bay," she says as she takes in her property, the plains that stretch on and on until they meet the hills on the horizon. "This place has been in my family for a long time. I'm the last that's left of them though." She considers me again. "You the last, too?"

Christ, this must be where Cypress learned it. That knack he has to ask the one question that'll put you on your ear.

"Thought so," she replies, not waiting for me to reply while shifting to take some of the weight off what I can only assume is her bad leg on the left. "How long ago?"

"Seventeen years," I say, and she looks as surprised as I feel that I said it out loud. *Seventeen years*. Can it really have been that long?

Fortunately, before she can ask me anything else, we both turn toward the barn when we hear Cypress coming out with the three horses— Cerberus in front, followed by a pretty bay mare that must be Dolly's, and then Helios in the back appearing bad-tempered as usual. Does fit, I suppose. The name. It's close to hell, although I doubt that's why Cypress picked it. More likely, there's some other meaning that delights him to no end.

"Always grinnin'," I say, shaking my head when he sees us waiting and gives an absurdly cheerful wave. "Even when it's over something that's probably going to get us killed."

"Perhaps you should try it," she suggests, not bothering to hide her answering smile at all.

"What? Getting us killed?"

"No," she replies, taking my arm and heading down the stairs. "Being happy."

CHAPTER 30
CYPRESS

Consult the local records, and they'll all tell you the same things about the town of Renas.

She's small. Barely more than fifty people.

She's got a mayor. A man named Rick.

And she's got a sheriff. A man named Stuart.

And she's quiet as a church mouse.

Consult the local citizens, and they'll *also* all tell you the same things about the town of Renas. The first being that Dolly *is* the town of Renas. That she is the mayor *and* the sheriff. That she is anything *but* quiet. And that the same can be said for her place.

Purposefully situated just outside the town lines, Dolly's place has more people coming through it on a daily basis than Renas does. All with various intentions and aims, most of which they prefer to keep to themselves. Which is fine, as long as they also keep to the rules.

"The rules?" Aiden asks as we walk inside, both of us following behind Dolly until she's immediately pulled into some conversation or other and we're left to our own whims. "And what might those be?"

"Generally?" I smile, catching the tune being played and the first flashes of color up on the stage. "Mind your business and mind your manners."

"Right," he mutters next to me, his brown eyes growing a bit bigger than usual as he takes in the room, and I try to see it too like it's my first time. The dark wood walls and floors, the long mahogany bar with the rows and rows of bottles that line the mirror on the wall behind it, the dozen or so packed poker tables, the women dancing in their flying skirts on the stage, the musicians playing the quick-paced music out in front, and more than one couple who didn't quite make it upstairs quick enough. "Right."

"Are you?" I ask him, watching his gaze catch and linger on a smitten pair on the stairs, on a woman in a dark green dress who has very little of her red rouge left on her mouth. "If you're uncomfortable, we can go. It's no—"

"Christ, you really think I'm that…what was the word you used? *Repressed?*" He turns his head toward me and rolls his eyes, though the tips of his ears have also gone pink, a color I find incredibly endearing. "Just wasn't imagining Dolly's bar to be so…"

"Diverting?" I offer, looking back toward the couple just in time to see them take off laughing up the stairs. "There are rooms on the second floor," I inform him. "Should the need arise."

"I'll keep that in mind," he mutters, shoving his hands in his pockets and glancing my direction a few times before he clears his throat and studies the room again. "Shouldn't be here. You heard what Dolly said yesterday. Talk about what happened in Soldana has already made it out this way."

"Not only talk," I murmur, immediately making his eyebrows shoot up beneath his hat.

"Meaning?"

"There's posters in town," I admit. "I was sort of hoping we might pass one or two on the way here. Would be a nice keep…" I trail off when I realize he's now staring at me like he might grab me by the shirt again. Not that I would mind. "Maybe later."

"There are posters?" Aiden snarls, voice low. "And you're only telling me this *now*?"

"Well, you didn't really give me the option of telling you earlier," I remind him. "So, *yes*, I'm telling you now." I glance toward a few of the tables near us and the eyes that are starting to drift our way. "Although, if you really are worried about us being spotted, perhaps we should stop drawing so much attention to ourselves."

"What we *should* do is leave." His jaw clenches, his teeth grinding together. "Fuck's sake, you make me fucking crazy, you know that?"

"No one here is going to say a thing, even if they do recognize us," I explain, trying to get him to meet my eyes. "It's as I said. Here, you mind your business. Or else. No one is going to want to risk—"

"Yeah, yeah, can't spend money if you're six feet under," he mutters, letting me know he's already had this conversation with Dolly. "Both of you are putting an awful lot of trust in other people, you know that? And you're asking me to do the same."

"I'm not asking you to trust *them*," I start to argue, waving a hand in the general direction of the room. "I'm asking you to trust—"

He shakes his head before I can finish. "You do what you want. But if you get yourself strung up again, don't be expecting me to cut you loose. Not this time. Our agreement isn't an excuse for you to be fuckin' careless."

With that he turns, the conversation apparently closed. I go after him before I can stop myself, though draw up short when he heads for one of the only empty seats at the bar instead of for the door. Without question, it's the better of the two outcomes, even if it ends with his back to me. *One step forward…*

I sigh, not sure now why I thought this would help.

It does for me. The noise, the excitement, the people—being in a lively place like this always makes me feel a bit more alive, too. But clearly it's not the same for him.

I should've anticipated. He hadn't been happy at the saloon in Soldana. He hadn't stayed at the hotel. He hadn't wanted to be around all morning. Time and time again, he has preferred to keep to himself, but the thing is…I suspect that doesn't make him happy either.

Riding seems to be something he enjoys. Something I enjoy, too, and I'd be more than willing to go with him even when there's no destination. If he'd let me…

"You plannin' on playing or not?"

I turn my head to find the man who spoke, currently sitting at the table closest to me and eyeing me with interest. I end up doing the same to him and the man beside him.

"Why?" I ask, giving him a friendly smile. "That an invitation?"

The man scoffs. "It's an invitation to either sit down or keep moving. You're hangin' around. And it's distracting."

"My utmost apologies," I say, taking a quick look around the table before putting all my focus back on him. "What's your limit?"

He gives me a number that barely registers. Because the truth is, I've already determined he doesn't have one, though I'd never be able to explain how. I just know. I can feel it, and I wonder if it's a matter of intuition or simply repetition. Of simply too much time spent with too many like him.

"I'll play," I tell him, pulling out the remaining empty chair at the table and sitting. "Name's Cypress."

He smirks, giving the dealer a nod to bring me in and letting the other few men at the table introduce themselves before he says, "I'm Tom. This is John." He tilts his head at the man next to him. "You passin' through?"

I nod. "Yourself?"

He shrugs, picking up the cards that have been slid in front of him. "We were planning to head out after this game, but…may have found something to keep us here a while longer." He smiles with far too many teeth before casting a look at the dancers who have recently come off stage, staying on one who's now leaning against the bar, chin resting on her palm while she gazes adoringly at the woman pouring drinks on the other side.

And I know. I always know.

CHAPTER 31
AIDEN

I watch Cypress in the mirror behind the bar as he sits to play, barely able to contain my agitation at him being so goddamn cavalier about this whole thing until I see it.

His hand is resting on the table over his cards, his thumb *tap, tap, tapping* the surface as he stares at the men across from him. There's five at the table plus a dealer, but I can tell it's these two that he's most focused on. Both dressed in dark colors, both with blood-red bandanas around their necks and beat-up wide brim hats on their heads. I can't make out their faces, but I don't really need to, because I can make out Cypress's. Especially as they turn more than once to look toward the other end of the bar.

There's a young woman down there, one of the dancers flirting with the bartender, who is so flustered by the attention that she keeps nearly dropping the glass she's polishing to within an inch of its life. I chuckle, covering my mouth so they don't think I'm laughing at them should they happen to notice anything but each other.

Funny how people can be so lovestruck. Poor souls.

My amusement fades, however, when I look back at Cypress, still tapping, still watching the men across from him as they watch her, and I start to get a feeling in my gut that I know better than to ignore.

"Dolly," I call quietly, turning in my barstool to where she's having a conversation with a few customers nearby. When she doesn't hear me, I get up, walking the few paces to her side and ducking down to talk to her without sparing a glance at her patrons. "Can I have a word with you?"

She peers up at me, clearly not pleased at the intrusion, but the moment she sees my face she seems to recognize I'm not going to go away easily and excuses herself.

"What's got you all in a tizzy now?" she asks as soon as we've stepped out of hearing distance. "You lose track of him already?"

I glower at her. "No, I know where he is, and I'm not—" She makes a gesture with her hand for me to hurry it along, and I roll my eyes before tipping my head at the table that's captured my interest. "You know them? The two across from Cypress?"

Her gaze flicks that way, but she shakes her head. "No, they're travelers. Almost everyone in here tends to be. Why?"

"They're making Cypress anxious."

"What makes you think that?"

For a brief moment, I almost tell her about the tapping, but decide against it since she might tell him and give away my advantage. "They keep looking at the girl down at the end of the bar."

"Looking how?"

"Not in a way that's friendly."

"See what you mean," Dolly mutters, frowning while she watches them. "I'll make sure Lou's not left on her own." Her eyes flit to me again, then to Cypress. "So much for keeping things *contained.* You probably ought to make sure he's not left alone either."

I don't need to ask why.

"Thought you were supposed to have rules in here," I say, even more irritated than I was before that barely *five* minutes have passed since we walked in the door and I've already got a problem to contend with.

"We do," she replies, tone icy. "As well as consequences for if they're broken."

I jerk my head in the direction of the men again. "They know that?"

She looks toward the table once more, her eyes fixing on Cypress, and if I were a betting man, I'd wager right there that she doesn't even need me to point out his tell to her. "I suspect they're going to find out."

CHAPTER 32
CYPRESS

"Room for one more?"

I glance up at the sound of Aiden's voice, tearing my focus away from the cards in my hand and the opponents at the table in favor of seeing him standing beside me with an expression that makes it quite clear he is not actually asking.

"This table is…" starts the distinguished businessman next to me before he also has a chance to look up and weigh the options looming over him. "As a matter of fact, I was just about to call it a night." He gives the rest of the table a nervous and apologetic smile while frantically gathering up his remaining money. "Here, you take my seat."

"Wise," Aiden mutters, pivoting to let the poor man scamper away before he drops into the newly vacant chair and fixes me with an intense stare. One that he still doesn't realize has the opposite effect on me than it had on the last man.

He's so handsome that it feels unfair. It really does. For him to look like he does and be who he is and be so damn close to me and yet seem to want absolutely nothing to do with me beyond what he feels is required. Actually, *fair* doesn't really seem to cover it…

"Aiden," I mutter under my breath as the game resumes around us. "Didn't realize you played poker."

"I don't," he mutters back, dropping his voice lower as he tilts his head away from the table and toward me to hide his words. "And I have a feeling that's not what you're doing either."

I glance at him. "Oh?"

"Whatever it is that you *are* doing…don't," he continues. "We don't need any more complications than what we already have."

"What makes you think—"

"She'll be all right. I already talked to Dolly about it. She's going to make sure she's not left alone."

This time, I don't think I manage to hide my surprise at all, which explains why Tom feels compelled to cut in. "Everything good?"

"Fine," Aiden answers, not taking his eyes off me, and even though I know it's my turn, the rest of the table waiting on me to either raise the stakes or fold, I can't seem to look away either. "Everything is fine."

Is it? I want to believe that as I look back at the man across from me. At his friend. And I know Dolly will be true to her word to protect her people, but what about the next ones? What about the next souls who cross their paths, not knowing what's coming? What if there's no one to protect them?

There wasn't for us. For me.

"You speakin' for him now?" Tom counters, giving his friend a grin before gesturing between Aiden and me. "Didn't realize he needed a handler."

"You're going to need one to carry you out of here if you don't watch your mouth," Aiden snaps, turning in their direction now. "You realize that?"

Tom's eyes narrow, his jaw clenching as he studies Aiden's face to determine if he's serious, only to find something else. "Hell," he says at last, then laughs. "I know you."

"You don't," Aiden replies, his tone another warning, because I suspect as well as he does that this man does not *know* him from the wanted posters.

"I do," Tom continues, saying to his friend, "You know who that is? That famous gunslinger. The one in Arizona."

Aiden's expression tells me he's ready to reach across the table, though I would guess it's nothing compared to my own as I tell the man, "*Careful.*"

"Why?" Tom laughs again as his friend grins. "From what I heard, he lost his nerve a while ago." He returns his attention to Aiden. "Isn't that right?"

Rather than answer, Aiden stands slowly then lets his hand hover near his revolver, waiting until the first flicker of uncertainty crosses Tom's face, the first whisper of fear.

When it does, Aiden smiles, turns on his heel, and walks away.

CHAPTER 33
AIDEN

I'm almost to the horses outside when he catches up, and I have to hand it to Dolly, she'd at least been right about one thing. Apparently, all I do need to do is walk the other direction.

"*Aiden*," Cypress says, reaching out for my arm right as I'm about to pull myself up into the saddle. "Hold on a minute."

I shrug him off, not trusting myself to face him. My chest feels too tight, my skin too hot, the music from inside still too fucking loud. "I'm fine."

"You aren't," he argues, and I can't tell if he's cross or if everything just sounds wrong right now. "I'm sorry. I shouldn't have made you come here."

I laugh. "You didn't *make* me do anything. My choices are my own."

Rather than try to swing up again, I start walking down the dirt path away from Dolly's bar and toward the house, leading Helios—because I suppose that really is his damn name now—behind me. Cypress follows a moment later with Cerberus, his long strides catching him up quickly until we're side by side.

"What that man was saying—"

I shake my head. "It's not important."

"It is."

"*No.* It isn't."

"It bothers you—"

"You don't think I've heard that before?" I ask, pausing and letting myself look at him now, at his frown that actually makes me miss the grin. "I've heard far worse. Far more times than I can count. It's the same thing everywhere I go. Here. Soldana. Doesn't matter. Everyone always wants to know the same damn thing." I start walking again, afraid if I don't, I'll reach for him. "You might as well get it fuckin' over with too."

His frown deepens, though this time it seems more in confusion. "Get what over with?"

"You know what," I tell him. "You've been saying since that first night in the alley that you know who I am."

"And I do," he replies, still sounding so sure of it. "From the moment I saw you in the saloon. Maybe even from outside the hotel—"

"Then why don't you ever ask me about it?"

"About what?"

"All of it," I snap, surveying the rocks and brush as if they're judge and jury. "The gunfights. The stories. The people I've killed. You've never asked me about any of it."

He shrugs. "Because I didn't think you were ready to tell me."

"Never seems to make a difference to everyone else."

"Well," he says with a sigh. "I don't want to be *everyone else* to you."

I stop again, turning to face him, still able to hear the music in the distance as proof we're not the only two people in the world right now. "What is it you want then?"

He opens his mouth to speak but then closes it, seeming to think better of what he was going to admit before he glances away. Another of his tells, though I haven't quite figured out yet what this one means.

"You really don't know?" he asks finally. "You didn't know me, too?"

"I knew you…" I begin, but now it's his turn to shake his head, smiling a bit.

"As a thief," he corrects.

"You are a thief," I remind him.

He smirks. "Only for you."

I roll my eyes. "You robbed Maddock in Soldana."

"I *conned* him."

"Is that not the same thing as thieving?"

"Not to me."

"Why?"

"Isn't theft if it never belonged to him in the first place."

"What didn't? His own money?"

"*His* money. *His* property. *His* land." He scoffs. "But taken from how many people? From how many more?"

There's an edge of something in his voice that I haven't fully recognized until tonight. It's the same as when he'd told those men in there to be *careful* or when he'd said Maddock already had too many advantages. It's not just anger. It's deeper than that. Darker. And it feels as familiar to me as the kitchen table had.

"You know, he didn't so much as hesitate when it came to wagering his men's money," Cypress continues. "When it came to wagering what he had already promised you. If I didn't do something right then—"

"Hold on." I raise a hand, stepping closer to him. "Are you saying you stopped losing just because he went back on our deal?"

He doesn't respond, not immediately, which is precisely how I know I'm right.

"Why?" I ask, trying to wrap my head around it all. "I wouldn't have told Maddock about the watch. Or that I thought you were playing him."

"I know."

"Then why? Why bribe me? Just because you wanted me as a partner? You could've—"

"*Bribe* you?" he asks, stepping closer now, too, so that only a couple feet separate us. "Is that *still* what you think I was doing?"

"Yes."

"Why?"

"What other fuckin' reason could there be? Nothing else makes sense."

He stares at me, appearing to be caught between laughing and tearing his hair out. "Aiden—"

"You knew who I was. You knew my reputation. That's why you wanted—"

"*Fuck*, Aiden, I didn't want your reputation," he nearly shouts. "I wanted *you*. I wanted you, and I thought maybe, just *maybe*, if I could give you the things you deserved, then you might actually…"

"I might actually *what*?" I ask him, my heart racing while I wait for him to tell me. While I watch his eyes search mine, only to switch to looking at the stars, as if he might find what he's searching for there instead.

"I should…" he starts to say. "I should go back."

"Go back?"

He sighs, his gaze returning to mine with his mask back in place. "Yes, I'll…I'll ride back with Dolly once the evening is over."

Without another word, he turns, guiding Cerberus in the direction we came from, and the fact that Helios acts like he wants to follow him, too, feels like insult to injury. *Traitor.*

"Cypress," I call after him when he's a few paces away, and he immediately stops, pivoting to face me again. "You go back and you'll stay away from that table? From those men?"

"You asked me not to lie to you, Aiden, so I won't."

"Damn it, *why?* Why can't you—"

"Because someone has to."

"Not you," I counter. "You think I don't get it? You think I don't understand that some men need killin'? But it doesn't have to be *you.* We don't need you getting involved and causing us more trouble."

His jaw clenches, and for a second, I think he's going to listen, but then he only smiles. "Like you said, wolf…" He turns away. "There is no me."

CHAPTER 34
CYPRESS

It takes Dolly longer than I thought it would to corner me, and if I let myself think about it, I might consider it's yet another sign that she's starting to slow down.

I don't though. As a rule.

"You want to tell me what happened?" she asks, slowly easing herself onto the barstool next to me, and I wonder how many nights we've sat just like this. How many we have left.

Suppose I really am not great at following rules. I should work on that.

"Cypress," she says, prodding me with her voice as well as with her cane. "Start talking."

I blow out a breath, purposefully avoiding my reflection in the bar mirror. "Not sure there is much to say."

"Oh, Lord, help us. You do have it bad, don't you?" She chuckles. "And what does your cowboy say about it?"

"Not much that's encouraging."

"That much I've noticed," she replies, raising a hand for Sammy behind the bar to bring us both a whiskey before she adds, "Also noticed that you call him *wolf*."

The observation hangs between us, an open door to a room I never wanted to step into again, because it feels like I'll be locked inside the moment I do.

"Thought it suited him," I say, shrugging as I purposefully avoid looking at her, too. "Doesn't have to mean anything."

She laughs again. "I never realized it…"

"What's that?"

"Always told me you didn't like lyin'," she says, giving Sammy a grateful nod when she sets one glass in front of her and one in front of me before moving back to the other end of the bar. "Now I see you just don't know how."

I smile, not having to fake it for the first time tonight, but I don't manage to sustain it long enough to ask, "Do you believe in fate, Dolly?"

Her expression shifts as she considers the question carefully, the thoughtfulness something I've always appreciated about her. Even now, when I'm so anxious to hear her answer.

"Suppose I do," she replies finally. "It's a big wide world. Like the idea of there being something helping us find our way. And seeing as how God and I aren't on speaking terms, I suppose I also like having something else to talk to."

"Still no apology?" I ask, knowing damn well what the response will be because I never received one either.

"No," she says, "but you can bet I'll be demanding one when I get up there."

I snort, shaking my head at her before I push the whiskey away and lean my folded arms on the bartop. "Maybe you can put in a good word for me while you're—*ow*." I straighten up when her sharp cane jabs my side, and I scoot my barstool away out of an abundance of caution. "What was that for?"

She narrows her eyes at me. "Since when do you need a good word put in for you? Since when do you want one?"

"Since…" My thoughts drift, but to no avail. They always land back in the same place. "Perhaps I'm simply planning for all possibilities? Only practical."

"You haven't been *practical* a day in your life," she says, sounding very serious now. "Besides, if there's anyone on this earth that doesn't need a good word put in for them it's—"

"As much as I love your flattery, Dolly, you know that's not true," I reply before she can finish telling me what she thinks I want to hear. "You know…" I lower my voice, even though I'm fairly sure no one is paying us much attention, not with so many other, more entertaining distractions to be had. "You know the things I've done."

"I do know." There's an edge of emotion in her voice now that makes me feel guilty. Not for those things I've done, but for upsetting her with them. "That's why I'm saying it. You don't need me to plead some case for you."

"Come on," I counter, trying for humor. "Who else is going to?"

Her voice is still quiet but also firm when she replies, "I know a few who would. Who would love a chance to pay you back."

I shake my head, as adamant on this topic now as I was a decade ago. "There's nothing to pay back. There's no debt. Never has been, and you remind them of that for me when you see them next. They're still all right?"

"They're all right," she assures me. "Are you?"

"I'm fine."

"That lie was even worse than the first one," she informs me, pulling me from that door again, from that room. "But since you're being so truthful, tell me this…it his looks? You can admit it if it is."

I let out a laugh. "Dolly—"

"I'm not judging you. He's a fine-looking man. In fact, if I were younger…"

"How lucky for me that you aren't then," I reply, smiling. "I'm not sure I could withstand the competition."

"Probably not," she agrees, smiling too. "I was a terror in my time."

"It's still your time, Doll."

"Course it is." She looks at me fondly, but I don't think I'm imagining the hint of sadness in her eyes. "But should that time run out before we see each other again…"

"It won't."

"*Cypress*," she says, gentle but insistent. "If it does…I'd like to go to my next life knowing you're being taken care of in this one."

"You don't need to worry about me," I try to reassure her. "I can take care of myself. Always have."

She scoffs. "Just an *atrocious* liar."

"It's *not* a lie." I let out a long breath. "I'll be fine. I…I want to be."

"And that cowboy—"

"Aiden."

"*Aiden*. You think he'll make you happy? Maybe make you more than *fine*? Again, I understand he's nice to look at, but…"

"It's not—I mean, he *is*, but it's also that he…" I examine my folded hands on the bar, noticing the way my left thumb is tapping against the back of my right hand, but I'm too tired to try to stop it. "He's part of what I've been searching for, and finding him made me think that it actually was worth it. That there was a reason for it. That I haven't been wrong to believe…"

There's a long pause after, and I'm not sure if it's her being thoughtful or her simply not knowing what to say this time.

"All right then," she replies finally, a slight waver to her voice when she says, "I'll put a word in for you, darlin'."

"Thank you," I say softly, knowing she's good to her promises, even if I'm not sure it would do any good at this point. Maybe there isn't anything that would.

I look toward the mirror at last, not to see myself but the same men from before as they move about the packed room. Thinking they're closing in. Not thinking for a moment that anyone else is.

"You tell Lula the plan?" I ask Dolly, not needing to see her to know she's watching them as well. "She know what she's supposed to do?"

"Mm-hmm, told Sammy, too, so she wouldn't be concerned," she supplies, and I glance down the bar to where Sammy is currently staring daggers at them between pouring shots. "She offered to do the honors."

"I'm sure she did," I reply, smiling briefly before standing as the men start heading for the stairs that Lula just climbed. "Tell her she can get the next round. I'll take this one."

CHAPTER 35
AIDEN

I try going for a ride. It doesn't help. Nor does it help to think about going back to the house knowing no one else is there.

There is no we.

Fuck.

I'd winced when he said it. Even knowing the words were, as he pointed out, my own directed back at me. But they'd sounded different out of his mouth. Cruel. And I didn't want to be. Not to him.

I wanted you.

God, the look on his face when he'd almost told me whatever was going to be the end of that sentence. *If I could give you the things you deserved, then you might actually…*

Maybe it had been for the best that he hadn't finished that thought. For both our sakes, maybe it had been better that we parted ways. Got a little distance from each other. A chance to think…

I don't feel like I can think sometimes when he's around. Like I can breathe or focus on anything else *but* him. And maybe it's simple self-preservation, to have had him *so* close that I could've reached for him but didn't.

Because I already knew what he wanted to say. I knew exactly.

Just like I knew, even as I was riding away, that I'd end up right back here.

"Where is he?"

Dolly's eyebrows shot up the moment she saw me walk back in, but her expression had become more pleased the closer I'd gotten, then just downright amused by the time I asked.

"He's not at the table. And neither are those men, so where is he?" I repeat, shouting now to be heard over the outrageous swells of noise. "I need you to—" I glance toward the stage when the line of dancers start to do some sort of two-step that involves an excessive amount of stomping, shortly followed by several rounds of cheering from the spectators when it's announced that the next round of drinks are on the house.

Still nowhere in the crowd do I see him.

"*Where?*" I try again. "*Where is he?*"

"Why should I tell you?" she asks, managing to time her answer to a lull in the volume. "I advised you earlier not to leave him alone."

My jaw clenches in frustration even though I know she's got a point, my teeth grinding together. "Never mind. I'll find him myself."

I start to walk toward the stage, only to feel her hand on my arm pulling me back. "You ready for what you'll find if I tell you?"

"I said I wanted to find him, didn't I?"

"That's not what I asked," she clarifies. "Be sure, because if you aren't—"

"*Look*, I appreciate the warning," I snap, my patience officially at its end, "but you can either tell me where he is, or you can watch me tear this place apart looking for him. You choose."

She smirks. "Well, how about that? I'm starting to like you."

"For fuck's sake, I'm sorry that I—"

"He's upstairs." She pats a weathered hand against my chest. "When you see him, can you remind him to be careful with my rug? It's new."

With that, she turns and walks behind the bar, headed in the direction of the bartender who is now watching that same young woman from earlier up on stage. I almost feel bad for her that she has to miss some of the show when I hear yet another call for a house round go out, right as I'm taking a look around, making sure no one has their attention on me before I slip up the stairs. My gun is already drawn before I round the corner at the top, then do a quick count as well as a quick check on my weapon.

Six rooms are split between two sides of the long hallway before the one at the very end, and although I can't hear anyone on the stairs after me, I keep my back angled to the wall so that I can monitor the space in front of me as well as what's behind as I progress. My grip on the revolver in my hands stays tight, my fingers flexing around the handle as I stop outside the first room on my left then the next, listening to confirm each is empty before moving on.

Should the need arise.

That's what he'd told me about these rooms earlier, when the ideas that flicked through my head were entirely different from whatever I'm about to walk in on here.

I don't have to. I could go. I could turn around right now. I could run for it until I reached the train yard Dolly mentioned. Take the line back to Arizona and be there in a matter of days. I could leave. No matter our agreement. No matter if he…

There is no we.

With my left hand, I reach into my pocket. Take out the watch and check the time. Either for my future alibi, or just so I know the precise moment I do something so colossally fucking stupid that it undoes everything I've been trying to accomplish these past few years.

As I reclose the lid, I remember something else—my father doing the same in the field before looking at me and telling me something that I don't have time to listen to. Not now.

"I'm sorry," I mutter, stowing the watch back in my pocket when I hear a solid thud from inside the door at the very end, as well as what sounds like a muffled cry. "I know I've a long list of sins to atone for but…" I reach for the doorknob. "I think you're going to have to add one more to it."

CHAPTER 36
CYPRESS

"How many? Tell me."

Tom shakes his head, saying something that sounds like, *I don't know*, but it's hard to make out on account of his own bandana smothering his mouth. Not the most appetizing, I'd guess, but I'm not terribly concerned about his comfort.

"You do know," I say, crouching in front of him as my heart beats a rapid rhythm in my chest. "Someone like you? I have no doubt you've kept track."

Tom shakes his head again, flinching away when my eyes narrow at him. Yet another mistake he makes, because it puts his friend John back in his line of sight, along with the pool of blood expanding out from beneath his unconscious, but likewise restrained, companion.

Tom's frantic gaze returns to me, but since it's nearly impossible to understand what he's saying, I'm mostly spared from whatever pleas come along with it.

"Will you yell?" I ask him. "If I take the rag out?"

He shakes his head.

"Promise? Because no one will hear you but me, and I don't really care to. Understand?"

Nod.

"All right. Don't make me regret my hospitality." I reach forward and yank the end of the bandana, letting it fall out of his mouth. Fortunately, he doesn't yell, although he does cough a bit before getting the words out.

"Name—name your price."

My head tilts. "My price?"

He nods adamantly, trying to adjust his position on his knees though his hands are still tied behind his back. "I can get you money. Lots of it."

"Ah, I see," I say, understanding now. "You mean that if I let you go, you'll pay me with the cash from under the bed in your room?"

His eyes widen.

"Yes, regrettably, that is a very poor hiding spot. Especially for that much money. Perhaps you should have spent some time coming up with something a bit more creative rather than being a disgusting excuse for a human being. Did you consider that?"

His mouth is open but he's not saying anything now.

"Thought not. Now, where were we…" I reach for the revolver in my right shoulder holster. "Hang on, better if I kill you during the next chorus. It's louder."

"You are fucking psychotic, you know that?" Tom says, trying to shrink away from me again. "You're insane."

"Sticks and stones…" I tell him, shrugging as I give my gun a fun little twirl. "While we wait, I did ask you a question. How many?"

"I don't—I don't know what you're talking about. I've never hurt no women."

"*Ah*, finally, a confession."

"What? No, I said I *haven't*."

"Actually…according to your statement…"

"I haven't hurt *nobody*."

"Well, that *is* likely correct. However, as much as I appreciate you being more truthful—"

"You're the one," he snarls, interrupting what would've been a useless lesson in proper grammar given that he won't be talking for much longer. "You're the one who attacked *us*. Without reason."

"*No*," I say slowly, my anger seeping back into my voice. "I attacked you because you followed a young woman with the intention of attacking *her* once she walked into this room. Already had weapons in your hands and smiles on your faces when you opened the door, and I have to tell you, the degree of comfort you felt in doing that makes me believe this was not the first time. So I will ask again, how many?"

"What…what the fuck does it matter? She your girl or somethin'?" he asks, still evading. "Look, I'm sorry. If we'd have known—"

"If you'd have known *what*?" I give the knife that's been resting in my right hand a spin now as well to remind him that it's there. "If you'd thought she belonged to me? That's the distinction for you? Her being my property would allow her more rights than she has on her own?"

Tom doesn't immediately answer, seeming to understand that his last statement might have been another misstep. "That's not…no. All I'm saying is, we didn't know she was yours. We didn't know this was your place. We thought you was with that one fella. The gunslinger."

I sigh, my head falling forward for a moment. "One, that's a sore subject at present, so I'd advise you to tread lightly. Two, this place does not belong to me. However, it *is* run by a group of women who would very gladly tear you limb from limb, so you really ought to count your blessings that you and your friend ended up with me instead."

"Bless—*blessings*? You want him to count his blessings?" Tom complains, jerking his head in the direction of his partner. "You fuckin' stabbed him. John's probably dead."

"He's being a bit dramatic if he is," I say, brushing the concern off… though I had hit the other one's leg pretty deep. "In fairness, he *did* try to stab me first."

"You ambushed us," he stammers, trying to blame me again as if this is all some misunderstanding for us to clear up. "People got a right to defend themselves."

"I could not agree more," I tell him, and for a brief moment, he looks relieved. "People *do* have a right to defend themselves. But if they don't possess the disposition or the means…I'm glad to step in."

No doubt sensing his impending peril, Tom tries to scramble back, but instead loses his balance and falls forward, the wooden boards and the sickening crunch of his nose conveniently muffling the sound he makes. Unfortunately, the floor's interference appears to have been useless based on the way the bedroom door promptly flies open behind me… then closes again with a few quiet and familiar murmurs of blasphemy.

"Now you've done it," I tell Tom, standing and giving him a light kick with my boot. "Better roll onto your side. I'll be upset if you suffocate before I can kill you."

He does as I say, likely more due to the pain in his face than my request. Or simply because he also wants to look at the figure I can feel hovering right inside the doorway. Given how much I like to do the same, I honestly can't blame him.

"You have to help me," Tom starts, appealing around me to Aiden. "He's a madman. He's crazy. He—"

"*Shut it,*" Aiden barks, and I hear the distinct click of his gun's hammer as he steps farther into the room. "Cypress." Reluctantly for once, I turn to face him, watching as he aims his gun at the man tied up at my feet, then looks to the one in the corner and then to me. "What the hell are you doing?"

"Well…" My eyes take the same path through the scene he just had, and given the evidence, I decide, as usual, honesty remains the best option. "Currently, I'm either at the beginning or"—I glance at John's unmoving form—"halfway through a double murder. How about you? What have you been doing?"

When Aiden only stares at me rather than respond, his brows knit together in concern, I really begin to worry. "You *did* say you understood some men need killing."

Aiden blinks. "What?"

"Earlier. You said—"

"I *know* what I said," he snaps, voice coming out rough. "I also said it didn't have to be you, didn't I?"

"You did," I hastily agree, despite the cold rage still simmering beneath my skin. "Feel like maybe we have a differing opinion there, but then, no one sees eye to eye all the time."

"Christ," Aiden mutters, apparently not ready to agree to disagree as he switches to his deity's full name. "Jesus *Christ*. At this point I'd settle for half the time."

"*Please, you have to—*" Tom starts again, believing now to be his potential opening, until both Aiden and I respond with a sharp, "*Quiet*."

"You see that?" I say to Aiden when the man immediately falls silent. "We agreed there just fine. All hope isn't lost."

I could swear that the corner of Aiden's mouth twitches before he reflexively adjusts his hat, uncocks his pistol, and places it back in its holster. "What's the plan here, Cypress? Besides ruining Dolly's rug?"

He nods at John, and I note how the blood has now unfortunately spread to the edges of her Persian rug. "Well, she's not going to be happy about that."

"She will not," Aiden confirms. "Even told me to remind you."

"I'll replace it again."

"*Again*? How many times—never mind. Don't tell me."

"This particular rug? Only—"

"I said *don't* tell me. Not tonight." Aiden sighs, sounding worn out, before he nods his head toward Tom now, who *is* still breathing but who appears to have passed out, too. "You really were just going to kill them both here?"

I shrug. "That was my plan."

"Then what?"

"What do you mean?"

"Then what would you do with *two* bodies on the second floor, Cypress?" he says, and not even the blatant irritation in his voice is enough to overshadow how good it sounds when he says my name. "You kill them and then what? You walk back out the front door?"

"Not exactly."

"Then *what?*" he asks again, scoffing when I angle my head over my shoulder. "Oh, I see. You wait for someone to catch you while you are fumbling about with the window."

"It's really not a concern," I tell him.

"Because?"

"Because I am not the type that *fumbles about,*" I say, holding his gaze until his cheeks start turning pink. "Are you?"

In response, Aiden clears his throat, adjusts his hat again. "Always so fucking arrogant."

"I prefer self-assured," I reply, putting my back to him as I turn once more toward Tom.

"Wait." Aiden is suddenly at my side, all my focus moving to the spot where his hand grips my upper arm as soon as he places it there. "Don't."

"Don't?" Once the word has a chance to sink in, I meet the intensity in his eyes. "What do you mean *don't?*"

"I can't—" His jaw tenses, teeth grinding together. "We can't kill him."

"Why the fuck not?" I ask, sounding more like him than myself, though it does nothing to help me understand his reasoning. "He and his friend followed Lula up here. Who knows what they would've done. What they'll do to someone else."

I almost start to move again, but Aiden's grip holds firm. "Cypress, I can't…"

"You don't have to. I'll do it."

He looks down, refusing to meet my gaze now. "Please." He huffs out a breath. "I'm asking you not to either."

Slowly, I nod as I reholster the gun, his single plea far more persuasive than the many that came from Tom. "All right, then what's the alternative?"

"I'm thinking," Aiden replies, still not releasing my arm as his other hand reaches for the knife. Without concern, I let him take it, let him wipe it clean with a handkerchief from my pocket and slip it into his boot.

"He's seen our faces," I remind him. "So has his friend, if he's still breathing."

"Pretty sure he isn't."

"But not *entirely* sure…"

"I know what dead looks like, Cypress."

"Fine, but Tom is a danger to others. We can't simply take him downstairs and let him loose."

"No," Aiden replies, tone thoughtful. "Suppose we can't."

I quirk an eyebrow at him. "So, any ideas?"

"As it so happens," he says, glancing once more in John's direction. "I think I do. Although, I think you might have to replace more than one of Dolly's rugs."

CHAPTER 37
AIDEN

Tom, or whatever the fuck his name is, finally comes to, about ten miles outside of Renas. Taking long enough that I stopped to check twice if he was still on this side of living.

Fortunately, he was. Or unfortunately, depending on how you looked at it, and to be honest, I wasn't looking too kindly.

"Welcome back," I say, crouching in the dirt near his head as he slowly blinks up at me. "We're going to have a little talk and then I'm going to be on my way. Sound good?"

The man starts to respond before he realizes his predicament, the rag in his mouth and the fact he can't move on account of the rug he's rolled up in, as if he were the makings of a tobacco cigarette. If I were in a better mood, I'd probably find it funny.

"I want you to take a moment to consider how you are still alive," I tell him. "And then I want you to take a moment to decide if you want to stay that way before you answer my questions."

He blinks at me again, but finally nods.

"Now, you know why you're in this position?"

He shakes his head, and I raise my eyebrows at him, not having nearly enough patience for this as I stand and press my boot over his chest through the rug, which I can only imagine doesn't make his confinement any more comfortable.

He groans, quickly nodding.

"Great," I reply, easing the pressure off. "You know what you've done?"

He nods.

"You know what will happen if you ever do something like that again?"

I can tell this time that he's only nodding because he thinks it's what I want from him. I smile, shaking my head. "It would be very stupid of you to think I can't track you down. Trust me, I've tracked men with far less."

He says something, and I sigh, debating for a moment before leaning down to pull the rag out against my better judgment.

"You'll regret it if you do," he immediately snarls. "You and…" He looks around as best he can, trying to catch a glimpse of Cypress.

"He's not here," I inform him, trying to sound apologetic. "I sent him to bury your friend. Afraid he didn't make it."

The man curses, continuing to tell me how much I will regret my actions as if I don't already have a lifetime of that behind me.

"Look," I tell him. "I'm giving you a chance. But if I hear of you hurtin' anyone in the future, you can bet I'll be the first to darken your door. You understand?"

"They'll find you first," he says. "I have more friends. They'll already be looking for us."

"Gonna have to look pretty hard. Not sure you're worth it."

"Maybe not," he replies. "But the money your partner took is." He laughs, likely seeing the first trace of uncertainty on my face. "Didn't tell you about that, did he?"

"We were somewhat busy," I say, hoping I'm getting away with a smile at least somewhat close to the one Cypress uses at the poker table. "Had to decide where to dump your friend. Maybe we made a mistake deciding not to roll you up along with him?"

I whistle to Helios and the mustang trots forward, dragging the rug behind him with the rope fixed to his saddle. Tom panics.

"No," he begs quickly. "No, I'm sorry. Don't."

I whistle again and Helios stops. Such a damn good horse. Wish I could say the same about more people.

"He's…he's going to betray you," the man starts to babble. "He will. Your partner…he's crazy. You…you didn't see him."

"I saw him," I say, thinking of how Cypress had acted when I'd come in the room, when I'd found him standing over one man while another lay dead, when I'd finally gotten him to look at me only to see *that* version of him.

He'd looked like he had that night in the alley. That night with the knife. Under the rage rolling off him, I'd seen it—how scared he was. Maybe better than he even saw it himself.

I'd seen him. And I never wanted to see him like that again.

"He'll betray you," the man is saying again. "Only a matter of time."

"And let me guess…" I reply slowly, ready to be done with this. "You wouldn't?"

"No." He shakes his head for added emphasis. "I won't. Not if—not if you help me. I saw the posters at the station. You're running from someone, too. You need people with you. There's safety in numbers."

"Not really partial to crowds," I inform him, suddenly thinking again of dinner at Dolly's house last night. "Three is nice, but any more than that would feel excessive."

"Isn't when it comes down to a fight," he counters. "He—you'll both wind up dead if you stay with just him. Let me go, and I'll take you to my friends. Knowing who you are, they'd welcome you. If you were with us, no one would stand in your way." Below me, the man smiles, my silence making him think he's finally getting through to me as he further explains, "Not with our resources. Not with your reputation."

Fuck, *Aiden, I didn't want your reputation. I wanted* you.

I sigh, putting my hand in my pocket to brush against the watch as I stare for a moment at the night sky. *Damn it.*

"You know, as tempting as you hope that offer to be," I start, smiling as I turn my head back to him, then bend to grab the knife from my boot. "I think I'm good where I am."

"*Wait,*" he tells me, trying to wriggle free as soon as he sees the glint of the blade, and I have to say, I'm impressed that he does manage to make at least some progress. Good sign for him. And for me, I guess, if I really don't want his name on my list. "Don't do this—don't—"

He stops begging when I reach forward and cut the rope tying him to Helios, letting it fall into the dirt like a rattlesnake before calmly setting the knife on his chest.

"You can't leave me out here," he calls after me when I begin to walk away, his voice echoing out into the stretches of empty plains on both sides. "You can't leave me to die."

"Not leaving you to die," I tell him as I swing up into the saddle. "I'm just leaving you. Whether you die or not is up to you. And God, I suppose, if he's interested."

"*Wait—*"

I click my tongue at Helios, taking in a deep breath as I guide us toward the right direction while the man continues to offer me bargain after bargain. None of them the least bit appealing, none of them enough to make me look back.

CHAPTER 38
AIDEN

By the time I make it back to the house, the moon is already high overhead, and though I'm tired down to my soul after getting Helios settled into his stall, I don't have my mind on sleep yet. Not tonight. Instead, I'm moving with a sense of purpose, so completely focused on it that I don't notice the person sitting on the porch waiting for me.

"Good evening, Aiden," calls out a soft voice once I'm already on the steps, making me jump before I see Dolly watching me from a rocker that appears as ancient as she is, a well-loved book and a lantern on the table beside her. "Eventful night?"

"You have to be related to him," I say again as I put my hands on my knees and try to steady my heart rate before she starts waving a hand at me as a signal for me to hurry up. She pushes to her feet, both the chair and her bones creaking from the effort.

"Come on in. I'll make you something to eat."

"Ma'am, it's late. You don't have to go to the trouble. I'll be fine with—"

"I'm not out here in the middle of the night for my health," she interrupts, prodding me in the side with her cane to move me along as soon as I'm within range. "Go on now. Besides, the food is only an excuse to make you stay still while I talk at you."

"Not sure the trade is worth it," I grumble, trying to evade the woman's continued jabs with her damn stick, as well as the swing she takes at my head with her other hand. Given that she is about half my height, the hit lands in the middle of my back.

"Sit," she orders, satisfied once she manages to successfully herd me into a chair in the kitchen. "Always such a grouch," she mutters, the ruckus she starts making with her pots and pans somehow still not chasing my exhaustion away. "Really must be your good looks that he likes so much."

I arch an eyebrow at her, but she only laughs at me. "I'm old. Not blind." She turns toward the stove, heating up what appears to be a vegetable soup she made earlier this evening. "And I have known Cypress a long time. Never seen him so smitten."

"That's not…" I start to say, shifting in my seat. "Cypress is *smitten* with everyone."

"Given what you saw tonight, I *know* you know that's not true." Her head tilts as she takes me in. "You sure it was smart to leave one of them alive?" When I give her a surprised glance, she chuckles again. "Nothing happens around here that I don't know about."

"Cypress told you," I guess. "Never does keep his mouth shut."

"He hasn't been back yet to tell me. But as I said, I'm not blind.

Neither of you came downstairs again, and you're arriving separately, which means you had different affairs to attend to. I'm also missing *two* rugs—which the two of you *will* be replacing. One would have been suitable if they were both dead, but they also can't both be alive based on the blood stain you tried to hide under that trunk. Let me guess, you went out the window and Cypress tossed each of them down like a rolled-up newspaper?"

"Or a cigarette," I mutter, impressed by how much she'd put together until my mind finally catches on the first thing she'd said. "Wait, what do you mean he's not back?" I start to stand. "I left him hours ago."

"*You* might have." She stares pointedly at my chair, and I sit again. "Doesn't mean he left you. Probably went looking for you as soon as he was done. Seems to prefer to be wherever you are, regardless of whether or not you're aware of it."

I lean forward in the chair, resting my elbows on my knees as I stare at the floor, not especially surprised by this observation even as I ask, "You're saying—"

"I'm saying he doesn't like to let you get too far out of his sight. As I said, *smitten*." She smirks, gives the soup a stir. "It's about time. He's been alone for too long. I'd wager you have been as well."

"I've been fine on my own," I argue.

"No one is fine on their own," she counters with a dismissive laugh. "And you both ought to stop pretending like you are." She looks back at me, smiling wryly. "He'll be good for you, too, I think. Need someone to give you a bit of trouble."

"Already have had plenty," I tell her, certain on that at least. "No need for more."

She's quiet for a moment as she finishes heating up the food and spooning it into a couple red clay bowls. For that empty span of time, I'm foolish enough to think that she'll drop the subject altogether. Even more foolish to realize I don't entirely want her to.

"He's a good boy, you know," she says at last, giving me an appreciative smile when I get up to carry the bowls to the table. "Far better than he ought to be."

"That so?" I ask, setting her bowl then mine in place at the table before I pull out her chair and wait for her to sit, her movements with her cane stiffer with the late hour. She must be tired, maybe even more than me. "I found your *good* boy with two men tied up tonight."

"Only two?" She looks up at me as she settles herself and lets me push her chair in. "A slow night for him."

"A *slow*—" I stare at her. "Suppose that's what you wanted me to be *ready* to see? Christ." I glance toward the door to see if we're still alone before I drop into the chair catty-corner from her, hanging my hat on the back of it and pulling an unsteady hand through my hair. "You want to help me out and tell me what I've gotten into here?"

"Nothing you can't handle. If you're wanting to," she replies easily. "Isn't that right, gunslinger?"

I go still, and she clicks her tongue at me. "I told you, nothing happens around here without me knowin'."

"I don't…" I start to say, her calling me that bothering me more for some reason than when I'd heard it a little while ago. Perhaps because I think I want this old woman to actually like me. "I don't do that anymore."

She purses her lips at me. "But you'd judge Cypress for killing?"

"I'm not *judgin'* him for anything," I try to explain. "I just can't be a part of it."

She nods, picks up her spoon. "He asked you to be?"

"No, but we're partners, aren't we?"

Her eyebrows rise again. "Are you? Just because you're riding the same direction doesn't mean you're doing it together."

"We have an understanding," I say with a frown, and since that description doesn't feel quite true, I quickly amend, "An agreement."

"An agreement," she repeats, pausing the spoonful on the way to her mouth to laugh at me. "So you've said. How romantic."

I snort, but my skin heats beneath my collar. "We aren't—it's not like that."

"Course not." She nods in the direction of my soup, directing me to eat before she takes another spoonful for herself, and I figure it's in my best interest to oblige her. "So, this agreement you keep hiding behind..."

"I'm not hiding," I argue, realizing how hungry I am once the first near-to-scalding bite hits my tongue. It's good. Real good. I eat another before I go on. "The two of us decided to be of use to each other until this thing with Maddock blows over—*if* it blows over. We split whatever money Cypress makes fiddling with his cards, and I keep him from finding an early grave. That's it. Pretty simple."

"Ah, but should the situation call for killing to keep him from that grave?" she suggests with a tilt of her head. "If someone had tried to kill him tonight, you'd have done what? Glowered at them?"

The furrow between my brow deepens, something that only seems to tickle her more. "I would've handled it."

Her smile shifts from amused to knowing, making me feel cornered even before she says, "I have no doubt."

"I'm not killin' someone just because he feels like being rash," I say, my irritation snapping a bit as I search the front of the house again and think about where Cypress could be right now. He *ought* to be back. God knows what he's gotten into. All he was supposed to do was bury the body and then head home.

"What happened in Soldana is one thing," I continue. "And I'll admit, I wasn't completely… I had my own reasons for intervening. But what happened tonight was different. He can't just go around killin' folk cause it pleases him."

When I look back toward Dolly, she's studying me, food seemingly abandoned as she reclines in her chair with her hands folded on the table, and I have the distinct impression I'm about to be scolded. "Is that what you think he's doing? Killin' cause it pleases him?"

No, I think, remembering again the way he'd looked. The way he hadn't smiled once the entire time we'd been in that room.

"Did it *please* you in your old life?" Dolly asks, as if sensing the direction my thoughts have taken. "The killin'?"

"No, it didn't," I tell her, and she seems to know that's the only response I'm capable of giving, too lost in some of my own memories before she starts giving me some of hers.

"You know, while I haven't aged a day, the first time I met Cypress, he was quite a bit younger than he is now. God, must be getting on about ten years." She smiles again, this time fondly. "He came through town with a group of train robbers that I knew at first glance were the type I wouldn't care to have stick around, but Cypress…he was different."

"Certainly is that." I smile. "Can be hard to ignore."

"He is. Was then, too. Bright. Kind. But also very…there was a watchfulness to him. He was always thinkin', always keepin' an eye on what the others were doing, even as he was talking away. Could tell he never missed a thing. Never missed a trick, nor a harsh word or action from the rest of 'em. He continually apologized on their behalf. Slipping us extra money when they weren't looking. And all the while, I wondered why he was with them, even if I was grateful that he was, too."

She pauses, stares pointedly at my still-full bowl, and I don't need to be told twice.

"He had a talent for defusing things," she explains as soon as I start eating again. "Whenever the rest of his group got too rowdy, he'd manage to step in the way in time, get everyone sorted in the end."

"He can be good at that," I agree with a slight shake of my head, thinking of him doing the same the night Maddock tried to draw a gun on me. "Maybe too good. Until he isn't. He doesn't know when to quit."

Her frown deepens. "I'm not sure he thinks he can."

It doesn't have to be you, I'd told him, and he'd told me we had a *differing opinion*.

"He thinks it's his responsibility?" I guess. "To intervene?"

She nods. "I didn't understand how much until…well, I'm sure you have no trouble believing all my girls took a quick liking to him. Every one of them thought he was sweet as pie. All half in love by the time the week was through." She chuckles. "Wanted to take him in like a stray cat."

I do laugh a bit at that, unable to think of a more perfect description for him and the nine lives he seems determined to burn through at an alarming pace.

"The people he was riding with," I prod, preferring to turn the conversation away from Cypress's demise. "You said they were a bad sort?"

"They were. Didn't really know how bad at the time." She looks down at her hands for so long I worry she's fallen asleep right before she says, "Cypress though…"

"He knew," I say, thinking of the way he'd focused in on those two men earlier tonight. The way I'd learned right then the sort they were and been able to tell he did, too.

"The night his old crew left town, they decided to take a few of my girls with them," she says, a sudden unsteadiness in her voice. "Took them right from their beds like cowards. I tried my best to stop them. Hit one of them in the back with my shotgun as they were taking off, but the bastard died before I could make him tell me where they were headed. I went after them as far as I could, but when I lost the trail…I didn't think I'd ever see them again."

I close my eyes briefly, knowing that pain all too well. How it feels to lose people and to feel completely helpless while you do.

"Where was Cypress in all this?" I ask, thinking of tonight's events, trying to marry them and Dolly's clear affection for him with the story she's telling now. "He wasn't part of—"

"I'll admit to you that I thought he was," she says, finishing my sentence for me. "I can still remember catching sight of him looking back at me before he raced off with them, and I wondered how I had gotten him so wrong. How I missed that he was playin' us all that time. For *weeks*, I cursed that boy's name and all the while…" Her voice tapers off, wearily. "I still feel sorry for it."

I've stopped eating again because of the look on her face, not sure if I can stomach it right now no matter how good. "What happened?"

She sighs, wincing with the effort of adjusting her chair so that we're better facing one another. "My girls showed up again three weeks later. They'd been let loose longer but…Cypress had warned them not to come straight back. Told them which way to go and where to lie low. Gave them food. Money. Everything he could to make sure they got home."

"But he stayed?" I ask, already suspecting the answer. "He freed them and stayed behind? Why?"

She stares at me long enough for an earlier part of our conversation to come back to me.

He doesn't know when to quit.

I'm not sure he thinks he can.

"Fuck." I stand from my chair, unable to stay still as I begin to wander back and forth, remembering how scared he'd been when I held that knife to his throat, when I'd hit him and he'd told me he'd experienced worse. "*Fuck*…he went back to deal with them." I feel like I want to break something…someone. "And they got the upper hand on him?"

She nods, watching me pace for a time before she tells me softly, almost gently, "He showed up another week after they did. Must have taken a more direct path, but when he did, I…I barely knew him."

Everything inside me goes quiet, a waiting tension ready to snap. I see the thin scars on his face now in a new light. "They hurt him?"

"To this day, I have no idea how he even made it here."

I swallow past the lump in my throat, surprised at how much it's bothering me to hear this, how much I want to go find people that are likely already dead for a man that a few weeks ago, I didn't even know. "He tell you what they did?"

"I can only give you my part of the story. He's never told me his.

Not all of it," she admits, neither of us missing the grim significance of there being something that even *Cypress* won't talk about. "As I said, he was hurt. Feverish for days. And what he did tell me didn't make much sense back then."

I'm grateful I don't have to ask this time for her to keep going, for her to know I want to hear it anyway.

"He kept saying he'd lost *them*. Over and over. No matter how many times I reassured him that all my girls were back. That he'd done right." Her gaze looks past me to another time completely. "I wanted him to have some peace. Just in case he didn't pull through. But he was *so* insistent on it. Kept trying to get out of bed. Kept saying he had to find *them*. That they'd met him in the dark, and he couldn't leave them. That they'd be looking for him, too."

"Did he ever say who?" I ask, standing near her again as I lean my hip and brace my hand against the table for support.

"I suppose he did, in a way." Her eyes flick to mine, searching my face, but her body is starting to sag in her chair, and I can see again how weary she's getting. "At the time, I thought it was nonsense. But he's never wavered on it after all these years anytime I've asked him. Imagine my surprise, then, when he walked up with you…" She chuckles. "I didn't get it then, but I think maybe I do now."

"Get what?"

She reaches out a wrinkled hand, patting the side of my face. "You'll take care of him for me, won't you? You and the little bird?"

The little bird?

"Dolly." I huff out a breath, sure now that I've kept her up too late since she's not making any more sense than she claims Cypress did.

"Maybe you ought to get to bed and we can talk about this later. It has to be past midnight. You should get some sleep. I'll clean up in here."

For a moment, she looks like she wants to disagree, but the telltale grimace when she shifts in her chair again seems to convince her. For now.

"Well, someone raised you right at least." She sighs, missing how I wince before she lets me help her to her feet and walk her toward her room. "Suppose I can see a little more why he's so taken with you."

I roll my eyes. "All these books in here are giving you too many ideas, Dolly."

"Mm." When we reach her door, she unlinks her arm from mine, leaning on her cane as she eyes me. "Let me know if you want to borrow one. Seems you could use some of those ideas."

"I don't—"

"Aiden," she says, her voice suddenly stern in a way that makes me fall quiet. "I understand. Really, I do. You've had not only a long road but a hard one, and up until now, you've done what it takes to survive, but… maybe while you're busy keeping Cypress alive, you could try to keep yourself alive, too, hm?" She pats my chest again as she adds, "Oh, and when you go searchin', you might want to check the roof."

"The roof?" I ask, looking up as if that'll help me understand the jump from the prior discussion to this one. "Why? It need fixin'?"

"Lord help me." She shakes her head and opens the door to her bedroom, muttering to herself as she walks inside, "Really must be his looks."

CHAPTER 39
CYPRESS

I'm quiet as I let myself inside, passing Dolly's bedroom and allowing myself a glance down the hall toward Aiden's room in the back before heading up the stairs. My intention not to wake either of them, though perhaps Aiden more so.

I'd been so set on finding him, knowing he faced far more of a risk dealing with Tom than I did dealing with a dead body. Though he had insisted on being the one to do so, it hadn't sat right, giving him another mess to clean up on my account. Bringing more *complications* to his door…

How many more times will he tolerate it before he decides he's had enough? Cuts his losses and moves on as he'd been planning to do with Maddock? If I'd been able to find him, would he have already told me as much?

When I reach the bedroom at the top of the stairs, I close the door behind me before grabbing the bedroll at the foot of the bed and a few blankets, putting both over my shoulder before walking to the window and pushing it up.

It squeaks loudly, and I pause for a moment, wishing I'd remembered to put some oil on it earlier today as I listen for the sound of stirring downstairs. Grateful that I hear none, I finally ease myself out onto the window ledge, turn to grab the lip of the roof, and pull myself up, crawling along the gentle pitch to reach the flat expanse at the top. There's not a ton of room up here, but I have no trouble unfurling my bedroll and the blankets before stretching myself out and staring at the clear sky. Looking to the stars for answers that they don't have.

What if he tells me in the morning that he's done? Worse, what if he leaves without even bothering to let me know? What if—

I hear the distinctive sound of the window squeaking again as it's pushed farther up, the creak of the ledge as someone puts weight on it, a low grunt of exertion, and then… "Jesus Christ."

I sit up, staring at the edge of the roof, and I'm still not sure I trust my eyes when I see Aiden's hat appear, shortly followed by the rest of him as he scrambles more than climbs to the top.

"You need a hand?" I ask him, biting the inside of my cheek when he glances over his shoulder toward the ground below. "I could—"

"No," he says, holding up a hand to stop me before smacking it back down on the roof. "You try to help and I'm liable to end up going over."

"I'd go after you," I offer. "If that's any comfort."

He takes his eyes briefly off the shingles to look at me. "Sort of is, I suppose." He huffs. "I'll be there. Just give me a minute."

Of course I do. Several, in fact, though he finally reaches me after feeling the need to crawl the rest of the journey on all fours, breathing fast and shaking a little as he peers back in the direction he came from.

"Can't honestly tell me…" he says, studying the flat square of roof we're sharing and scooting a bit closer to me. "You actually prefer this to a bed?"

I shrug. "Better view."

"Yeah." His eyes flick toward the stars before he slowly surveys the ever-evolving Texas landscape rolling out all around us, plains giving way to pockets of trees, to rock formations and to a well-known canyon in the distance. "Suppose it is."

He tucks his knees up near his chest before cautiously putting his hands behind him, bracing himself as he leans back in what must be an attempt at relaxation.

"You don't have to stay," I offer, trying not to laugh at his expense. "I can come down."

"*No,*" he says quickly. "No, I'm not sure I want to think about how we get back down. Not yet. Getting down at Dolly's place was bad enough."

"All right," I say, leaning back in an imitation of his own posture, except I leave my legs sprawled out in front of me. After another moment, he notices and does the same.

"Did you…" I start to ask, worried about what could have possibly brought him up here. "Did everything go as planned?"

He nods, seeming to grow a bit more at ease now that he can look out instead of down. "Left him rolled up a good way out there. Suspect it'll take him a bit to get free but he should be able to if he wants it bad enough. Hopefully will give him plenty of time to do some thinking."

"And if he thinks to come back?" I ask.

Aiden sighs. "Then we'll cross that bridge when we come to it. He said he's got other friends. Should stay here a few more days in case he really does. Don't want Dolly dealing with it on her own."

If he were looking at me, he would see the affection on my face, but since he isn't, I'm able to cover slightly better when I tell him, "Thank you."

Now, he does glance my way. "Nothing to thank me for. It was my call not to kill him."

"But I was the one who got myself *involved*. Got you involved and…" I take a deep breath. "And I am sorry for it. You told me that you wouldn't kill anyone for me, and I want you to know it wasn't my intention to try to force your hand. I would've taken care of it. It's only…I couldn't just let them go. And if that changes things for you—"

"It doesn't," Aiden replies, and I feel my pulse skip then full-on race once he corrects, "Well, it does, but not in that way…I should have explained before. I haven't been fair to you, asking you not to lie to me and then not giving you the same courtesy."

"You've lied?" I ask. "You really do play poker then?"

"No," he says, laughing slightly as I hoped he would, breaking some of the increasing tension in the air. "We should definitely leave the gambling to you."

We. It's the third time he's said *we* since he climbed up here, and I'm beginning to hope it's intentional.

"I've omitted things," he continues, peering briefly over the roof again before deciding better of it. "About my past. About who I was before, and there's things you ought to know if we're really going to be partners."

"You don't have to tell me," I remind him. "If you don't want to."

"I do. Want to," he replies, tone firm. "I think maybe it would help if I did."

"All right." I stay very still on the off chance that one wrong move might spook him into either falling or changing his mind. "I'd like to hear it then."

"I *was* a gunslinger," he says after a few more moments pass, his eyes back out on the midnight horizon. "And I was…good. Very good. Enough that I made the newspaper headlines more than once."

"Doesn't surprise me," I tell him, hoping he doesn't mind me saying it. "You have a steady hand. And a quick draw."

"Not like I did," he says with a slight smile. "I'm not sure I'm the fastest out there anymore. Maybe not even the fastest on this roof."

I grin, undeniably pleased he'd noticed. "I've had a lot of time on my hands."

"So have I," he agrees, his expression shifting into a frown before he picks up his story again. "I ran away from the orphanage when I was thirteen and I suppose, when you're that young and that scared, you tend to latch on to whatever it is that lets you survive. For me, that was shootin' well. Shows, marksmanship contests…anything that would give me enough to get by. Wasn't until I was older that my targets started becoming people."

"How much older were you?" I ask, wondering how similar our stories are but also wondering when he'll decide I'm prying too far. "The first time you killed someone?"

"Sixteen," he says after a long pause. "You?"

"Fourteen," I admit, making Aiden one of two people in this world that I've told. Maybe the only one left. "He was… My father died before I could even walk, and my mother worked hard to make up for it. I…I wish I could say I always made things easier on her." I clear my throat, glancing at Aiden to see if this will make his opinion of me even worse than it was before. "When I was eleven, she started thinking I needed someone to look up to, and when a wealthy gentleman took an interest in her, she really believed our prayers had been answered. That he would make our lives easier. But he didn't. He…he started to hit her right after they were married. Then one day, I made it so he couldn't anymore."

Beside me, I see Aiden hang his head before he nods. "Then you did right."

As soon as he says the words, it's as if a burden has been lifted from my shoulders, one I hadn't even realized I was still carrying. My understanding for why he could be, perhaps, the only one to absolve it coming to me a moment later when he keeps going.

"Mine was…a thief. Someone my father had caught stealing on the farm and let go. I was supposed to be helping fill in, but I lost track of time playin' with my friends. I'd just come back when the man showed up, and he…" Aiden's eyes find mine in the dark as I think back to the first time he'd followed me into the alley, to how angry he'd seemed when he'd called me a thief.

"Your parents?" I venture. "He took them?"

"When I was nine," Aiden mutters. "Spent years thinking I might never find him. But I did."

I hesitate only for a second before shifting closer, my shoulder lightly brushing against his as I tell him that I'm sorry, and I feel him brush mine back when he repeats the words a moment later. Both of us holding each other up for a while in the dark.

"My parents were *good* people," he says when he eventually starts speaking again, his voice even lower than usual. "Honest, hard-working. They didn't deserve…I tried to run for help, but I wasn't a particularly good rider at the time. Law eventually found me. Sent me off to an orphanage without letting me go home. Probably wouldn't have wanted to with everything already sold or gone, but…after a while, I started thinking that if I killed the man who did it…maybe I'd get *something* back."

"But you didn't."

"I didn't," he confirms. "Not until…" He glances at me again, and I think I see one of his hands go to the pocket of his coat before he clears his throat and puts his hand back where it'd been, empty. "After I killed him, I thought if I helped other people…helped other good folks who'd crossed paths with the bad in the world…"

I think of Clayton back in Soldana, how adamant he had been that Aiden was a hero for something he'd done for a family he knew. As well as, I suspect, why Aiden didn't have all the "earnings" from his time as a gunslinger, the ones Maddock believed he'd already spent.

"Did you charge them? A fee?" I ask, already knowing the answer even before Aiden's head whips in my direction.

"*No*," he snarls, as if the idea is abhorrent to him. "They'd already lost enough without someone trying to make a profit on it."

I nod, pleading uselessly with the stars again before I fall back against the roof. "Thought that was what you were going to say."

"Do you?" Aiden asks, looking down at me while I stare up at him with what can only be described as pining devotion. Not that he notices.

"Do you ever charge? For the people you kill?"

"Nope."

"But you keep the money you take from them?"

"Sometimes," I tell him truthfully. "I keep some of what I win. Use it to keep up appearances. To get myself from place to place. To get *us* from place to place," I test.

That full mouth of his presses into a thin line, but he doesn't correct me before he asks, "To buy watches?"

I grin. "On one occasion…"

Aiden rolls his eyes. "And what do you do with the rest of it?" He pauses, hesitating. "What did you do with the money you took tonight?"

I frown, wishing I'd been the one to bring it up first. "Tom tell you?"

"Mm-hmm."

"And you're concerned I'm keeping it from you?"

Aiden considers. "Strangely enough…no, I'm not. Figure we had more pressing issues at the time, but I'd like to know now."

"It's hidden in the barn along with Maddock's money, stashed behind the loose sideboard in the empty stall," I tell him, relieved he chose to trust me on this at least. "Of course, half of it is yours, so I wanted to discuss it with you before I do what I usually do."

A cautious look comes over his face. "What is it you *usually* do?"

"You might not like the answer."

"Tell me anyway."

"All right." I take a bracing breath. "I burn it."

His mouth falls open. "You what?"

"I *burn* the money."

"*Why?*"

"I've heard it's the root of all evil."

He snorts, shaking his head. "Thought you weren't religious."

"I never said that."

"Oh?" He arches an eyebrow at me. "You're telling me you believe in God?"

I cock my head, still staring up at him, and I really could get used to this view. "Why? Still wondering when you'll be able to see me on my knees?"

"Fuck's sake." He huffs out a laugh then drops down next to me, still close but not so close that we're touching as we lie side by side. "You ever think about what's coming out of your mouth before you say it?"

"Always."

"I'm not sure if that makes it better or worse."

"Better," I say, turning my head toward him. "Because then you know I mean it."

I see his jaw tense, the way he swallows as he keeps his eyes on the sky, and I bet that if the sun were up, I'd be able to see him blush. My *favorite* of his expressions, which is why it's so hard for me to do anything that would make it go away.

"What made you quit?" I ask. I need to know the ending as much as I do the beginning, and I'm not sure when this opportunity might present itself again. "What made you believe it was enough?"

Beside me, he breathes slowly, a deep in and out that catches once, twice, before he manages, "No matter how many I killed, it wasn't helping. Wasn't bringing them back. No more than it was bringing back anyone else, and… After a while, all it felt like I was doing was losing more. Like one side of my balance sheet was just getting longer while the other stayed empty."

"Your balance sheet?" I ask. "As in, your list of sins? Do you believe there is one?"

"Sometimes. That orphanage I was sent to after my parents died… It was Catholic."

He shoots me a look, daring me to say something, but though I feel extremely satisfied at being right, telling him so doesn't feel important at present. "Go on," I simply say.

"They were pretty clear there about what happens to sinners, and I guess, I figure if there really is a heaven, it might be my only…" he continues hesitantly, although when he pauses again, I suspect the sentence ends differently in his mind than what I get to hear. "Figure at some point I should start trying to earn forgiveness."

"I see," I say, considering the idea. "In that case, can I ask you something?"

He eyes me warily. "I suppose."

"Do you regret it? Doing what you did? The families you helped get justice?"

He blows out a long breath. "No, I can't say I do. At least, I don't regret doing what I did, so much as I maybe regret what it cost me. But, even if it didn't bring me peace, each of those men…"

"Needed killing?" I offer.

"Yeah," Aiden says, the ghost of a determined look on his face. "They did."

"You know, wolf," I start to say, and even though he doesn't turn his head to acknowledge me, I can tell he's listening. "I am not religious."

He closes his eyes. "You just said—"

"Hold on, let me finish," I interrupt, nudging his side. "I am not religious in a *traditional* sense. However, to play devil's advocate—"

"You would."

"—my understanding is you have to repent in order to be forgiven."

He mulls that over, too. "Suppose you do."

"Something to consider." I shift on the bedroll, intending to have the stars be the last thing I see before I close my eyes. "Not that I would mind you keeping me company in damnation, wolf."

"Cypress."

"Hm?" I turn my head to him, only to find him already staring at me this time, making me increasingly aware of the space where my hand is resting between us, his own near enough that I can feel the heat from his palm.

"Why do you call me *wolf*?"

"Maybe because it suits you," I hedge, even knowing now would be the time to tell him the rest. But I don't want to lose him again. "Or maybe because I've just always wanted to be friends with a wolf."

He laughs. "Friends. I'm not sure I would call us— the fuck are you grinnin' for?"

I shrug, still smiling. "Because you're right...we are not friends." His eyes search mine, but I'm the one that sees the flash of disappointment in his. "What we are, Aiden...I hope the appropriate word is *inevitable*."

"An inevitable pain in my ass," he mutters back, but he's smiling now, too.

Right up until I suggest, "Do you want me to help you back down the roof?"

He shakes his head. "No. Not ready for that yet. Might stay up here for a bit and go down later."

"All right." My heart thunders in my chest as his eyes find mine again, and if I could choose, this would be what I see before I close my eyes every night. "Tell me when you're ready."

He nods. "Okay, Cy, I'll tell you."

CHAPTER 40
CYPRESS

When I wake up, the first thing I notice is that I've slept soundly once more. The second is that I'm warm. Almost to the point of discomfort but also not nearly, because everything about this feels so *good*.

The third thing I notice, in addition to being well rested and nicely warm, is that everything feels *heavy*. Again, not in an unpleasant way, but certainly in a way that I can't really move. A sensation that should be far more alarming than it is, and perhaps would be had I not cautiously cracked one eye open and seen…*him*. Well, part of him anyway.

Rather than making his way back down the roof last night, Aiden appears to have decided to stay put, apparently also deciding at some point during the night that I should too.

What I can see *and* feel is that his right arm is draped over my abdomen, his corresponding hand gripping my shirt around my chest as we both lie on our sides, his right leg similarly flung over both of my own to keep his body as close as he can get it. I don't even need to see his face to know exactly where that is, too, the warm, steady current of his breathing brushing against the ends of my hair on my neck.

I'm afraid to breathe myself, afraid that even fully opening my eyes could wake him, make him realize that he is currently wrapped around me and, worse, make him stop, and that is the *last* thing I want. Except…

Though I managed to stay still, Aiden is shifting, and I wonder again if it's simply that he can feel my heart racing in my chest, can hear—

I bite back a quiet sound when the bridge of his nose brushes against my hairline, his whiskers scraping rough across my nape. He groans, the arm he has around me tightening and pulling me more firmly against him, and I…I was not wrong in my judgment of his size.

"Fuck's sake," I whisper, borrowing one of Aiden's expressions as I debate my options. On one hand, I could pretend to be asleep, and in doing so also torment myself with how it feels to have him pressed up hard against me. Which is *exceptionally* tempting, since I have never been opposed to a little delayed gratification. However, I also know that if I allow this to progress, once Aiden does wake up and realize what he's doing, he's going to startle out of some misplaced sense of decorum. Potentially even to the point of *actually* falling off the roof, and then I really will have to go after him, because the idea of not having this again is going to make me *want* to.

Which brings me to the other option I am not super enthused about but…does have the better chance of eventually achieving that delayed gratification, since we'll both be alive.

I squeeze my eyes shut, take a deep breath in—an egregious mistake since all I can smell is his personal combination of campfire and leather— then move.

Not a lot. But enough to make it seem as if, while I'm not awake yet, I'm about to be.

Behind me, I feel the moment Aiden stirs enough to notice, his whole body going extremely still while I continue to keep my eyes closed and my breathing slow. While I wait for him to pull away and dread the moment he will. Only, he doesn't.

Aiden doesn't move.

I know he's awake. I can hear the way his own breathing has changed. But he still hasn't moved.

"*Cypress.*" He says my name so softly I'm not entirely sure I really hear it, and I tell myself that's my excuse for staying quiet before I feel him take another deep breath, only this time his forehead presses between my shoulder blades, the fabric of my shirt muffling the low groan that escapes his throat, and I can't help it. I don't even actively think about it before I push back against him in response.

We both tense now, neither of us moving apart even though his breathing hitches and grows shallower. "Cypress," he repeats, deeper this time, more authoritative, his fingers bunching more firmly in the fabric of my shirt. "Is this…"

I nod, not knowing if he was going to ask me if this is okay or if this is something I want. Both of which I would say yes to without hesitation.

"This…" he begins again. His hand releases my shirt but thankfully shifts lower to grip my hip, his fingertips pressing in to keep me right where I am. "This is not a good idea. For a lot of reasons."

"Really?" I say, fully dropping the pretense that I'm anything but wide awake. "None of them are currently occurring to me."

He huffs out a laugh, his warm breath on my nape again. "We're business partners."

"Still can be," I argue, finally letting my own hands roam, my right moving to cover his over my hip, our fingers interlocking, and my left reaching back to find those wavy curls I'm so infatuated with. "In fact, one could argue we might be able to achieve a much deeper level of partnership this way. Think of how thrilling this could make our negotiations…"

He laughs once more, but the tail end of it shifts into something else when my fingers tangle in his hair and give a gentle tug. Not so different from how I've seen him do it so many times, although I would wager the effect *is* quite a bit different.

"We're on the run," he says, and I have to remember what it is we're talking about because he chooses to shift his hips at that precise moment, subtly grinding himself against the curve of my ass. "We're fugitives."

"All the more reason…" I say, moaning when I become aware of the distinct scrape of teeth on my shoulder as he does it again. "Better take advantage while we can."

"Is that what we're doing?" He's laughing, but only for a moment before I match his rhythm, before I lead the hand on my hip to where I really want him. My reward is the low, needy sound that leaves his throat when he feels the outline of me through my slacks. "What about…what about the fact that you already make me crazy?"

"Wolf," I say with a chuckle. "I haven't even *begun* to drive you crazy. But I will…" My hand is still over his as he continues to feel me, feel exactly how hard I am from this, how much this is affecting me, how much *he* affects me. "I will if you let me."

He groans, and I think he's going to give in and put both of us out of our misery until the moment he finally moves, pulling his hand from mine so that he can yank me beneath him. He stares down at me, eyes wild, chest heaving, and his mouth…*that mouth*. There are so many things I want to do with that mouth.

"*Cypress.*" He drops his head, letting it hang for a moment between his shoulder blades. The sudden shift in his demeanor makes me question if I'm still allowed to touch him, if he still wants me to…

"We can't do this," he says finally. "We can't."

"Is it the roof?" I ask, trying to keep the tone light, my fingers digging into the blankets so I won't succumb to the urge to dig them into him. "Not ideal?"

He looks up, shakes his head, but I breathe a little easier when I see his eyes are soft. "Not ideal," he repeats, though the way he slowly peers over the edge makes me think he's just remembering where we are. "We also need to get our plan together."

"Our plan?" I ask. He's still caging me in like he's afraid I'm going to make a break for it. "Our plan for…?"

"Fugitives," he says, as if he can't understand why that's not at the top of my mind. "We're still fugitives."

"Right," I say slowly. "And…?"

"That's bad, Cypress. That's a problem." He quirks an eyebrow at me, clearly amused. "Interesting."

"What?"

He smirks, those wavy strands I just had my fingers in partially covering his brown eyes. "Not as sharp when you're horny, are you?"

I narrow my eyes at him. "It would be a mistake for you to assume

I'm not *always* horny. But, forgive me for not immediately following the switch from you wanting to fuck me to you wanting to discuss us being wanted criminals."

"I didn't—" he starts to say before I shoot a meaningful glance toward his cock, still making itself known through the bulge at the front of his pants. He rolls his eyes. "Fine, but the point still stands."

"Well, something definitely does," I mutter. "Impressively, might I add."

"I felt you, too, Cy," he reminds me, leaning lower so that his face is inches from mine. "Can even now, so don't act—"

"*I* wasn't," I interrupt him, unflinchingly meeting his gaze. "I have never once pretended like I didn't want you. Anytime, wolf. Any place. You just say the word."

His eyes drop to my mouth and hold there before coming back up. "We can't just pretend... We need to figure out our next move, remember?" he says, voice strained. "We need to know what we're doing here."

"And apparently what we *aren't* doing." I finally touch him again, but only to ease him off me. Something he appears as reluctant about as I am as I gather up the blankets and bedroll.

"Are you coming?" I ask him, turning to start backing down the roof.

He studies me, then the roof. "I don't think that's a good idea right now."

"Why?" My head tilts, my face the picture of innocence. "Are you also not as sharp when you're horny?"

He glares at me, but a few moments later when I swing myself through the bedroom window, he follows right behind me.

CHAPTER 41
AIDEN

Well…*fuck.*

I think…I think I may have lost my grip on this situation. Not that I ever really had one, but…I sure as *fuck* don't now.

This is…this is a problem. This is…*not* good.

"Aiden?" My head shoots up when I hear Dolly call my name, and I realize I've been staring at the same section of wood on her kitchen floor for God knows how long instead of eating my breakfast, something she's probably noticed. Cypress certainly has.

When I look to where he's seated across from me, the only thing obscuring his giant grin is the cup of coffee he's bringing to his mouth. Everything else about him, from his styled hair beneath his hat to his black clothing, is back to flawless after he'd cleaned himself up this morning at the same time I did. Albeit separately. Which was *wise.*

If he's got his hat on, I suppose I could, too. Might make me feel less like all of my thoughts are being read by the two people at the kitchen table with me. Although, it might also seem odd to put it on now when I've had it off and I'm not on my way out the door. Maybe I should be. Maybe I need some air. Maybe…

My eyes sweep Cypress up and down as he leans back in his chair, looking perfectly at ease. God damn him, but *God*, he looks good.

Does he always look this good? *Yes*, murmurs a voice in the back of my head, the same one that a moment later says, *Yes, you fucking have* when I wonder if I've simply not noticed before today.

Should've found someone while I was in Soldana. That would've taken the edge off. Although *when* I would've done that, I'm not sure. From the moment I saw him in the saloon, the vast majority, if not *all*, of my thoughts and my time have been taken up by Cypress. And that is unlikely to change in the immediate future if he keeps…

He takes another sip of his coffee, watches me track the swallow right down to the couple open buttons at the top of his shirt where some of his chest is exposed.

"Am I going to have to spray you two with water?"

Both Cypress and I turn our heads to Dolly. "What?" I ask first, catching Cypress brushing a few drops of coffee off his shirt out of the corner of my eye. Serves him right…and maybe he'll have to change again now.

No, thinking about that is not helping.

"Lord help me," Dolly snaps, getting up from her chair and pointing a finger my way. "You go anywhere looking at him like that and you're going to be fined for public indecency. And you…" She turns her finger on Cypress. "Stop tormenting him until he figures out how to do it back."

She switches again to me. "Aiden, you're still welcome to my books."

"Why does everyone think—I *know* how to do it back," I argue, feeling my face heat.

"He certainly does," Cypress says around a chuckle.

In response, Dolly gives an exasperated sigh. "Well, I'm happy to hear that's not the problem, but since I can barely hear myself think in here with you two panting at each other, should I lock you both in a room until you figure out what is?"

"Aiden? Thoughts?" Cypress turns to me, a perfectly polite expression on his face as if it's completely normal for a woman old enough to be our mother implying we should fuck some sense into ourselves.

"Confinement won't be necessary," I assure them. "Unless it's what's needed to come up with a serious plan."

"A plan?" Dolly repeats, glancing at Cypress, who for some irritating reason only shrugs.

"You're the one who said running isn't a strategy," I remind him.

"Did I?" he says, sounding contemplative. "Hard to recall. Been so long."

"It was two days ago."

"Was probably sharper then."

I put my head in my hands, praying for patience before I say, "*Cy*, we need a plan. We've got our friend from last night out there somewhere, along with *his* friends, *and* we've got Maddock looking for us."

"Speaking of which…" Dolly says, bringing herself back into the conversation. "While you two boys were sleeping in this morning, or"—she glances between us—"*whatever* it is you were doing, I went into town." Her gaze focuses on Cypress. "Got a telegram back from the friend I was waiting on. She said rumor is Maddock's mama and daddy cut him off."

Cypress and I exchange a look. "They did what?" I ask.

"They cut him off. Reached their limit from the sounds of it and disinherited him after the mess in Soldana. Now everything will go to his younger brother. I'll bet the reward they're offering on those posters is more than he even has left."

"Maddock has a younger brother?" I try to think if he ever mentioned a sibling, although it's not as if we spent a lot of time chatting. "How old?"

"No more than four by the sounds of it," Dolly replies. "Must have made a backup when their firstborn started proving rotten." She catches my expression and gives me a sympathetic smile. "Might sound harsh but that's the way some of them think. Babies are part of business."

I frown, though I suppose she's right, then look to Cypress who is watching me with interest. "What?"

"Do you…" he starts, setting his mug down before folding his hands in front of him. "Do you want children?"

"Oh for God's sake," Dolly says, taking the words right out of my mouth.

"You said we were supposed to be planning," Cypress mutters, picking his mug back up and taking a sip, sulking. "We can talk about it later."

"Getting quite a list, aren't you?" I ask, choosing to focus on the part of me that was caught off guard by the question rather than the part that would like to know his answer. "Of things to address later?"

"Growing by the minute," he replies with a wink.

"All right," Dolly says. "The both of you, out." She starts shooing

Cypress and me from our chairs and toward the back door, apparently not even wanting to risk taking us through the house to the front.

"Go cool off. Go for a ride. Go for each other," she recommends, resorting to her cane when we don't move fast enough. "I don't care, so long as I'm able to walk around without tripping over one of your libidos."

"What a lovely picture you paint, Dolly," Cypress replies, making me grin as we get effectively shoved outside. "Are you sure you don't need our help with anything?"

"Not until you help yourselves," she mutters, then slams the door.

Cypress and I stand there for a moment, staring at the house and then at each other before we both start laughing.

"Now look what you've done," he says after a while when we've both calmed down.

"Me? You're the one who got us thrown out."

He shrugs. "Bound to happen." His blue eyes shine with amusement. "So, how about it?"

"About *what?*" I ask, even as I feel the heat start to pool low in my stomach, even as I think about how much I'd like to reach for him again, to hold him.

I've never held someone like that. Every experience I've had before has always felt…impersonal. A mutual satisfaction of a need. But this morning, while I have no doubt it would have been mutually satisfying…nothing about it felt impersonal. Nothing about the way I feel about him does.

"How about a ride?" he suggests, clarifying his statement. "How about we take Cerberus and No Name—"

"Helios," I say.

"Helios," he repeats, grinning. "How about we take them for a ride?"

"If you want," I say, afraid to admit how much I like the idea before falling into step beside him. "Where *did* you come up with the name Helios, by the way?" I ask him as we head for the barn, thinking to take at least one thing off our list for later. "And Cerberus?"

He glances at me. "Are you familiar with Greek myths?"

"Not especially," I admit.

"Cerberus is Hades's dog. A guardian," he tells me. "Hades is—"

"God of the underworld," I finish for him, knowing that much at least. "Really do like that *distinctive brand*, don't you?" His grin widens. "And Helios?"

"God of the sun."

My steps slow as I smile, shaking my head at him. "They're opposites."

"In a way." Cypress slows too, keeping pace with me while moving a bit closer so our shoulders are almost brushing. "You know, I've been told they attract."

"You know, I've been told that, too. If they don't kill each other first."

Cypress laughs, giving me another wry smile, and I can't remember why it ever bothered me that he does it so much.

"Another thing about Helios?" he asks, likely confident he already has my full attention, but I still nod for him to continue. "He was also all-seeing."

"All-seeing?"

"Mm-hmm."

"As in…?"

"As in he liked to watch…" Cypress pauses just long enough to make my stomach tighten before adding, "Over *everything*."

"Right," I say, but there's that fucking grin again. "Cy," I warn, immediately going after him when he takes off for the barn. "*Cypress.*"

Even after I catch him, we don't stop running. Not for days.

CHAPTER 42
CYPRESS

I think this must be what people who believe in God feel like. Only, I have no need for blind faith when the subject of mine exists right in front of me.

All those years waiting…I'd do it all again.

Aiden and I stand toward the back of the room at the end of what has been a perfect day, close enough that I can feel the warmth rolling off him more than I can feel it from the rest of the bar. Both of us watch the dancers up on stage, grinning as we see Lula give Sammy a cheeky wave whenever she looks up from behind the bar.

"How long have they been together?" Aiden asks between songs.

"They aren't."

"Why not?"

"Sammy is shy," I explain, biting the inside of my cheek at Aiden's sudden concern with local gossip. "Or so I've been told."

"She obviously likes her," he argues. "She doesn't look at anyone else all night. What's she nervous for?"

I shake my head, my eyes straying toward the ceiling in search of a more perfect display of irony. "Couldn't tell you, wolf."

I glance around the room, for once not because I'm looking to join a game, just looking for a couple open seats. When I spy a few, I tentatively place my hand on his lower back and point their direction. "You want to have a seat?"

He frowns. "Someone could see us."

"Someone could see us here, too," I point out, removing my hand from him since our current spot, while inconspicuous, is not invisible.

"I don't want people to…" He sighs, and my stomach drops, leaving me wondering if he's going to say he doesn't want to be seen with me. If, as much as I'd like to tease him for feeling nervous with me, I'm much better.

He's going to see. If we keep going like this, he's going to end up seeing that I'm—

"I don't want people to see me," I hear him say as I stare at his perfect face. "I don't want to deal with the questions."

"The questions?" I repeat, not following.

"About who I was before," he explains, and I swear my knees almost buckle from the relief as he leans his shoulder into mine and keeps talking. "This is nice. Back here. Just us."

I love you, I think, still staring at him though his attention is back on the stage. *I'm so much in love with you that I feel like it could kill me, and I don't even care.*

"It is nice," I say instead. "Just us."

If only it could last… My gaze is drawn away from him as I see Dolly striding across the room while talking to someone, clear concern etched into her expression before she grabs for her shotgun behind the bar and walks toward the front door.

"Aiden," I mutter, and he immediately turns, seeing the same thing and already reaching for his own gun.

No one else notices us go, the music and the party still in full swing behind us while we pause on opposite sides of the main door to listen and check our weapons. Outside, I can hear talking, raised voices, one of them Dolly's.

Aiden and I exchange a glance, and for a moment it looks like there's something he wants to say before he nods and holds up three fingers to count. *Three. Two. One.* When he lowers the last one, we burst through the door in perfect sync with guns drawn, one in Aiden's hand and two in mine, but based on the crowd already assembled, it's not nearly enough.

While Dolly stands alone, there's fifteen men on horseback facing her out in front of her place, all of them armed and all of them looking particularly unhappy to see us, although none more than the one near the middle…who still has a good amount of earth on him.

Upon seeing us, Tom starts for his gun, but another man holds up his hand for him to stand down as Dolly does the same with us. Both sides begrudgingly follow orders, but Aiden steps closer to me, positioning himself so that he's slightly in front.

"That was fast," Aiden murmurs, looking at Tom, too.

"They must have already been searching for him as he said," I guess.

"Him, or the money," Aiden agrees. "You burn it yet?"

"Not yet."

"Should have burned it all with the body. Two birds…"

This time, I can't help myself. "I find you incredibly attractive. Do you know that?"

Aiden smirks as he shakes his head, about to respond when Dolly turns toward the two of us. "Finished?"

I give her a small smile. "Hope not."

The look she gives both of us is once again exasperated but also undeniably adoring.

"Dolly," the man in the center who had held up his hand calls her back, and I'd guess he's the boss, based on how he's the only one not in the strict brown-coat-red-bandana-brown-hat uniform. Well, he is, but his hat and coat are far, *far* nicer. "As much as I respect you, I won't allow one of your people to steal from me."

"Afraid you will, Jim," Dolly replies easily. "You know the rules."

"I have my own rules."

"Then you ought to start enforcing them. Or use better discretion when picking your people," she counters. "Two of them came into my place last night and thought to attack one of my girls. Whatever they misplaced while being escorted from the premises is not my problem."

"*Escorted?*" Tom pipes in before pointing over Dolly's shoulder in our direction. "That one killed John. And the other left me for the coyotes."

"Could've done worse," Aiden replies, voice chilly. "Still can."

"I do like him," Dolly murmurs, looking back toward me. "He surprises you."

"Thanks," Aiden mutters, not sounding sure if it's a compliment.

Ahead of us, the men on horseback appear to be growing antsy, exchanging glances as the boss moves a bit closer. "I'm not leaving without my money."

"You will be, as I don't *have* your money," Dolly says, sounding tired. "But I do have it on good authority that your boys were planning on skipping out on you." She tips her head toward Tom. "The only reason that one ended up crawling back is because he had nowhere else to crawl. You want someone to blame, then you have him right there in your ranks."

"That true?" Jim asks, turning to Tom, who seems less brave than he had a minute ago. "Were you and Johnny skipping out with my money?"

"No, boss, wouldn't do that. She's lyin'. We were on our way back like I said. Just stopped here for the night is all. That one—" Tom points a finger at me. "He's the one who took the money. He told me he swiped it from under the bed."

"Under the bed." Jim's tone is full of barely concealed rage. "You hid my money under a bed while you went drinkin'? How *stupid* are you?"

Tom shrinks into himself, and I mutter, "Told you," loud enough for him to hear before Aiden and Dolly both give me warning looks over their shoulders.

"Dolly," Jim calls. "I know none of us want this to end in a massacre." Quite a few of his men appear to disagree with that, something he doesn't notice as his gaze slides to me. "Get him to turn over my money, and we'll be gone. No retribution."

Once again, Jim's men look like they would very much like to disagree but Dolly beats them to it, simply saying, "No."

"No?" Jim questions.

"No."

"You're really going to—"

"No, *you* are really going to gather up your band of morons and leave. Now. Unless you want to make an enemy of me." Dolly fixes each of the men on horseback with a glare as they sneer back. "That clear?"

"This is not a discussion," Jim replies, raising his voice rather than getting the hint. "You *will* turn him over."

This time, Dolly doesn't reply. She simply raises a hand, and on cue, every window on the first and second floor of her building opens to reveal the long barrel of a rifle in each, all aimed and ready.

In response, Jim's face pales, he and his men finally taking a wise step back.

"You come for him…" Dolly says, coldly. "You so much as harm a hair on his head, and I will make sure that every single one of you dies a very slow and very painful death. Whatever death your man received last night will look like a mercy. Clear enough now?"

Without hesitation this time, Jim nods. The rest of them do, too.

"Enjoy the rest of your evening, boys," Dolly tells them, all smiles again. "And get the hell off my property."

CHAPTER 43
AIDEN

However lively the atmosphere had been in Dolly's place before, it's far more now. Far past celebratory after a standoff was successfully diverted.

It's hard not to be taken in by it. Or by Cypress, who like me was relieved enough to actually indulge in a couple of shots of whiskey from Sammy. But who, unlike me, is not able to hold his liquor.

"You're so…" he's saying as he leans against the bar next to me, one arm braced on top to hold himself up. "*So* handsome."

I laugh, thoroughly entertained by his good mood and by the hum in my blood that I'm grinning almost as wide as he is. "You're handsome, too, Cy."

His eyes widen a bit. "You think so?"

I cock my head, genuinely confused that he seems confused. "Of course I do."

He smiles at first but then it falters. "Maybe you won't. After."

"After what?"

He looks away, but comes back wearing a sly smile. "After…I let you have your way with me."

"After you *let* me?"

He nods, suddenly very serious now. "I would let you do unspeakable—"

"All right." I reach forward and clamp my hand over his mouth before shouting, "*Dolly.*"

She turns, making her way down the bar. "Aiden."

"I think I'm going to take him home," I tell her, keeping my hand on Cypress's mouth and able to feel him grinning again beneath my palm. "Seems safest."

She laughs, giving Cypress a knowing look. "You need me to come with you?"

"No," I say, about to stand. "I've got him."

She smiles, reaching out a hand to pat my cheek much as she'd done the night before. "I'd say you do, wolf. Let me know when you find the little bird."

I pause, half off my barstool as other things from the night before begin falling into place. However, before I can get the words out to ask her, someone else is calling for her and she's turning away while Cypress is using the distraction to make a break for it.

"Where are you *going?*" I ask, quickly following him as he heads for the stairs. "The door is that way." I tilt my head in the direction of the front entrance.

"Ah, yes, but there are rooms that way," he replies, tilting his own head the opposite way. "They have doors and everything."

"*Cypress.*" I grab him by the arm and give him my best stern voice while trying not to laugh again. "There are rooms at Dolly's house, too. Ones we haven't already committed crimes in, might I add."

He frowns, pouting. "But those are so far away."

"They're also far more private," I suggest, leaning in close to his ear and trying not to get taken in by his proximity to where *I'll* end up leading us upstairs. "Might come in handy? With all the unspeakable things you're going to let me do."

His eyebrows shoot up as he rears back to give me an appraising look. "You know, wolf, I'm really starting to think maybe you're not so *repressed* after all. Next thing I know, you're going to tell me about a time you took part in an orgy or—"

"Not sure I would call it an *orgy*, but I suppose, there's been a time or two where it was more than just two…" I say innocently, waiting for his reaction, and, God, if there is one memory I could keep…

"A time or two?" Cypress repeats, eyes wide. "With *more* than two?"

I shrug, enjoying every bit of this. "I'm not sure if you know this, but I was once a very famous gunslinger."

Cypress stares at me for so long that I worry he's going to pass out before he shouts, "Dolly, we're leaving!"

"I already told…" I trail off, not seeing the point since he's already escaped back to the bar. I shake my head, laughing as I follow after him.

"Dolly, we're heading out," he says again, in case she didn't get the message the first time while he leans against the bar directly in front of her. "Aiden and I are going."

Dolly is laughing now, too, neither of us able to contain it in his current state. "I know you are."

"Good," Cypress says, boosting himself up to reach across the bar, give her a kiss on the cheek, and steal a bottle of whiskey in a surprising display of dexterity for his drunken state. "You know I love you?"

She smiles, her eyes soft. "I do. You know I love you, too?"

He nods, and she says, "Good. Go on then."

Cypress gives me barely any time to say my own goodbye before I'm after him again, both of us spilling out into the night with much less care than we had a few hours ago. Fortunately, however, there also does not appear to be fifteen men waiting on horseback to kill us this time.

"You know, Aiden," Cypress is saying as we walk down the stairs, heading for the horses. "I think this is my very favorite day."

I glance at him, smiling. "Oh, since when?"

"Since always," he says, as if such an admission didn't just crack my chest in two.

"Mine, too," I murmur, though I'm not sure he hears me, already too busy making a dash for Cerberus at the hitching post.

"Hold on," I tell him, grabbing him around the waist and pulling him back just as he's about to swing up. "Let's stay on the ground for a while."

Rather than break out of my hold, he sinks into it, his head falling against my shoulder, and he smells so fucking good. Like mint and pine and something so uniquely him that it would be so fucking easy to give in. So fucking easy to kiss him right now, but once I do, I'm not going to want to stop.

"You think I won't stay on my horse?" he asks when I let him go, looking almost wounded as I take the whiskey from him and stash it in my saddlebag, but he rallies quickly, his expression turning suggestive again. "I'm an excellent rider."

"Cypress," I warn, moving around him and giving my hands something else to do other than grabbing him by collecting both horses' reins and setting off in the direction of Dolly's house, hoping he will follow. He does.

"Never been unseated," he's going on. "Not once."

I laugh again, not sure I've ever done it so much in my life even if I am sure now what Dolly meant when she said just because we were going in the same direction didn't mean we were doing it together. But I think we're starting to…

A half hour later, Cypress is still talking away, and I don't even know what all he's talking about, only that I like the sound of it. I think I like everything about him, even the parts that make me crazy. Maybe *especially* the parts that make me crazy.

"Cypress," I start to say, despite the rest of the words feeling stuck. "I wanted to…"

He stops to listen, and I stop, too. Those blue eyes on mine the way they have been since the first time I really saw him. "Cypress," I try again. "I'm…"

I want to tell him. Want to apologize for not telling him sooner. I believe I would have.

Only, that's when we hear them.

Eleven men on horseback this time, and while it's not the full fifteen like before, this does not feel much better.

I pull my gun, moving myself in front of Cypress as best I can when they form a circle around us. At the same time, I feel him turn behind me, his back lining up to mine as he pulls one of his own revolvers.

Before I can wonder why he kept the other hidden, one of the men dismounts, the bright moon revealing the now-familiar face of the man I should have left dead.

"Drop your weapons," he orders, cocking his gun, his men doing the same when we hesitate. "Drop them. Both of you."

Currently not seeing another choice, I let my gun fall, then Cypress does, too. They're quickly collected them along with our horses, but I at least get to hear the other man yell out in pain when Helios tries to take his arm in return. Unfortunately, however, the moment of satisfaction is fleeting.

"Tom," Cypress greets warmly, as if we're not participants in a standoff for the second time tonight. "Don't take this the wrong way, but I was actually hoping we'd seen the last of one another."

Tom glares at both of us in turn. "Change of plans."

"I'll say," Cypress mutters, and it's a terrible time for me to laugh, but I still struggle.

"Pretty certain you were all told to get gone," I tell Tom once I've put myself back in check. "Something about long, painful deaths sounding familiar?"

Tom snorts, rolling his eyes. "The old lady's scare tactics might have worked on Jim, but they won't work on me."

"Ah, I think you're going to find those tactics work just fine when you're begging for your life," Cypress replies, tone still conversational. "Jim can likely tell you some stories—"

"Jim is dead," Tom says shortly. "We are under new leadership."

Cypress and I both look around for someone else to step forward.

"*Me*," Tom snaps. "I'm the new leadership."

I glance at one of the men with him. "You mutinied for *him*? Really?"

"*Enough*," Tom snaps, taking a step forward with his gun still raised. "Start telling me where my money is or *our* painful deaths are not the ones you're going to have to worry about."

Behind me, I can practically hear Cypress thinking, hopefully the same as I am. Hopefully understanding that if we tell them where the money is stashed, it'll lead them to Dolly's house, where she—as far as I'm aware—does not have a rifle ready at every window like she does at the bar. She could get hurt. Although, so will we if we tell them nothing.

I reach back with my hand, subtly grabbing Cypress's and squeezing, willing him to realize that he needs to stay quiet. That he needs to let me handle this. In answer, I feel Cypress's hand turn, his palm to mine when he squeezes back, and I breathe a little easier through the next part.

"Your money is with your buddy," I say to Tom, deciding to make a slight but important change to what I'd told Cypress he should've done with it earlier. "Buried it with him."

"I don't believe you," Tom replies, looking as doubtful as he sounds. "Why would you leave it with John?"

I shrug. "So the buzzards can help us find it later. Suppose *buried* may have been overstating things."

Tom's lip curls. "Well, how fortunate for the buzzards that they'll get to eat again so soon." He turns to his men. "Grab him. Five of you will stay here with the crazy one while the rest of us take the gunslinger. If we're not back in a few hours…" He smiles at Cypress. "Kill him."

Several men dismount, ready to start closing in, and everything in me wants to fight. But I know how it'll end if I do. Least this way, Cypress will have a chance at getting free while I lead them away, at getting back to Dolly where he'll be safe. He's still armed. He's fast. He'll survive, and this time, I'll have done—

Cypress squeezes my hand once more before he lets go, stepping out from behind me and saying to Tom, "He's not telling you the right location."

"That so?" I feel Tom's eyes shift between us, but I don't see it, because I'm too busy looking at Cypress, willing him to look back, to see that I *need* him to stand down like I had in Soldana. He'd done it then. He'd trusted me.

Only this time, he doesn't.

"You already know he wasn't the one who buried your friend. I am. I'm the one who knows the location. I'm the one who hid the money," Cypress is saying as he takes another step away from me toward Tom and his men. "And not just *your* money. There's more."

Tom arches an eyebrow, undeniably intrigued. "You offering somethin'?"

"I'm offering what you want," Cypress replies simply. "So I get what I want."

"Which is?"

Without hesitating, he says, "The gunslinger goes free."

"Cypress," I warn, needing him to *know* this time when to quit.

Surely he knows. Surely he's realized the odds if they turn me loose and all go with him. Even if they leave me, they're not going to leave me armed or with Helios, and by the time I'm able to get back to Dolly's for a weapon, he'll be too far ahead without me knowing which way he led them.

He can't do this. We already agreed. I protect *him*. We already agreed. "*Cypress.*"

He still isn't looking at me, his focus on Tom, who is starting to smile at him. "Well, isn't that noble."

"Is it?" Cypress argues. "Or is it self-preservation? You make it all the way out there and see it isn't where he says it is…" He shakes his head. "Well, I imagine you would end up coming back to me regardless. I'm telling you now in hopes of saving us all a lot of time and earning your trust."

Tom scoffs. "Trust? You honestly expect me to *trust* you? After you already stole from me? After you already killed my friend? After you nearly killed *me*?"

Cypress doesn't waver. "Our previous interaction only means you know what I'm capable of, what I could be capable of for *you*."

"For me?" Tom sounds doubtful again. "You want to work for me?"

Cypress shrugs. "Been a while since I've been on a crew."

"You were on a crew before? Which one?"

"The Levi Gang."

A murmur ripples through Tom's men, glances exchanged as the name registers with them even if it doesn't with me. I remember Dolly saying that though she knew Cypress's crew was bad, she didn't realize how bad. But Cypress did. And something about their reaction tells me these men do, too.

"The Levi Gang?" Tom asks, now surveying Cypress with even more interest than before. "Haven't heard tale of them in *years*."

"You wouldn't have," Cypress responds, his voice absent its usual humor though I think I'm the only one that can tell. "Afraid we disbanded after Levi stopped seeing reason. Stopped seeing anything soon after." He smiles. "You understand."

Tom huffs out an almost laugh, looking to the rest of the crew, who all nod. "That I do. But I'm still surprised to hear you want to leave your partner to come join us." He glances between Cypress and me. "You two seem…attached to one another"

"Our partnership came about as a result of necessity," Cypress replies easily. "He's no outlaw." He sighs, tilting his head. "And, to be honest, I wouldn't call us friends."

We are not friends. What we are, Aiden…I hope the appropriate word is inevitable.

He'd said he hoped we were inevitable, and I hadn't realized until now how much I was hoping for the same. "Cy," I murmur, practically pleading with him now. "Don't."

Finally, *finally*, he looks at me, searching my face as if he's trying to memorize every detail. My gaze falls to his left hand, fully expecting to see it tapping against his leg, to see the sign of his tell, but his fingers are still. His hand steady. Far steadier than my own when he finally murmurs back, "I'm sorry, wolf."

A few feet away from us, Tom laughs, clapping his hands together as if this is all for his entertainment, and I almost miss what he says next over the rushing in my ears, over my thoughts repeating, *No. No. I can't. I can't do this again.*

"Well, this *has* been a change of plans," Tom is saying, still chuckling as he steps nearer to me. "I said he would betray you. Even told you that you should join us, and now it'll be him…," Tom pauses, tilting his head and considering before he puts his gun away in favor of a knife from his belt, the same one I left him with last night. Immediately, Cypress's whole body goes completely still. "Well, maybe it will. Depends on how he takes this."

I step toward Cypress again, my hand raised to caution Tom. "You'll never get a chance to spend that money if you're six feet under," I remind him. "Dolly said she'd hunt you down."

"Oh, but that only applied if I hurt *him*," Tom counters, tilting his head toward Cypress, who hasn't moved. "And since, as he so kindly pointed out, I don't need you to find my money…"

"But you *do* need me," Cypress argues, and I can hear the fear he's trying to keep from breaking into his voice. "I gave you my terms."

"And I'm telling you mine. Because I'm going to need more than your word if you actually want my *trust* after what you've done. Afraid it's going to have to be eye for an eye." Tom comes closer. "Shouldn't be a problem though, right? If you truly aren't friends?"

Cypress doesn't respond, not before Tom stops directly in front of me. "You should've accepted my offer, gunslinger. Could have seen your name in the papers again. Now you'll die like a nobody."

I meet his gaze as I assure him, "There are worse things."

Tom's lip curls as he raises the knife, and I brace myself to move, to grab for my own knife to defend myself. Even knowing I have the rest of his men to contend with. Even knowing I've likely run out of places to run. Quickly, I glance toward Cypress, wanting to see him first, wanting to—

He's not there.

In the second between Tom raising the knife and bringing it back down, *Cypress* is the one who moves, stepping in front of me and pushing me away. The sudden change in target causes Tom's aim to land higher on him than it would have on me…or so I think for one heartstopping moment until, rather than giving any sign he's been hit, Cypress *keeps* moving, taking advantage of Tom's surprise to grab for his gun at the same time I reach for Cypress's. The revolver comes free from his right holster just as he pivots behind me again, already aiming and firing.

I do the same, my first shot to kill in years going straight through

Tom's chest. As soon as it hits, he falls in an exaggerated arc, but I'm firing again before he even fully drops.

One, two more go down next. More names for my ledger, and I'm about to add another when the third tries to dive behind their horses for cover. At my back, I hear Cypress's stolen gun going off a second time, hear the accompanying thud of a body hitting dirt before—

"*I'm out*," he shouts. "Chamber wasn't full."

I turn, shooting toward the three men in front of him without taking time to properly aim, sacrificing accuracy in exchange for the chance to sprint for our horses let loose in the chaos.

There's two bullets left in my gun, only one after I blast another over my shoulder. Enough to make one man fall but not the remaining five men who are regrouping, climbing onto their horses as Cypress and I take off at a gallop.

"We lose them," I yell to Cypress as he thunders after me on my left. "Then we double back. Head for Dolly's."

He nods, already reaching for the rifle strapped to his saddle that I'd seen him use in Soldana. Despite the speed, he lets go of the reins and turns to fire, and I don't need to check to know the aim was true, don't dare risk it when a bullet whizzes by my head and sends my hat flying. *Fuck.*

I urge Helios more, Cerberus keeping pace and slightly leading as we target a grouping of trees interrupting the landscape ahead. Faster and faster until we reach them, far enough ahead of the men behind us that when the undefined path splits, we veer left and hope they'll think we went right.

It buys us time, only a little. But we get a chance to do it again, winding our way through more tree pockets, cutting ravines, and scattered rock formations. *Anything* that might widen the gap between us until eventually we lose sight of them, although I don't think for a moment that they've given up.

Still, I start to wonder if we're actually going to make it out of this, to feel that frantic hope again that we are *that* lucky when I look at Cypress flying across the terrain beside me.

He looks back, smiles. But then he sways. His eyes drifting shut.

"*Cypress*," I yell at him. "Cy, are you—"

For one terrifying second, I think he's going to fall while we're still galloping at full speed, barely giving me time to grab Cerberus's reins to pull him up as I signal Helios to slow. "*Cypress*, what are you—"

His body sways again, toward me, and I reach out a hand to steady him, pushing against his shoulder to keep him in the saddle. He winces immediately, flinching from evident pain before I pull my hand back.

It comes away red. And right then, I remember all the reasons I don't believe in luck.

CHAPTER 44
CYPRESS

"Goddammit, Cypress." Aiden's voice has a sharp bite of reproach to it as he pours good alcohol over a wound that I hope only looks bad. "The hell were you thinking?"

I flinch as the burn hits, my head dropping back against the tree we made it to after I nearly fell off Cerberus.

Did I fall off? I feel like I did. Groaning at the pain, I take a sharp breath right as Aiden presses a cloth hard over the wound in my right shoulder. *No, Aiden was there…*

I wish he'd speak up, because I think he's scolding me, shaking his head as he pulls the cloth back and examines the wound. There's a dim light coming from a lantern hanging on the branch above to help him see, only I don't remember putting it there. *I don't remember getting here…*

"It's deep. There's so much… Fuck, Cy, there's so much blood." I nod, sure he's right. Usually is. "You need stitches. I'm going to do it, okay?"

I nod again, and he presses the cloth once more on the wound, staying like that for several long minutes while he searches through a saddlebag with his right hand, producing a tin with a needle and thread that I can only presume is for this exact purpose. Or for clothes. *Bet he's good at sewing…at mending things. Suppose I'm about to find out.*

Aiden stands briefly, holding the end of the needle into the flame of the lantern until it glows red, then drops into a crouch in front of me, threading the opposite end and nodding at the bottle of whiskey that has appeared in my left hand. "Drink."

As directed, I take a long pull and that burns, too, making me flinch again, but I reopen my eyes in time to see Aiden unbuckling his belt. "Wolf…while I have certainly been looking forward to it, I'm not sure now is the best time…"

His head jerks up, and he gives me an incredulous look before whipping the leather belt the rest of the way free and holding it out for me. "Take another drink, then bite down."

Ah, that makes sense. Still…

"I'm going to go fast," he's saying when I lower the bottle and grab for the belt. "Might not be the prettiest."

I shrug. "Will match the rest." Biting into the strip of leather, I wait for him to start as he hovers over the wound with the needle, his jaw clenched as tight as mine, and I want to tell him it's all right. That this is nothing…

"You shouldn't have gotten in the way," he grits out, taking a deep breath in and then pushing the needle through my skin. "I would have been fine."

I remove the belt from my mouth, swallowing a grunt of pain as he moves to the next stitch. "It wasn't…something I was willing to risk."

He makes another stitch. Then another.

"It's not your job to protect me," he argues. "That's not the deal we made."

"I made my own deal." Another stitch. Another. It *hurts*. I forgot how much it hurts. "And neither—neither matter if you're dead."

"And what about if *you're* dead?" he snaps. "Did you think of that?"

Tears sting my eyes when he hits a particularly angry spot. "Not—not really."

"*Fuck.*" Aiden finishes off the last stitches and then knots the thread, my shoulder throbbing like he's still going. I close my eyes and lean my head back again to try to get myself to believe he isn't. "Cy, I need you to…I need you to think about it."

I crack my eyes back open, watching him as he rips a clean black shirt, folds the strips carefully over the fresh stitches, and then uses a few more to secure them. Will be good…the black…can't see the blood that way. "Aiden."

His hands are shaking now as he checks his work over, again and again. Again and again and again and— "*Wolf.*"

When Aiden looks up, his eyes are glassy. "Don't." He lets out a shaky breath, maybe the same one he inhaled before he started, then leans forward, pressing his forehead against mine. "Don't fucking do that again."

I savor him touching me, savor knowing he's unharmed. "It's going to be all right. Had worse." I'm so tired. I know we need to keep going, but maybe if I could just rest for a bit…"It's nothing, wolf."

I feel Aiden shake his head before his mouth brushes against my forehead, where he murmurs, "Not to me."

He pulls away, and I'd like to pull him back, but he's looking toward the way we came. *Or maybe it was the other way?*

"They're still searching for us. I don't...we can't cut over to Dolly's," he's saying. "Can't risk running into them when I won't be able to shoot."

I want to ask him why, but then I remember—he'd swung up behind me in Cerberus's saddle, hanging onto me so I wouldn't end up on the ground until we found a place to stop.

On the ground? In the ground? Probably amounts to the same thing.

"We..." Aiden is breathing hard, bending down to help me get back on my feet. "We need to get out of here, Cy. We need to get some distance. I have a place we can go, but it'll take us some time to get there. Need you to stay with me, okay?"

I nod again. Sure I won't care where we're going as long as he's there. It was okay when he was there. When she was...

The dark didn't scare me. Not when they were there in it with me.

PART THREE
OUTLAWS
SALOON

CHAPTER 45
AIDEN
TWENTY-SIX YEARS OLD
ARIZONA

It's still dark by the time we make it to the train yard, the same one Dolly said she'd been trying to keep at bay, but I can't help feeling grateful for it now as I stow us away in an empty stock car about to head west. Locking the door behind us and hoping they already did their checks to leave at sunrise, hoping, too, that they won't notice a little extra food and water going missing when I hear the yard begin to stir.

I wait for them to find us even after the train starts moving. And I don't really stop over the two days it takes us to get to Arizona, nor do I stop waiting to see if Cypress is going to survive until we do.

By the time we jumped on board, Cypress was already in and out of it, anywhere from a few minutes to a few hours. I try to make him eat something every time he wakes up, drink something. Afraid that if he doesn't he won't wake up again.

Sometimes he talks. Sometimes he doesn't. I have a hard time stopping him when he does, even if I can't understand everything he is saying, even if the things I can understand make me wish I couldn't.

Being on the train bothers him. Makes him tell me how he messed up joining them because he didn't want to be alone anymore, how they used to rob trains and the people on them. How he hadn't minded when they were taking from people who could afford to lose. How much he *had* minded when they started taking from people who couldn't.

I remind him it's just us now. I tell him he doesn't have to do that anymore.

Being in the dark bothers him more. Makes him tell me how dark it was while they had him locked away, how they would hurt him to try to make him say where he took them, how he used to listen to the water dripping from the roof to distract himself. *Tap. Tap. Tap.* How he used to wait to fall asleep because then he'd see *them* and the sky again.

I tuck him against me and cover his ears before I shoot holes in the ceiling of the train car. I tell him the light streaming in is stars.

He's awake again to get off the train when we finally roll to a slow stop, the horses jumping off before us into the blinding daylight with a lot more grace than I manage while I'm carrying, more than holding, Cypress. I turn us in time so that I absorb the worst of the fall. Then I get back up, and we keep running.

I steal a wagon in the first town we reach, too desperate to care they see both our faces. Too desperate to care I'm a thief now, too.

He comes to while we're heading north beneath a midnight sky, and if he were to ask me this time which stars are my favorite, I think I'd finally be able to tell him. Instead, he asks me where we're going, and I tell him we're going home.

Now, he's quiet.

I think that's the worst of it. He's so fucking *quiet*.

I hadn't realized how much I'd gotten used to it. His constant, ceaseless talking. The way he'd have something to say from the moment he woke up in the morning to the moment he put his head down at night. The way he'd even talk in his sleep.

But not now.

I keep pacing the room, waiting for something to do, for there to be something I *can* do, but for the past several days, I've run out of options by mid-morning. Only so many checks clean shirts I can rip up for bandages, only so many times I can put my hand to his forehead to see if he's still hot, only so many hours I can spend wondering if he's stopped breathing.

When I can't take being in our tiny one-room cabin anymore, I go out to check the horses, then go and chop firewood until my hands blister, enough to last us through the next several winters despite it being the middle of summer, but it's something I can do close by. Even with our food rations running low, I don't risk leaving to hunt.

Maybe getting here was too much. Maybe I should've taken him to the doctor in Troy's Hill, but I'd been afraid with both of us wanted that if he did live, it would only be to see a jail cell. That I'd be taken to one, too, and never know if he was all right. That he'd wake up alone.

This is all my fault. I was the one who insisted we leave Tom alive. I was the one who suggested we leave Dolly's. As soon as there was trouble, I should've realized Cypress would put himself in harm's way. He *always* does. Never knows when to quit. Never thinks he can.

I was the one supposed to keep him safe, and maybe the old me could have. I told Dolly I would. I told *him* I would. That was our deal.

You'll take care of him for me, won't you? You and the little bird.

Another time I didn't do right. Another time I wasn't where I was supposed to be. Another time when I didn't hold up my responsibilities.

"Cypress." I resist the urge to nudge him as I sit in the wooden chair I've kept next to the bed. "Cy, I need you to wake up. Don't leave, okay? I can't… I need you to wake up and talk to me."

He doesn't move. Doesn't show any sign at all that he hears me, but just in case…

"There's things I need to tell you," I say to him, hoping that's tempting enough to keep him here. "But you gotta wake up first."

Nothing.

I try again and again over the next several hours, tracking his pulse with a silver watch in my hand until I finally let sleep take me, too.

When it does, I dream I'm running again. Looking back at everything I've lost.

CHAPTER 46
CYPRESS

The first thing I see is Aiden. Or at least, I think it's him.

The person who is currently asleep at the foot of the bed, his front half uncomfortably slumped over the mattress while the rest of him sits in a kitchen chair that looks far too small for him, has a beard that's a bit longer than the one I last saw on him.

His hair too is especially disheveled, his brown waves falling into a disarrayed half-circle on his head that matches the dark bags beneath his eyes. Yet he's still so painfully, heartbreakingly handsome that I almost don't trust it.

Slowly, I try to sit up without considering how difficult that might be, only thinking to touch him. Just to make sure he's real, that we really did survive, that I don't need to realign my belief system after another near-death experience. *Very* near, if memory serves. Although I can't say that it serves particularly well...

Still, what I *do* remember is him.

I try again, and manage pretty well this time, getting myself propped against the wooden spindle headboard without issue, except for the low grunt of effort I'm unable to bite back in time. As I figured it would, the effect is immediate. Aiden's head pops up so fast I feel my own spin, one of his hands flying out to grip the bottom of his chair so he doesn't topple over with the sudden movement.

"You could have stayed in the bed, wolf. More room than the roof," I tell him, my voice coming out raspy and my grin faltering when he only stares at me for a few moments too long. "Aiden?"

His eyes close briefly, blinking fast when he opens them again as if coming out of a daze. "Cypress." He starts to reach toward me then pulls his hand back, pulls *himself* back, getting up and looking around the room as if he's the one who's never been here before. "You—I should—" Aiden clears his throat, then even removes his gaze from me before he says, "I should get you some water."

With a sinking feeling in my chest, I watch his back as he crosses the cozy one-room cabin to a table in the opposite corner, feeling envious of the breeze drifting through the wide-open windows for the way it gets to rustle his hair and clothing as he passes.

"Not sure if you recall," he's saying, still turned away from me as he fills a tin cup from a matching pitcher. "But we're in Arizona. In the mountains. This is…"

"Home?"

He nods. "You've been out for the last few days. Been quiet. But you must have needed the sleep after what happened."

What happened… I'd seen Tom go for him and I had stepped in between, giving Aiden a chance to reach for my second gun. He'd hit Tom square in the chest. Hit a few of the others, too, before we ran.

He'd killed. For me. After I'd told him he wouldn't have to. After he'd told me he regretted what it had cost him.

"Wasn't how I imagined receiving my invite," I say, trying for a smile again when he crosses back over to the bed to hand me the cup, still somehow managing to do so without touching me or looking at me. "But I did say you'd hardly notice I was here."

"Right." His jaw clenches, his now-free hand dragging through his hair, and I wonder where his hat has gotten to, even if I'm not complaining about seeing him in nothing but a loose white shirt and a comfortable-looking pair of brown trousers. "Are you—you're okay? Does anything hurt?"

"Not like it could." Before I take a sip of water, I finally think to look down at myself, noticing for the first time my own lack of clothes, my torso bare except for a fresh bandage over my shoulder and then…the scars. He's likely seen all of them now.

I bring the cup to my mouth, downing its contents and wishing they burned again before setting it on the little side table by the bed. As with most of the other furniture pieces in here, it appears to be carefully handcrafted. Beautiful. Perfect. Nothing broken.

"Now that you're awake, I should probably go hunt," Aiden says, and for once I hope he'll leave, because I'm not sure how much longer I can keep the smile in place. "We are getting low on food. I did bring some water in this morning if you feel up to cleaning up. It's over by the stove. And there's some clothes here." He gestures toward a pile of folded things at the end of the bed. "A few blankets, too, in case it gets cold while I'm gone. You want help getting up?"

I shake my head, not looking at him either now. "I'll manage."

"Cypress."

My tired eyes find his own, red-rimmed and nearly hidden beneath a few too-long, stray strands that I ache to brush away. To be allowed to.

"I wanted to tell you…" Aiden takes a deep breath…and swallows whatever he was going to say. "You should try to rest more. You were…" He shakes his head, already turning away. "I'm sorry, Cy. I'm so sorry."

Then he's gone. And all I can think is that maybe we didn't survive after all.

CHAPTER 47
AIDEN

Fuck.

CHAPTER 48
CYPRESS

Running is not a strategy. Unless you're Aiden. Then, it's a battle plan.

Over the next week, I barely see a trace of him. His ability to avoid me in Soldana and at Dolly's apparently a faint glimpse of his talent.

One room. We're in one *single* room, and he still manages to never be in it at the same time as me while simultaneously lingering in every corner of it.

In every neat little pile of clothes and blankets set out. In every warm meal and pitcher of fresh water left on the table. In every book set out in a place I'll see it. But perhaps nowhere more so than in the chair that has not moved from the end of the bed.

Oddly enough, I think it's the chair that does it. That reminds me that while running may be Aiden's strategy, it has never been mine.

CHAPTER 49
AIDEN

The lanterns in the cabin went out about an hour ago, the light that was streaming out dimming until it's completely pitch black inside.

I've been leaving the windows open in hopes that they'll let enough moonlight in so that he won't be afraid if he wakes up in the middle of the night. He hasn't been. Not yet. Not as long as I'm sitting there by the bed, keeping watch.

Seems to help. Or maybe I just like to tell myself it does.

I know I'm being a coward. Know I need to face him but I don't know how to tell him one thing without telling him all of it, without asking him for things I have no right to ask, for things I don't deserve.

I just have to get a grip on things again. Get both my feet back on solid ground, like they haven't been since I walked into that damn saloon and saw him that first time. I just have to get some control on this...and then we can talk. Have a calm, clear-headed conversation about where we go from here. Have a plan.

I open the door to the cabin and slip inside, my carefulness making me think about that night on the roof and wondering how it could already feel so long ago, wondering, too, when he'll feel strong enough to try pulling himself up on this one.

I'll need to check it before he does. Make sure there's no holes or loose shingles that could hurt him or could hurt me when I once again follow him up there like a goddamn—

"Good evening, wolf."

I turn on the spot like I just heard someone say *draw*, facing the bed in time to see a lantern flare back to life, illuminating both the room and the person sitting in the very chair I had been planning to spend another night in.

"I have to say," Cypress says, reaching over to set the lantern on the bedside table. "This does alleviate any guilt I might have felt over sneaking into the stable to watch you sleep in Soldana."

"Didn't realize you were feeling guilty over that," I reply, not seeing much point in denying why I'm here.

Apparently he doesn't either, because he quickly assures me, "Oh, I wasn't really."

"Great." I shake my head, eyes falling to the floor before I finally stop fighting the urge to just *look* at him. "See you found the clothes I left for you," I tell him, noting the head-to-toe black but also the fresh shave and styled hair, and finding comfort he's looking like himself again. Even if I doubt I look half as good after quickly cleaning up down by the creek. "Sorry to say we used quite a few of both of our shirts for bandages, so you might need to source a few more from whatever undertaker you buy through."

He smiles slowly, although the fact that he doesn't further take my bait has me shifting my weight from foot to foot. "Are you all right? You hurtin' at all?"

"No, no, good as new."

"Are you sure? There's some salve there on the bedside if—"

"This really is a nice chair," he continues, abruptly taking the conversation in an unexpected direction. "Not as comfortable as the bed, but…" He tilts his head, and I could swear he appears more amused with me than angry. He *should* be angry. "I noticed there are three."

I frown, confused. "Three what?"

"Three chairs."

"Yes," I say slowly, worried now he's not entirely level-headed. "Why?"

"Why what?"

"Why three?"

"Because…that was how many I thought I needed?" I respond. "Why are you asking me about chairs?"

"You thought you needed *three*? Interesting. Not two? Or four?"

"Are you sure—"

"*Large* bed, too," he observes. "Wide. Spacious. Think you needed that, too?"

"Christ." I huff out a breath, leaning against the door and dragging a hand down my face. "This what you want to be talking about right now? The furniture?"

Cypress shrugs. "Seems relevant."

"Does it?"

"I think so."

"Course you do," I say, caught between whether I want to laugh or shout at the ridiculousness of this conversation after everything this last week. "Why wouldn't it be?"

"You don't think so?"

"No, I don't."

"Why not?"

"Because the number of fucking chairs isn't important."

"Isn't it?" He smiles again.

I open my mouth, but nothing comes out apart from, "I'll go back outside. Let you—"

"Sounds great." Cypress stands as if there were never a time when I had to help him up. "I'll go with you."

"No." I'd take a step back if I wasn't already against the door. "You should stay in here. Get some more rest."

"Why?"

"Because you're still recovering," I remind him, unable to forget it myself no matter how perfect he looks now. Unable to forget watching him slip away no matter how much I want to reach for him. "And because you're probably going to keep talking to me about chairs."

"We can talk about something else."

I need to get out of here.

"Simply name it."

I can't do this.

"Could be anything."

Not now.

"Whatever is on your mind."

I can't.

"Because—"

"How about that you almost *died*?" I snap, irritation and exhaustion and *hopelessness* burning through whatever tether I had left. "How about that you didn't wake up for *days*? How about that I lost count of how many times I thought I lost you? That I can't sleep without seeing you almost fall again? How about that the entire time we were on that train, I was asking God if my punishment for the people I killed would be watching you die? Or how about that I had already figured out the spot where I was going to have to fuckin' bury you?" My chest is heaving when I finally stop, my eyes burning. "*Fuck*. How about that? Want to talk about any of that?"

Cypress frowns, folding his hands as if carefully considering. "Was it nice?"

I stare at him. "Was *what* nice?"

"The spot where you were going to bury me. Was it nice?"

Shouting. Shouting is definitely going to win out. "*Yes*, it was really fucking nice, Cy," I tell him, flinging my arm out toward the open window. "Right next to the fucking river I was going to consider jumping in when I was through. That sound *nice*? Christ."

"Aiden."

"No, you know, I'm so—I'm so fucking *angry* with you." I start pacing near the door simply because I have to move, my voice getting louder and my words coming faster. "Why the fuck would you get in the way like that?"

"*Aiden.*"

"We had a deal. I protect you. Not the other way around. That's what we agreed to, and I need you to hold to your fucking end of it. I need you to *never* do that again. Because I can't—I can't lose someone else, all right? I fucking *can't* lose another person that I love, and I swear to fucking God if you die on me, I'll kill you."

"*Wolf.*"

"What *now*? What do you—" I turn and he's right there, right in front of me, and I don't know how I even missed him getting so close. "I can't—" His eyes are on mine, his hands up as he comes even closer, a sign that he poses no threat to me, but he *does*. He does because I can't bear this, just as I can't even be angry with him because… "It's my fucking fault. I didn't stop it."

"Aiden." He's almost pleading, willing me to listen, but what if he doesn't understand? What if he wouldn't want me if he did? "It wasn't your responsibility to stop it."

"No, I should've—I should've stopped it. You weren't supposed to get in the way. I can't—I can't do this again. I couldn't stop it. I just ran. She told me to run and I ran."

"I ran, too. It's okay," Cypress says, his expression turning sad, but I don't need his pity. I don't deserve it.

"You ran after you did what needed to be done. I ran, because I was doing what I was told. Because I was too scared to do anything else. I should've fought. It was my fault. I let you get in the way. I let them get in the way. It was my fault. I was supposed to be home on time and I wasn't. If he hadn't been so tired, he wouldn't have—"

"Aiden, you were *nine*," Cypress says. "What happened wasn't your fault."

"I didn't protect them," I argue. "I didn't protect you. It was my responsibility to be the one—"

"I didn't want you to be," he says simply. "And I can promise, neither did they. I don't *want* you to die for me, Aiden. Just like I don't want you to kill for me, and I know you had to…" He searches my face again, the regret clear on his own. "I'm sorry…for making you add to your list of sins—"

"I don't care about the fucking list," I tell him, meaning it. "I don't care how long one side gets, so long as I get to have you on the other. I don't regret killing them, Cypress. I'd do it again. What I care about is that I didn't protect you in time."

"You did," he argues. "I'm here. I'm alive."

"But if I'd—"

"You can't change what happened, wolf," he says softly. "All you can do is try to change what happens next."

I drag a hand through my hair. "I don't *know* what happens next."

Cypress shrugs. "No one does. But *we* can figure it out, all right? No matter where the road leads."

"We?" I look at him warily.

"Yes, *we*." He smiles. "You said you're in love with me. And I have been in love with you to the point of madness for nearly ten years, so—"

"You haven't even known me ten *weeks*," I remind him.

"Semantics."

I roll my eyes, but I also take a deep breath in as he takes another step forward. "I didn't say I was in love with you."

"You did, wolf. It was right before you threatened to kill me if I die, which seems overly complicated, not to mention a waste to pay the ferryman twice. Though, I believe it's the thought that counts."

He's so close, so close now I could touch him. "Why would you love me? How do you even know me well enough to decide?"

Cypress sighs, then grins, always finding everything so fucking entertaining.

"Loving you is not something I needed to decide, wolf. I was looking for you for so long. In every face I passed I looked for you, hoping that when I saw you, I would know. And I did. I saw you and I knew who you were in this life and in the next and in all the ones that came before, because you were mine in every single one of them. I saw you and I knew that I would gladly go through it all again, that I would relive every single moment of my life just to have one single moment where I mattered in yours. To have one single moment where you let me."

I reach for him, finally pulling him to me so that my body is flush with his when I push him up against the door. As I hold him there, his hands grip my forearms and his eyes meet mine like they did that night in the alley, only maybe neither of us are afraid anymore.

"You matter to me, Cy," I murmur, my mouth hovering over his. "Pretty sure I've been looking for you, too."

CHAPTER 50
CYPRESS

I meant it. Every single moment. Every single one. I'd face them all again knowing this was waiting for me. Knowing *he* was…

The *relief* of Aiden's mouth crushing against mine, the feeling of his hands on me, the pressure of his body. Him. After all this time. After *so* long waiting, but I would have waited lifetimes more.

He touches me as if he knows how much I need it, knows *precisely* how much I need his hands dragging down my chest, how much I need his fingertips digging into my hips as the desperate edge of teeth turns a hesitant, searching kiss into a hard, hungry suck of my bottom lip.

"*Cy.*" He says my name on a moan that makes me want to start begging. His breathing already heightened even before I start trying to take his air, kissing him back just as hungrily, drinking him down as if I'm drowning when this is actually the first moment I'm beginning to think I see land. "Fuck, we shouldn't…"

"We should," I argue, my own hands skimming up over his broad shoulders then back down his body, loving how strong he feels, how solid, even if it takes nothing more than the brush of my fingers above his waistband to make his stomach muscles tense. "We *really* should."

"You're still hurt." Despite his words, he makes a low sound of disapproval in his throat as soon as I move my hands away from the button of his slacks, although he seems to forgive me when I cup the back of his head, burying my fingers in his hair and tugging on the wavy strands so I can press a kiss to the racing pulse beneath his jaw.

"You need rest," he protests again, half-heartedly, and going willingly when my other hand kneads into his lower back to pull him even closer to me. I'm careful not to let him see my wince at the slight twinge of pain in my shoulder at the movement, knowing he will care far more about it than I do. "You…you could've died."

"But as we've discussed, I did not," I remind him, smiling victoriously when he practically lunges to kiss me as soon as I angle his head to take his mouth again. "I'm very much alive," I murmur to him between kisses, between answering groans as I grind my hips into him and feel him as hard as I am. "And so, it would seem, are you."

His fingers flex around my hips, his body moving to match my rhythm so perfectly that I actually start to worry I could come just from this, just from the friction and this small taste of him, but I don't want to. I don't want it to be over that quickly. I don't want just a *taste*.

"Aiden." I will beg. If he needs me to, I will. Even if he doesn't, I will. "*Please.*"

"*Fuck.*" His forehead presses against mine, rolling back and forth as if he's shaking his head, but his hold on me only tightens. "You'll tell me if I hurt you."

It's not a question, but I answer it like one.

"You won't. You don't want to hurt me," I reassure him, smiling again as I draw back to study his face, to clearly see that while there are plenty of things he does want at this moment, that isn't one of them. "At least, not anymore."

Aiden huffs out a laugh, the sound somehow better than when he moaned my name. "Never really wanted to hurt you," he murmurs, his right hand finally leaving my hip to cup my face in a way that feels reverent, his thumb brushing across my cheekbone, across my mouth. "I wanted to…"

"You wanted to…?" I repeat back to him, meeting his gaze as I part my lips and let him press his thumb inside, taking him as deep as I can so he has no trouble imagining how well I will take anything else he's willing to give me. No trouble imagining how *good* it will be.

"I wanted…" he starts again, making it sound like another broken plea before his eyes close on another moan. "Fuck."

"Could've done that a while ago," I reply, placing a far too gentle kiss on the tip of his thumb given how rough I'd like him to be.

I want to feel it. To feel him. So I'll never have to question if it's real. "Told you I—"

"Wasn't just that," Aiden says, his eyes still shut, his whole body still wound so impossibly tight that he's practically trembling. "I wanted to understand why you were so hellbent on making me crazy."

"And?" I ask, not doing much better given how my hand is shaking a bit as I clasp his and guide it back down, pausing when we pass over my chest. "What conclusion did you come to?"

"That I don't really care as long as you don't stop." Aiden's eyes open, and everything goes still. My breath stalling in my lungs as I see how the amber-flecked brown is nearly swallowed up by the black in his pupils, and I would probably think my heart had stopped, too, if both of us couldn't feel it racing.

"I won't stop. I promise…*please*," I ask him, leaning in to kiss him again and hoping this time he's ready to let it consume us. Hoping that my voice sounds steadier to him than it does to me, that he won't interpret my weakness as physical rather than spiritual and send me back to bed without him. "Please, wolf, let me make you crazy."

He exhales on another soft laugh, but rather than kiss me back, the hand he has on my chest switches from holding me to pushing me more firmly against the door. "Good as that sounds, Cy," he murmurs, a breath away from my mouth as his other hand moves from my hip to my waistband. "Think it's my turn."

At the statement, two of his fingers slip beneath the band before he gives a firm tug, the clatter of the button falling to the floor accompanied by the distinct sound of ripping fabric. Not that I fully register either, not when I'm too busy taking in the sight of Aiden dropping to his knees in front of me.

"What?" he asks as I lean against the door for support, his thumbs hooking inside the torn slacks so he can drag them down. "Nothing clever to say?"

I open my mouth, but no words materialize as I watch him push the clothes to the floor in one smooth authoritative motion, as I watch him take in the sight of my cock with his tongue resting along his bottom lip and his palms skating appreciatively back up my thighs.

"*Aiden.*" I'm begging again, my hands braced against his broad shoulders and my thoughts unable to focus on anything beyond the fact that I need him. I need him to—

His eyes find mine, staying there as he raises a hand to his mouth and spits into his palm, and despite my ongoing silence, I must manage to say plenty because he gives me a satisfied smirk before he says, "Shirt."

Shirt… I recognize the word but not its meaning. Aiden shakes his head, smiling when he lifts the bottom of my shirt over my stomach and nuzzles his face into my bared abdomen, the whiskers of his beard scratching the sensitive skin in a way that feels so unbelievably *perfect*.

"Cy," he says in a low tone, right before a sharp warning bite of his teeth. "Shirt. Off."

Understanding breaking in, I scramble to comply, trying to push away any remaining fear I have over him seeing the marks on my chest, knowing he's already seen them and seems to want me anyway, but my fingers fumble on the first button at my collar when he finally wraps a wide, warm hand around my length.

"Fuck," I murmur, somehow managing to unbutton more even as my head tips against the door and my eyes close at the first long, gorgeous stroke. At the first moment when I get to feel him touching me after so many nights lying awake thinking about it. "*Fuck.*"

Aiden chuckles. "Really aren't so sharp when you're horny." He removes his hand, and I'm certain that I actually whimper before I hear him spit into his palm once more. "If I'd known all it took was my hand around your cock to stop you running that mouth…" He puts it there again, slicker this time, and it really doesn't help with the whimpering.

"Can think of another—" I moan when he picks up the pace, stroking me faster, his other hand brushing up the inside of my thigh to cup the rest of me. Testing what I like most yet at the same time seeming to have no doubt. All the while, I grip his shoulders as if I'm going to pull him up and reverse our positions, as if I'm going to strip him just as bare. And I will…I need to. I need to see him, too.

But for now, he stays on his knees and gives me another look, the warning in it only softening when I make it to the last button of my shirt and let it fall open at my sides.

"Good boy," Aiden praises, his gaze sweeping up and down, and somehow this feels even more intimate than anything else he's done in the last few moments. "So fucking pretty."

I wonder if he notices it. The immediate heat beneath my skin. "Could be prettier. If you'd let me show you another way to stop me *running my mouth*…"

"Not yet," he murmurs. "Had enough quiet for a while." His eyes momentarily flick to the fresh bandage before he meets my gaze again. "Which is why you're going to be nice and loud for me, all right?"

I nod, not capable of more than that. Then he takes me in his mouth.

"*Aiden*, you—" I groan, feeling him around the width of me, bringing me deeper and deeper until he has almost all of me, his head bobbing while I bury my fingers in his hair. And I'm so afraid that I'm going to come already that it's almost a relief when he pulls away again.

"Cy." He says my name in a low gravelly tone, one of his fingers sliding inside his mouth and releasing with a wet pop. "Louder."

Another nod is the only response I can manage before he wraps his lips around the head of my cock and sucks before guiding me deeper to the back of his throat. At the same time, I feel his hand slip between my legs so he can place that finger against my entrance. I groan and his eyes flash to mine, the question clear.

"Yes," I murmur, and then say louder just as he asked, "*Please.*"

He starts to brush his fingertip there while he continues to work himself up and down my cock, slow circles at first until he eases his finger inside, appearing just as desperate when I notice his other hand palm himself through his slacks, when I am able to *feel* him moan more than I even hear him.

"Please," I say, my eyes squeezing shut as the pressure at the base of my spine builds higher and higher. "Aiden, I'm going to…" I tighten my grip on his hair and pull him up, not nearly ready, and this time he goes, his mouth immediately seeking mine when he's standing in front of me again.

"Can I fuck you?" he pants against my mouth. "Can you—do you want to? If you're hurtin'…"

"I think I'd be hurting a lot more if you didn't." My fingers are flying across his own buttons far faster than I'd handled my own, pushing his shirt down over his shoulders so that he's temporarily bound by the sleeves. I moan at the image, biting into my bottom lip, but decide to save that idea for later. Although not *too* much later.

"You want it like this?" Aiden asks as soon as his hands are free to grip my waist while I move to the button of his slacks. "Your favorite position?"

I grin, my chest aching. "You remember."

"That you told me you liked to be fucked against a wall?" he mutters, a hiss of air passing through his teeth when I finally manage to slip my hand down the front of his pants and wrap my fingers around him, and, *fuck*, while I'm certain no one would ever describe me as small, he really is impressive. My stomach flips even before he adds, "Hard to forget something like that."

"Wasn't the wall," I inform him, pressing my forehead against his as I touch him. "Was being at your mercy. Being with you," I explain, the crease between his brows deepening as I squeeze the base of him. "That's my favorite."

"*Christ*," he mutters, moving to cup my face and kissing me so hard that I really think he might draw blood. "Can't believe you're mine."

I nod. "Yours. For a long time."

I expect to see confusion on his face when he eases back to look at me, but I don't. All I see is determination before he rids himself of the rest of his clothes with my help, then bends slightly, grabbing the backs of my thighs to pick me up and carry me the small distance to the bed.

"I wouldn't have minded the wall," I tell him, after he puts me on my back while he stays standing between my legs.

He shakes his head. "Want to be able to see you." He leans over me, bracing himself there and kissing me as his hands roam my body. Still so worshipful in the way he touches me that I already know he's condemned me to wanting it forever. Even more than before. So much so that I find myself wishing I really was his god just so I could absolve him of whatever sins he thinks he committed. Of whatever ones he'll end up committing for me…

My pang of worry is quickly eclipsed by Aiden straightening, reaching for the chair still nearby and dragging it behind him with a slow scrape along the wood floor before he sits. I lift myself up on my elbows so I can look down at him, wincing at the pain until I've adjusted to something I can bear, and I know he sees it this time because his eyes narrow.

"I know, I'm a terrible patient," I acknowledge with a smirk that shifts to a grin. "Lecture me later. Fuck me now."

Aiden rolls his eyes, but he also grips both my thighs and tugs me closer to him at the edge of the bed, spitting in his palm again before taking my cock in his hand, and there is something incredibly arousing about him stroking me while also glaring at me. "Maybe I'll do both. Maybe then you'll actually listen."

My head falls back as the need starts to build again, a single word escaping on a sigh. "Doubtful."

He feels *so* fucking good, his palm and his fingers rough, his grip firm as I feel his mouth kissing up my inner thigh. He pauses to suck a mark into my skin, another farther along as if leaving a path for himself to follow next time, and I hope that's precisely what he's doing as he releases my cock to wrap both his hands around my thighs and drag me even closer, giving himself better access before his mouth is on me.

At the sensation of his tongue at my entrance, I surrender any attempts to hold myself up, dropping onto the bed as I moan, gripping my own cock to keep myself from coming. Squeezing harder when the pressure of his tongue becomes one of his fingers, then two after he grabs for the salve and starts using it for an entirely different purpose than I believe was the original intention..

"Aiden." My hips roll, driving him deeper, his other hand spanning across my stomach to pin me but I only grip it in my own, my nails digging in to his skin to once more leave crescent marks. "Fuck, *please*."

"So pretty," he groans, momentarily pressing his face into my inner thigh before pressing a third finger in and giving me time to adjust, still not wanting to hurt me. "Cy, are you—" I drag the hand he has in mine higher, back up toward my face, forcing him to stand once more as he frames my jaw then kisses me hard. "Ready?

"Yes." My whole body feels lit up already, so overwhelming that I'm not sure how I'll survive him, but I will. So we can do this again. And again. And again. "Yes. Stop making me wait."

He grins as he replaces his fingers with the broad head of his cock, the pressure building until he at last pushes himself inside, kissing me and moaning into my mouth every time he sinks forward a bit more. Overtaking every experience I've had before this one until I can no longer remember them.

"Fuck," Aiden groans, sounding just as overcome. "You feel so fucking good. I'm—Cy, baby, need you to come. I can't—."

"It's okay," I reassure him, already astounded I've made it until now, already not sure how I can take more of him, but I really always have loved a challenge. "We've got time."

So much time. Please, let it be so much time.

Aiden pulls out and when he thrusts in again, I roll my hips with him until he's as deep as he can be. He stays there and lets me feel him, lets himself feel me until he can't help but move. Until he can't stop kissing me as he fucks me with one hand framing my face, his grip firm as if he's still afraid I could slip away.

"I'm here," I murmur to him. "You're not alone anymore."

He smiles against my mouth. "Neither are you."

And a few moments later, when it finally does consume us, I think both of us actually believe it.

CHAPTER 51
AIDEN

There's sunlight streaming in through the trees as I sit by the river, bathing the world in a warm haze that matches the one humming in my blood. Sated, drowsy…happy. I think I'm happy for the first time in a really long time. I stare at the silver watch in my hand and rub my thumb over its surface, unable to stop tracing the three interlocking floral rings like I've been doing since he gave it to me.

Only this time, it's different.

I'm starting to remember some things, I think. Little things. The way my mother would smile at us when we came home for the day, the way my father would laugh until his sides hurt, the way it felt to be part of something. And it doesn't feel as painful as I thought it might—to remember.

I think they'd be happy, too. I think they'd understand. Loving someone so much that you'd follow them anywhere. Even if it takes you farther away from what you knew before. Even if it means letting go of what you've lost.

Beside me on the bank, Cypress is lying on his back fast asleep after we had finally stopped going at each other long enough to decide that we needed some fresh air—for our own well-being as much as the cabin's—and I'm glad he seems as comfortable here as he had in bed. Perhaps even more so, sprawled out with his left arm thrown above his head and his other against his chest, although it's his face that I can't stop studying once I stow the watch in my pants pocket. Memorizing his dark hair in a tangled mess from my fingers, appreciating the tinge of pink on his cheeks and neck from where my whiskers had scratched his skin. A few bite marks, too, and not just there.

I'd called him pretty earlier, but what I'd meant was gorgeous. In a way that fucking *aches*.

I should let him sleep for a while. I know I should. He needs it even more than I do, but it's so hard to resist touching him now that I've finally let myself. Carefully, I lie down next to him before my fingertips dust over his cheekbones, trace the bridge of his nose, the bow of his mouth, the scar along his chin. There's several on his face but this one is the one I notice most. Probably because it runs closest to his smile.

"It *is* nice here," he murmurs, his voice a low, raspy drawl before he starts humming that familiar song, letting me know I've been unsuccessful in my attempts not to disturb him. But I struggle to feel guilty for it, so lost in the sound of it, so lost in the memory of him murmuring in my ear, over my skin only a couple hours ago, that it takes me longer than it should to understand what he means when he says, "Would've been a good spot."

Cypress cracks an eye open to see me glaring at him. "Not ready to joke about that?"

"I will never be ready to joke about that," I growl before continuing my slow perusal.

"Do you…do you mind them?"

"Mind them?" I ask, my thumb now dragging across his bottom lip, down his throat, over his collarbone. Brushing the outline of the bandage lying high over his right shoulder through his—*my* unbuttoned undershirt, reminding me of how close he came. How close *I* came to not getting this. To not taking what is mine because I was so afraid. Won't make that mistake again.

"The scars," he says quietly, and I momentarily stop what I'm doing, looking up at his face to find him looking back at me with that rare vulnerability he sometimes lets me see. "Do you hate seeing them?"

"No," I tell him, keeping my eyes on his so he can see I'm not lying, so he can be sure there's not a single thing about him that I hate. "I like having the proof."

"The proof?" he asks, surprised. "Of what? That I'm broken?"

I sigh, leaning over him to press a kiss to a thin raised line over his chest, then another, then another. "You're not broken, Cypress. Not to me. All I see is proof you've got nine lives. That you survive."

I hear him chuckle while my mouth is against his throat. "Was your own intervention in a few of those lives, wolf. At least three."

"Three?" I shift so that I'm braced over him, careful not to rest too much of my weight on his upper body where he's still healing, but less careful in other areas.

Neither of us are wearing more than undershirts and sleep pants, in part because getting fully dressed seemed impractical and in part because we are both running dangerously short on intact clothing. Through the thin fabric, my eyes flutter closed at the feel of him against me, but I don't need to see him to know he's grinning. I can hear it in his voice when he murmurs, "Wake up ready, don't you?"

I huff out a laugh, no sense in denying it, but I still try, just so I can tell myself I have some semblance of control here. "You're the one who's been sleepin'. I've been awake for a few hours."

Cypress chuckles, lifting his head and kissing my jaw with such intensity that I don't need a mirror to know I'm as marked up as he is. "How fortunate for you that it won't take me nearly as long to catch up."

To prove it to me, he lifts his hips, grinding against me, letting me know the extent to which both of us are already hard, already needy. And suddenly, I'm not so sated after all. I'm not sure I ever will be.

"What's the third?" I ask him, distracting myself by burying my face into his neck. Right over where I can feel his pulse. Strong, but starting to race. "I only remember two."

His pulse picks up. "Hm?"

"I remember Maddock. Then the last one." I lift my head and stare down at him before asking again, "What's the third?"

That vulnerability is back in his eyes, a wariness, too, as if he's not sure he should say, but part of me is nearly sure he already has, that he's tried. *I have been in love with you to the point of madness for nearly ten years.*

Ten years. Same amount of time that had passed since Dolly met him, since he wandered back to her place wounded. It's not possible, and yet…

You ever think about what's coming out of your mouth before you say it?

Always.

I'm not sure if that makes it better or worse.

Better. Because then you know I mean it.

"Cy," I murmur, tracing the scar on his chin. "Why do you call me wolf?"

"Suits you," he whispers, eyes searching my face as he gives me the same answer he did on Dolly's rooftop. "Told you that."

"You did," I reply, not saying more until I've rolled us so that we're lying side by side and facing each other. "But you didn't tell me why."

He hesitates. "Didn't think you wanted to know."

"I do now," I reassure him. "You remember being on the train?"

He frowns. "A bit."

"You told me some things. And before we left, Dolly did, too," I say slowly, still watching him closely. "About what happened to you." I brush some of the messy strands from his forehead, clearing my view of his stunning blue eyes. "She said you've never told her all of it."

His mouth presses into a tight line. "Didn't want to burden her with that."

"Cy…" I murmur, inching closer so that my forehead is pressed to his as I wrap an arm around him, tight enough to hold us both together. "Will you tell me?"

"Why?" he mutters. "So you can be burdened instead?"

"So I can keep my word to you," I tell him. "I want your future, Cypress, but I want your past, too. So when you go back to visit it, you're not alone there anymore either."

He takes a deep breath, lets it out. Then another. "I do go back sometimes. Even though I don't want to."

"I know." I sigh. "I do, too."

For a time, both of us stay as we are, breathing each other in and taking comfort in the fact that there are some things we don't have to explain. Not to each other. Makes it easier then, I think, to ask for the things we do.

"Dolly said you told her there were people you lost. That you were trying to find them? People that *met you in the dark*. And on the train, you mentioned you see them when you sleep."

"Not anymore," he says, his voice quiet like a whisper even though there's no one but us and the water running by. He shifts, somehow getting closer. "Dolly told you? About some of the young women being abducted from her place?"

My hand starts brushing up and down his back. "She did."

"Those girls were the first ones they decided to take. But I knew they wouldn't be the last. Over those last few months, things within the group had been…escalating, and I'd known we were heading for something. Was part of the reason I stayed with them as long as I did."

"You wanted to prevent it. Whatever they were heading for," I say, already knowing too well by this point that would've been the case with him. "How many of them were there? In your group?"

"Eleven. Apart from me."

I pause, thinking about how hopeless it had felt when the same number had surrounded the two of us. Yet Cypress had gone back on his own.

"I didn't realize at the time, but one of them had already grown suspicious of me," he says, his voice a little stronger. "And when I came back, they were waiting." He takes another deep breath, his thumb tapping against his chest where it's pressed between us, keeping time with another source of water that no longer drips. "Next thing I knew, they locked me up in some small shed nearby and…they held me there for a time. Not really sure how long. They kept hoping I'd eventually admit where I took them. They…"

"They hurt you," I say for him, suddenly having to fight off a rising tide of rage, a rising desire to hurt them back when I know I won't get the chance. "They're the reason for the scars."

Cypress nods. "They would come in and attempt to get it out of me until they'd give up for a while, and after they were gone, I'd try to sleep just so I could be somewhere else. When I could, I'd have these… dreams, I suppose you would call them."

My hand continues its path up and down his back, an attempt to soothe myself as well as him, to remind both of us that it's over. "What kind of dreams?"

"I remember being in a field," he says, sounding almost wistful despite everything he'd just confessed. "And I could see the stars again. Always the same ones. After a while, I started to talk to them…since no one else was listening."

I smile even as my chest feels like it's going to split open. "They talk back?"

"Sometimes," he says, and I think I can hear him smiling, too. "They sent me them."

Them. My heart hammers in my chest as more of his words from the train return to me, along with Dolly's. "Who is *them*, Cy?"

He's quiet again for a while, and I wait. Wait for what I already know is coming. "There was a wolf and—"

"A little bird," I finish.

"Yes." His head draws back so he can meet my eyes. "They stayed with me until I made it out, but after, I didn't see them anymore. I told myself it was because they escaped, too." His gaze searches mine. "So I went looking for them and hoped…I'd get lucky enough to find them."

I was looking for you for so long. In every face I passed I looked for you, hoping that when I saw you, I would know.

And he had. He'd called me wolf the first night we met. He'd known, but…he can't have. Things like that don't happen.

As if he can hear my thoughts, Cypress smiles. "You don't believe me."

I let out the breath I've been holding and roll my eyes. "Give me a minute to wrap my head around it, would you?"

His smile broadens. "Take all the time you need, wolf. Although, I would like to point out, you did say you thought you had been looking for me, too."

I did. I had said that. And in truth, I believe it. For so long, I've felt like I've been looking for *something*, but I'm also not one to…

"I've never put a lot of stock in fate," I say, glancing down to where his hand is now clasped in mine, his thumb no longer tapping. "Or in luck."

"But you choose to believe in God?"

"Suppose I do."

"You choose to believe an unseen being can take things from you."

My jaw ticks. "Yes…"

"But not that the universe might give you something instead?" he asks. "You only believe in divine providence when it's to your detriment? Not when it's to your benefit?" He frowns. "Rather pessimistic view of things, don't you think?"

I open my mouth to respond, close it, then restart. "Are you the benefit in this situation?"

Cypress grins. "Of course."

I roll my eyes again, but since I also start kissing him right after, I'm not sure I make much of an argument. Not until a few minutes later when we've both broken away panting for air. "Wait." I put a hand on his chest to keep him at bay. "The little bird. If you think I'm the wolf, then you think there's another person out there, too?"

He nods while trying to chase my mouth.

"That you'll love?" I confirm, staying just out of his reach.

"*We*," he corrects. "That *we* will love. It isn't them unless we're both infatuated." He sighs, still smiling. "You'll find her first. That's what I saw in the dream. She appeared with you and then came to me."

"She?"

"Just a feeling."

"Cy, it was a dream. It wasn't…" I start to say, then immediately regret it, not wanting him to think I'm belittling whatever he had to believe to survive.

"And yet, here you are."

I frown, unable to dispute that point even if I want to dispute the argument as a whole. For the most part.

I *had* been honest about being with multiple partners before. Helped, sometimes. Made everything that was overwhelming a bit quieter. But even so, none of those times were for more than a night, me moving on before the sun was even up. None of them were like Cypress, and I have trouble imagining that there could be another person I could love the same way…that could love me.

"A bit greedy, don't you think?" I ask him, the hand I had against his chest skimming lower. "Not that I would mind some reinforcements."

"There's *three* chairs," Cypress mutters, taking my cue and moving to help with our clothes. "You may not believe in fate, Aiden, but it seems you have been planning for it all the same."

I shake my head, sitting up so I can tug my shirt off, then his. "Would you stop talking about the chairs?"

"Sure," he obliges, letting out a heady sigh when I lunge for him, lifting his hips so I can rid him of his pants, too. "What do you want to talk about?"

"Right now?" I ask, kissing him once more before lying on my back again so I can free myself. "Nothing that doesn't end in you saying *please.*"

"Ah, well, you see…" He rolls, quickly straddling me in a surprising show of speed for someone who had another brush with death not more than two weeks ago, though I suppose nothing at this point should surprise me about Cypress. "I think it's my turn."

"Your turn?" I ask, watching him reach for my discarded shirt and twist it into a makeshift rope. He holds it out in a line over my chest, eyes on mine while he waits for me to place my hands in the center. Once I do, he wraps the fabric around my wrists and knots it.

"Quick release," he murmurs, guiding my bound hands over my head. "You want me to stop…all you have to do is say."

I nod, a bit of nerves but mostly anticipation pooling in my gut as his hands trail slowly back down my arms and chest, exploring in a way that someone who didn't know him better might interpret as lazy. "Why do I have a feeling that nothing else about this is going to be quick?"

"Why rush things?" he asks, taking me in as his teeth press into his bottom lip.

My thoughts skip, darting around for something to do, because surely there's *something.* "We should—we should plan out our next steps.

Go into town. Resupply. Get word to Dolly."

Cypress makes an affirmative noise, though he doesn't seem to be focused on anything other than my eager response as he skims his fingers lightly across my abdomen. "Dolly will have figured out what happened to us. Just like she will have already punished those responsible. She'll trust us to make our way back."

"Even so," I argue, not sure why. "We need to—"

"Wolf?"

I realize that I've closed my eyes, arching my back to try to guide him. "Hm?"

Cypress grins. "Thought you didn't want to talk."

We don't for a while after that. Not until it really is his turn to hear me say *please*. My knees and my still-bound hands in the soft dirt as he takes his time in taking me from behind. His chest against my back, his mouth once more against my ear, as he murmurs in return, "That's it. Just like that, wolf. So perfect."

Never like this, I think again. *It's never been like this.* I've never let it be, never could have. With anyone but him.

"You liked that, didn't you?" Cypress continues, running that damn mouth again as he thrusts into me hard and deep. "Watching me?"

Fuck, I had, and I'd like to tell him just how much I'd liked watching him work himself up while he straddled me, how much I'd liked waiting for him to put me out of my misery, to let me touch him while I was completely at his mercy. I understand now exactly why he'd said that position was his favorite.

"You want to come?" he asks, his hand between my legs stroking my cock at the same pace with which he's fucking me. "You had enough?"

Against all reason, I shake my head, and he actually laughs. "Fuck, you really are perfect."

Perfect. God, it really does feel like he's right. Like nothing could be better. And I decide right then that even if I don't believe in dreams, I believe in him without question. I believe he's mine. That I belong with him and he with me.

And I would do anything to keep it that way.

CHAPTER 52
CYPRESS

A few months pass by before Aiden and I do make it back to the front steps of Dolly's place, waiting for the last of our belatedly assembled plan to fall into place. None of which involves running, and all of which has Aiden fidgeting where he stands.

"He's late," he mutters, verifying it on his watch before glancing to where the sun is hanging high overhead, albeit slightly to the west. "Least he could do is be on time."

I shrug. "Can you fault him?"

Aiden glares at me. "Yes. Yes, I can, seeing as how he is largely to blame for most of this mess."

I grin. "Almost feels like we should be thanking him."

"Wouldn't go that far," Aiden grumbles, though the corner of his mouth twitches. "You're *sure* everything else is taken care of?"

"Yes," I tell him, not minding repeating the details if it will soothe him. "The first part is done. Clayton got the money we sent, and he's handled paying off Maddock's friend in the stagecoach business. Already stopped his stations distributing the posters."

"Turned awful quick."

"No more than they usually do," I reply, shrugging.

"Right," Aiden says, letting out a breath. "Keep forgetting this is the *usual* way."

I grin. "You know what they say…no honor amongst gentlemen."

Aiden quirks an eyebrow at me. "That is *not* what they say, nor is it how that phrase goes." He considers momentarily. "But it probably should be." He goes back to fidgeting. "Won't people ask questions?" Aiden asks, still dubious. "Want an explanation for why the posters are coming down?"

"As eye-catching as we are, I doubt anyone will notice. Not when there's plenty to take our place," I point out. "If they do, they'll be told it was all a mistake. A clerical error—"

"A *mistake?*" he questions. "The word of more than two dozen witnesses is a mistake?"

"If the right people say it is."

"Christ," Aiden mutters, looking like he would ask more questions on that point if he weren't so concerned elsewhere. "And what about the law? You're sure they've also been paid for and settled?"

"*Not* paid for, in this case. We didn't have to," I remind him. "Simon still had the agreement he found in your pocketbook. Wanted to keep it as an autograph, but Clayton paid him off as well. Kid drove a hard bargain."

"I'll bet," Aiden mutters. "Still not sure what it even proves. I didn't exactly hold my end."

"It proves that Maddock didn't either. And that he didn't *hold his end* first by gambling what he shouldn't have. That covers you. Plus, Ben also has Clayton's word that I wasn't cheating on the last game. Seems to hold a lot of weight with him."

"Who is Ben?" Aiden asks, pulling his revolver from its holster and opening the chamber to check rounds even though he did the same thing five minutes ago. "Do I know him?"

"The sheriff? In Soldana?"

Aiden scoffs. "The one whose deputies probably helped chase us out of town?"

"Well, you know law enforcement…" I reply. "Hard for them to see chaos and not want to contribute. Clayton said Ben feels sorry, though, for the inconvenience."

"Funny thing to call being hunted on horseback with guns."

"They both send their best."

Aiden chuckles. "Well, tell Clayton I wish them a long life together."

"All right," I say, pleased that he isn't holding a grudge in this case. "He did also say that, as of now, Maddock has refused to lodge an official complaint that states I was letting him win before, so we don't have that to worry about either. There's nothing on record. See, told you I'd fix it. Besides this last part…which I still would."

"No," Aiden murmurs, giving me a look. "You've done plenty."

I smirk. "Hardly anything."

"We were nearly shot *twice* on the way here."

"Well…it was a long journey. Might have been dull otherwise," I defend. "I did offer to take the train."

Aiden shakes his head. "No more trains." He sighs. "We should probably get a wagon."

"We had one."

"One that's *ours*."

"Right."

"Just so we're not carrying everything with us all the time," Aiden further explains. "You hide the rest of the money this morning?"

"Depends on your definition."

"That mean you burned it all?"

"Most of it. Should be enough left for your wagon and anything else that might catch your fancy." Aiden shakes his head again, but I can tell he's trying not to smile.

"Oh," I say before we leave the topic entirely. "I did also send some money to Charley."

"Who?" Aiden stows his gun again—formerly *my* gun since he had been kind enough to offer to hang onto this one while I obtained a new matching set. Something about how it *made good sense*, and nothing at all about how he thought it might be good fortune, since he doesn't put faith in such things. Similar to how one of my black hats *just fits him better* and *why bother getting a new one if what we have will do?*

My response, that the *bother* was that he deserved to have things from someone who loves him, was met with a long period of tight-lipped silence before he responded, "Well, now I do."

That, along with him spending the night showing me what types of things he felt *I* deserved, had managed to mostly put an end to the topic. Although, we had at least agreed for the sake of common decency and self-restraint that I could buy him some new clothes.

"You probably wouldn't know that name," I admit, giving him a pass in this case on his typical reluctance to learning more than a select few people. "He was the old cowboy at the poker table in Soldana. Honest sort. Good man like Clayton. Gave Maddock a hard time whenever he could, so while I didn't end up taking any of his money, I felt like giving him something for that at least."

Aiden nods. "Not taking from men like that should be considered one of our rules. Not that either of us would."

"Our rules?"

He shrugs. "Was thinkin' we should have some. Like Dolly does. Rule one can be that we don't take from good men. Rule two can be…"

"That they think they're untouchable," I offer, watching as a hired coach comes into view.

Aiden straightens, head high as he subtly leans into my shoulder. "I still can't believe he agreed to this."

"Pride goeth," I murmur, leaning back.

"And idiocy before that."

The coach stops directly in front of us, the door promptly swinging open as the three occupants shuffle out before the coach is gone again. The driver apparently not eager to be a witness, and seeing the assembled party, I can understand why.

"Nice of you to finally come out of hiding," Maddock says to Aiden, the former heir looking quite a bit less pampered than the last time I saw him. Also looking quite a bit less influential, since the only people he now has tailing him are an extremely anxious-looking Arty and another equally uncomfortable man with a notepad. When Aiden doesn't immediately respond, Maddock's eyes flick to me. "See that you're still associating with criminals."

"Better company," Aiden replies coolly, folding his arms across his chest as he meets Maddock's gaze. "Better morals, too, more often than not."

His former employer sneers, his fury intensifying when I politely offer my own greeting. "Hi Maddock, how's the family been keeping?"

He takes a step forward but when Aiden does the same, putting himself between us, Maddock seems to think better of it. "I've brought a reporter here from Galveston," he says, gesturing to the tidy man with the notepad. "He will be acting as a witness to these events."

The man offers a nervous smile, then approaches as Maddock had done, only he comes all the way to the stairs. "I must say, it's an honor to meet you, sir," he says, holding out his hand for Aiden to shake and absolutely beaming when he comes down the stairs to take it. "I feel as if I'm meeting a legend."

Aiden shakes his head, still uncomfortable with the attention, as well as with the idea that anyone observing could see what we are to each other and use it as leverage the way Tom did.. "Appreciate that, but—"

"I don't have all day," Maddock snaps, actually going so far as to stomp his foot. "Let's get on with it."

The reporter gives Aiden an embarrassed smile before moving away to take his place, giving me time to take mine at Aiden's side before he announces, "Cypress will be serving as my second."

"Fine," Maddock replies, then gestures toward Arty. "He'll be mine."

Aiden and I both look toward Arty, and I have the distinct impression that the young man would *much* rather be *anything* but Maddock's second.

"Hello," he says quietly, appearing even more beaten down now, and I can only imagine how much of a role Maddock has played in that.

"Sorry about…" Arty jumps when Maddock calls his name and scurries off to stand near the journalist on the other side of the road.

"Think we should probably have Cypress call it," Aiden offers, frowning after the young man before turning to Maddock, who is already waiting in the middle of the wagon path out front. "That fine by you?"

"Yes, fine," Maddock says, waving his hand. "Stop stalling."

Aiden rolls his eyes, but then says quietly to me, "Just in case…"

"Wolf—"

He gives me a look and I fall silent, knowing I won't want to miss whatever he thinks he needs to say.

"Just in case things don't go the way we planned…" he says, appraising me with so much open affection in his eyes that it's tangible. "I'd follow you again."

I smile, not believing for one instant that this moment will be our last, but I tell him anyway, "So would I."

With one last long stare, Aiden turns, walking out to stand back to back with Maddock and looking every bit the legend he'd prefer not to be.

"Ten paces," I call out, my voice steady.

"One." Aiden and Maddock both take a step forward.

"Two." Another, and the space between them widens, Aiden's shadow behind him.

"Three." How did he do this alone for so long?

"Four." How can I make sure he never does this again?

"Five." He'll be all right. I know he will.

"Six." Fate would not make me wait so long only to take him from me so soon.

"Seven." This isn't the end.

"Eight." It's a beginning.

"Nine." Aiden takes a step, and Maddock takes…off, absolutely *sprinting* in the same direction as the coach, and as fast as he's going, he might just catch it.

"Well, guess that's that," Aiden says as soon as I come to stand next to him to watch the rest of Maddock's retreat. "Bet he's wishing he hadn't brought that reporter now."

"Somewhat anticlimactic," I agree, having to squint now to see the small man in the distance. "Must not think he's so untouchable after all. Too bad. Really was hoping you were going to shoot him."

"Waste of a bullet," Aiden mutters, shaking his head. "Plus, I think we've had plenty of climaxes for a while."

"Well…maybe a few more wouldn't…" I trail off as he rolls his eyes.

"Suppose I set you up for that one."

"You set me up for most of them."

"Only because my mind doesn't work the way yours does."

"How fortunate for me and my desire to corrupt you."

He snorts, turning with me as we move out of the street. "That what you're doing?"

"God willing."

"Sadist."

"Masochist."

I look in time to see Dolly stick her head out the door with an expectant expression. "Show's over, I'm afraid."

Frowning, she glances up and down the street. "Where's the body?"

"Running for the hills."

"Sounds right." She gives a whistle that causes every window in the front of the building to close at once. Noticing the sound, Aiden looks up, then at me.

"What?" I say. "While I have no doubt in your abilities, there's nothing wrong with having an ace up your sleeve. Just in case."

"Cheat," he mutters, shaking his head again, but he's fighting a smile when the reporter makes his second approach in under five minutes.

"I think I'll start walking back to town," he says, already scribbling away in his notepad. "Want to get this into the Sunday edition." He glances once more at Aiden, holding out his hand. "Been an honor."

Aiden blows out a breath, then takes it. "Sure." He waits until the man is out of earshot before adding, "Least he didn't take any pictures."

"I could run after him and give him one of the cutouts from the wanted posters I saved?" I offer, helpfully. "The sketch isn't bad. They really captured your roguish cowboy-turned-outlaw charm. Would pair wonderfully with the article."

He gives me a hardened stare. "Don't you dare."

"It's no trouble. I have extras. Plenty to go around."

"Cypress, I swear to—"

The sound of someone clearing their throat interrupts what I'm sure would've been a tantalizing threat, both Aiden and I finding Arty still lingering on the other side of the road.

"What's that one's name again?" Aiden asks, and now it's my turn to shake my head.

"How can you not know? You worked with him. For *weeks*. For nearly as long as it took you to fall in love with me."

"Didn't take me that long," Aiden mutters, starting to cross the road with me. "What's the point in getting names? Not everyone feels possessed to talk to every person who crosses their path. Remembered yours, didn't I? And Dolly's? I remember the ones I like."

"Along with Maddock?"

"Right, the people I like. And the people who would like to kill me. The important ones."

I laugh, unable to debate the efficiency before we come to a stop in front of Arty.

"I'm sorry," the young man says again. "I'm sorry about Soldana. I was—"

"Scared," I answer for him, and he nods.

"Yeah." He takes a nervous step away from Aiden. "Still am a bit."

Aiden sighs something unintelligible before giving Arty a look that likely doesn't help. "You the only one left of Maddock's crew?"

Arty nods.

"You didn't take that as a signal?"

"I did," he replies, twisting the bottom of his shirt in his hands. "But I didn't really have anywhere else to go."

I look at Aiden. He looks at me, then hangs his head before grabbing me gently by the arm and leading me a couple feet away. "Would Dolly take 'im?"

My eyebrows shoot up. "Take him?"

"Give him a job. Give him some people around him, so he doesn't end up…like us."

"Why *wouldn't* he want to end up like us?"

"Or a lot worse."

I fold my arms, pretending to mull over the options. "Probably. At the very least, she'll need someone to bury bodies for her once we go back to Arizona."

"Not that."

"I could teach him to play poker before we go."

"Not that either."

"You could teach him how to be menacing."

"Cypress."

"*Fine*," I say, not wanting to push him too far on what has already been an eventful day. At least, not until later. "I'm sure she could find him something *boring*." I glance back at Arty. "Go on inside and get something to eat."

He only stares at me until I tilt my head toward the door once, then twice when he doesn't move. His expression shifting from flustered to tentative hope as he walks up the stairs to be ushered in by an intrigued Dolly, who I have no doubt will find a place for him as she does everyone else. As she once did for me.

"He'll be all right," I tell Aiden, noting the way he also watches him. "Might not turn out to be a gunslinger or a gambler as you said, but not everyone is destined for that sort of greatness."

Aiden chuckles. "My father used to say, there are a lot of things you can be in this life, but the most important is a good man. Hopefully he still has a chance at that."

He starts to head for the door. "Aiden," I call, waiting for him to turn before I say, "You are one, you know? A good man."

His eyes fall. "Not sure some would agree with you."

"Doesn't matter if they do." I walk over and grab his hat, lifting it off before I snag his shirt and pull him to me, kissing him hard enough that he blushes, the color deepening after I remind him, "You are to the important ones."

He nods, smiling and kissing me back before he murmurs, "Think I can live with that."

CHAPTER 53
AIDEN

Nine Years Later

I pull myself up onto the rooftop of a boarding house in Preston, Arizona. The sky above clear and carrying a breeze that reminds me the temperatures are going to keep growing colder as we get closer to winter. I frown thinking about it, letting out a long sigh as I drop down onto two bedrolls and a few blankets that are already spread out, wasting no time before turning my attention toward where it most often resides.

"Hello, wolf," Cypress murmurs, those striking blue eyes of his searching my face from where he lies next to me. "Everything all right?"

"There's a girl in the stable," I tell him, seeing no point in trying to conceal what's on my mind after all these years. "She's staying up in the hayloft."

He immediately looks intrigued. "Oh?"

"Could hear something when I walked in," I tell him, immediately feeding his curiosity rather than teasing him with it, since I feel as much a need to tell him as he does to listen. "First I thought it was a bird up in the rafters, but then she slammed the hatch down. Think she must've seen me and startled."

"Why? Were you being broody?"

"*No*, I wasn't…" I hiss out a breath, because while I might not have been *broody*, I also wasn't friendly. Not after a long day getting here and not when towns like this one still tend to put me on edge no matter how many times we pass through. "I told her to come down, and she didn't, so I went up."

"Hm," Cypress hums, clearly amused. "Have a nice talk?"

"Not exactly…" I drag a hand through my hair. "I may have pointed my gun at her."

Cypress gives me a look. "I take it you're not speaking metaphorically…"

"No, damn it," I bite out. "I didn't know who was up there, and you know the reputation Preston has. Better to be careful."

"True," Cypress agrees, nodding. "So, you pointed your gun at her, and then you…?"

"Was fine," I inform him. "We came to an agreement."

"Did you?"

"Yes."

"And what does that entail?"

"We mind our own business."

Cypress laughs. "How sweet."

"More feisty," I say, turning to stare back at the sky and quickly clearing my throat when I realize her temperament likely was not what he was referring to. "I suspect she doesn't know how to defend herself properly. Also think she's on her own. Not saying she needs looking after, but she seems like maybe she hasn't had much kindness. No people around her. I might…I might go check on her later." I can feel Cypress looking at me, can practically *hear* what he's thinking, but he's wrong. "Just something for us to be aware of as we're getting into things here."

"Indeed," Cypress agrees. "And what does she look like? So I can be *aware*, too, if I run into her."

"Pretty," I say, deciding to keep things short and simple, since there's no reason to be going on about it. "Green eyes. Freckles on her nose. Long auburn hair put up. Think maybe it's a bit curly, kind of. She's not very tall, but you might not know it for how she holds herself. She's feisty, as I said, but I think maybe she's got a softness to her, too. She has a horse there that looks well and cared for…" I clear my throat again, trailing off. "Anyway, not sure that's much to go on."

"Hardly anything." Out of the corner of my eye, I can see him grinning. "Although, I have a feeling I will know her when I see her."

"Cy…" I say, looking at him now.

"Aiden," he replies, the picture of innocence.

"Whatever you're thinking…"

"I'm not thinking anything."

"You're always thinking *something*."

"I am merely open to possibilities."

"You open to the possibility of not causing trouble for just the span of a few hours?"

"I'm not sure." He frowns, appearing to think carefully before his eyes drop to my mouth. "A lot can get accomplished in a few hours..."

I roll my eyes. "I'm still not gonna fuck you on a roof, Cy. Not when there's a perfectly good bed downstairs."

"What if I fuck *you*?"

"Sure. Downstairs. In the house. In the room we are paying for. Where the farthest we can fall is to the floor rather than several stories."

"Fine," Cypress says, letting out a resigned sigh that makes me chuckle.

"You going to be okay?" I ask him, worrying about leaving him up on this roof. "If I go check on her? I know you don't sleep well if I'm not..."

"I'll manage," he says easily, then smiles again. "Small price to pay."

"Cypress," I warn.

"You really thought she was a *bird* when you walked in? That's interesting."

"Cypress."

"Just think, wolf..."

"*Cy.*"

"What if we finally get to use that third chair?"

"I'm closing my eyes."

"I'm really looking forward to meeting her."

"Fuck's sake," I groan. "Go to sleep."

"When I'm this excited? Impossible."

"I never should have told you. Getting all worked up, and all it's going to amount to is a headache."

"What's her name?" he asks, not remotely deterred.

"I didn't ask."

"You should have. She sounds important."

"Important enough that you probably won't even see her."

"Care to wager on it?"

"No."

"Fine. But when I'm right…"

"You are *not* right. And I don't just mean on this."

"We'll see…" he says, grinning wide, and I know there's no point in trying to rein in his enthusiasm now. No matter. Nothing will come of it. Might as well just listen to him talk. Because no one…*no one* gets that lucky *twice*.

Cora. Her name is Cora.

The Midnight Gang will return in

PROSPERITY

ACKNOWLEDGEMENTS

First and foremost, to my readers, who read *Adversity* and told me over and over again that they needed to know how Cypress and Aiden ended up together as much as I needed to tell them. Thank you for loving these characters like you do and for going on another adventure with me.

To my own talented and amazing gang. To Makenna, who wrote *CYPRESS* over and over in her notes on this book and honestly if that doesn't about sum it up. To Rachel, who continues to work magic with her covers and with all the other million things she does for me. To Kat, who got real weird about this book. To Em, for loving cowboys as much as I do and providing me with the kind of live updates that authors dream of. To Lemmy and the Luna fam, who help me manage the chaos.

To my friends and family. To my mom and to Kayla, who continue to be some of my loudest and most unhinged supporters. To my dad, who read poker scenes and then traumatized us both by reading the rest. To my in-laws, who are never more than twenty seconds away. To Kirby and Bee and our group chat with the weird name. To CiCi, who tells me that I'm crazy but then tells me to do it anyway because so would she. To Kelli, who still has to tell me if things are hot.

To my grandfather, who first made me love westerns, and to my grandmother, who kept us all in line in a way that would have made Dolly proud.

To my babies, who still make me believe in magic. And to my husband Kyle, who continues to walk side by side with me no matter where the road leads. I love you.

ABOUT THE AUTHOR

Ren Browne is a lifelong romantic, cowboy enthusiast, and rumored woodland spirit. When not reading or writing, she can be found spending time with her husband, who is the living embodiment of Ron Swanson, their two outdoor-loving children, their silly dog, and a growing flock of chickens.

Other Books by Ren Browne:

Adversity

The Crush

For updates on future releases, including bonus content, consider signing up for her newsletter at RenBrowne.com or following her on:

Instagram: @renbrownewrites
TikTok: @renbrownewrites
Threads: @renbrownewrites

www.ingramcontent.com/pod-product-compliance
Lightning Source LLC
Chambersburg PA
CBHW031957150726
47990CB00005B/1742